M000086486

Praise for *Alpha Bette*

"Against a vibrant New York City backdrop, this playful novel reveals a constellation of quirky characters, all interconnected around an eccentric wealthy matriarch. Blending humor and heart, each character comes alive through their distinctive voices and internal dialogues in the orbit of the dowager. It's a master class in how lives intersect and will remind readers how seemingly small encounters shape bigger destinies."

—ROBERTA BASKIN, **award-winning investigative journalist and nonprofit leader**

"*Alpha Bette* is a fast-paced story that details the lives of Bette's diverse family and friends who mirror so many families across our country today. Jennifer Manocherian finds both the frustrations and the magic within everyday circumstances and offers each of us the hope that we, too, can live all our days with style, grace, and in as delightful and happy a manner as possible."

—MARCIA BRADLEY, **author of** *The Home for Wayward Girls*

"*Alpha Bette* pulls you in from the first line. Its marvelous cast of characters are complex, and their stories are warmly relatable. You won't want to say goodbye, but you don't have to because they will stay with you long after you read the last line."

—PATRICIA "T.M." DUNN, **author of** *Rebels by Accident, Last Stop on the 6,* **and** *Her Father's Daughter*

"A vividly written character ensemble. Insightful and witty, Jennifer Manocherian explores themes of love and family in an extraordinary debut."

—LISA O'DONNELL, **author of** *Closed Doors, The Death of Bees,* **and** *I Love You All the Same*

"How essential are the bonds we form with one another? Change one life, and will the rest fall apart? That's what I was thinking as I read Jennifer Manocherian's new book, *Alpha Bette*. Quirky, entertaining, and surprisingly profound, *Alpha Bette* will leave you thinking long after you've read the last page."

—**BARBARA JOSSELSOHN**, **author of** *The Cranberry Inn,*
The Lily Garden, The Lilac House, The Bluebell Girls,
The Last Dreamer, **and** *Secrets of the Italian Island*

"Poignant family scenes, rich character development, and ongoing familial traumas make Jennifer Manocherian's debut novel, *Alpha Bette*, a compelling read for any student of humanity. Manocherian's depiction of multigenerational entanglements and human foibles is searingly honest while maintaining a strong degree of sweetness and empathy for all the characters. Insightful and empathetic, *Alpha Bette* is an exquisite book written by an exquisite author."

—**LIS WIEHL**, *New York Times* **best-selling author**

"A riveting, intergenerational New York City novel that focuses on unique 'families' that are created in an urban neighborhood, where everyone depends on one another and knows one another's secrets—or thinks they do. Jennifer Manocherian has written unforgettable characters with breathtaking surprises."

—**JIMIN HAN**, **author of** *The Apology* **and** *A Small Revolution*

"A deeply moving family drama about love, regret, and hope, *Alpha Bette* reminds you of your family ties and the choices you might have made that not only changed your life but those of your loved ones."

—**READERS' FAVORITE** (five-star review)

ALPHA BETTE

a novel

Jennifer Manocherian

RIVER GROVE
BOOKS

This book is a work of fiction. Names, characters, businesses, organizations, places, events, and incidents are either a product of the author's imagination or are used fictitiously. Any resemblance to actual persons, living or dead, events, or locales is entirely coincidental.

Published by River Grove Books
Austin, TX
www.rivergrovebooks.com

Copyright © 2023 Jennifer Robbins Manocherian

All rights reserved.

Thank you for purchasing an authorized edition of this book and for complying with copyright law. No part of this book may be reproduced, stored in a retrieval system, or transmitted by any means, electronic, mechanical, photocopying, recording, or otherwise, without written permission from the copyright holder.

Distributed by River Grove Books

Design and composition by Greenleaf Book Group and Kimberly Lance
Cover design by Greenleaf Book Group and Kimberly Lance
Cover image: Joaquin Corbalan / Adobe Stock

Publisher's Cataloging-in-Publication data is available.

Print ISBN: 978-1-63299-718-0

eBook ISBN: 978-1-63299-719-7

First Edition

To my husband, with love and appreciation.
He married a very young woman a very long time ago and wound up
with a different me along the way and hung in.

ONE

The Old Lady

Bette's bowels woke her. Glancing at the digital clock on her bed table, she saw that it was only 3:30. She didn't want to get up; she was too warm and cozy, plus which going to the bathroom entailed calling the night aide to help her into her wheelchair, then onto the toilet. Such a hassle. Too much hassle. No, her bowels would just have to wait until morning to be emptied.

Bette lay in bed, trying to will herself back to sleep, but something was blocking her, some nagging thought that just would not surface. She racked her brain, trying to come up with what she might have forgotten. *Did I take my blood pressure pills last night or fail to return a phone call or neglect an overdue bill or forget someone's birthday, possibly my daughter's? I'd never hear the end of that. How am I supposed to remember dates anyhow when my days all drift uneventfully into one another?* Trusting that whatever it was would eventually surface, Bette turned her focus toward falling back to sleep. She almost never had insomnia. Her doctor had prescribed Ambien after her husband died in case she had trouble sleeping, but she never used it. She believed all it took was willpower. However, she kept the pills anyway, viewing them as insurance.

What usually put her out like a light was revisiting the memory of a happy experience. This morning she chose to imagine herself at eight, seated in the rumble seat of her father's new yellow Model A Ford on the way to her oldest brother William's oceanfront home in Deal, New Jersey.

Adjusting the rearview mirror, her father glanced back at her. "All set, my little Bette Boop?" he called.

"All set, Daddy," she replied. Whenever he called her by that pet name, Bette knew it was one of his good mood days.

As soon as they crossed the George Washington Bridge, the car gathered speed. Bette tucked the skirt of the pretty new dress her nanny had bought her under her legs, then closed her eyes as the wind whipped her pigtails into her face. She loved the feel of the wind and sun on her body, loved the sound of the motor, loved the anticipation of the day ahead playing with her brother's two sons, who were about her age. She stretched out her arms, palms flat, playing with the force of the wind, wishing the ride would never end.

Before she could fall asleep, reality crept in when she remembered that both nephews were dead. One died serving in Korea, the other a year ago in a nursing home in St. Petersburg, Florida.

She started over. This time it was the late 1980s, and she and her husband were in Paris, sitting at a café on the Champs Élysées.

George, who was on the board of the International Intellectual Property Law Association, had just given a speech at the Grand Palais. Bette was watching the passersby as George studied the menu.

"Sweetheart, if you can take your eyes off the handsome French men for a moment . . ."

"Not sure I can."

"What're you having?"

"What're my options?" Bette said, fumbling blindly with one hand for the menu as she continued to view the scene.

"Crock Messer, Salad Nusus, Soup ah Lunion, Craps Suzette," George said, reading from the menu.

"I hope your speech wasn't in French," Bette said, laughing.

"Ma cherie, what's wrong with my French?"

But then, the screeching tires of cars in the street fourteen floors below, followed by loud honking, ended the virtual trip.

Bette began yet again, this time drawing from their honeymoon in Bermuda in 1950.

Wearing the new midnight blue Cole of California bathing suit she bought for her trousseau, she visualized herself sipping a piña colada as she lay on a lounge chair on Elbow Beach, soaking up the warmth of the sun, her senses heightened after a night of lovemaking. She could feel and smell the salty sea air and hear the crashing of the waves and the laughter of children as they chased sandpipers by the water's edge. Daphne du Maurier's latest book, *The Parasites*, was open across her lap, but as much as Bette wanted to know if at the end Niall made it back to Maria, it would have to wait; she was too relaxed to read. She didn't even have the energy to respond to George calling, "Come on in, the water's perfect."

Just as she was drifting off, the wailing siren of an ambulance tearing down West End Avenue on the way to Roosevelt Hospital brought an end to that memory.

Giving up, Bette slowly moved her right arm across the bed and reached for George, even though she knew he wasn't there. God, how she missed him. She started wondering, as she had done every single day since he died, why he still had not contacted her.

Decades ago, when they were in the early glow of marriage and wanted to believe they would be joined for all eternity, they made a pact that whoever died first would signal the other if there were such a thing as an afterlife. They didn't get into the specifics of what such a sign might be, as the notion of death back then seemed almost hypothetical.

In the five years since George's death, nothing had occurred that Bette could take as a sign. Did he forget their pledge? After all, he had been one hundred years old when he died, and his mind had been slipping. Or had he sent a signal that she mistook for something else? Doubtful, since she was always on the alert for it. Or maybe communication between the before and after was not possible. Or, worse still, could life end with death?

Such an idea was too unsettling for Bette to even contemplate. She fully expected to rejoin George; meet her mother, who had died giving birth to her; see her father, her three older brothers, and their families; embrace her granddaughter who had died so tragically in her twenties; and in time be joined by her descendants. Together forever.

Then Bette had an even more troubling thought. What if life did continue in one form or another but George had met and fallen in love with someone else, someone in the prime of life, someone with whom he didn't have a history of nagging him about getting exercise or watching his diet or turning down the TV or turning off the TV or any of the myriad of other small things they bickered about? After all, even in old age, he was still a catch, so charming, so handsome, with a full head of great hair, pure white, and a lean, upright body. He would have his pick of billions—no, trillions—of women who had passed on before him. So much competition. Too much competition.

Bette was startled out of her reveries by the sound of breaking glass. Her heart started pounding so loudly she wasn't sure she would be able to hear it if someone was in her bedroom. As her breathing slowly settled down, she lay still, listening for an intruder. But it was completely quiet—there wasn't even any street noise, a rarity in Manhattan.

Suddenly a quiver of excitement coursed through her body. Could this finally be the sign she had been waiting for?

"George, are you there?" Bette shouted into the darkened bedroom, hoping, praying, for an answer.

Silence.

George hated it when she raised her voice, so she repeated it more softly. "Georgie? Dear? Is that you?"

Again silence.

Bette began weeping, then just as quickly stopped, worried that her night aide might have come into the bedroom to check up on her and was the source of the noise. The last thing she wanted was for her to hear her crying. Bette assumed that her night aide and her housekeeper talked about her. She could just imagine the conversation:

"Poor Mrs. Gartner. Last night I came into her bedroom and heard her crying. I felt so bad for her," the night aide would say.

"Did she know you heard?" her housekeeper would ask.

"I'm not sure."

"Well, better not let her know. Ever. She does not want to be pitied." Rosie, her housekeeper, knew her well, as she should after having worked for her for over twenty years.

Bette doubted that her night aide was in the bedroom, but she needed to be sure.

"Venera, is that you?"

When there was no answer, Bette shouted, "Is someone there?"

She reached over and turned on the bedside lamp. There on the floor by the bed lay shards of glass next to a framed photograph of George and her in costume for a fabulous New Year's Eve party they had given in the early 1950s. In it, George, as Tarzan, was holding Bette as Cheetah. It had taken two martinis and a lot of persuasion to get him into that loincloth. She had come upon the photo one day when, burrowing through the desk drawers in George's study for no particular reason other than to feel connected to him, she discovered it buried beneath a stack of papers. She had laughed, realizing that even though George had hidden it, he hadn't discarded it.

Now she stared down at the broken frame for a long time, struck by the timing. Just as she was wondering why she had not heard from George, the picture fell. It had to be more than a coincidence.

At that moment, Bette made a decision she had been considering for a long time.

She pressed the intercom on her nightstand that connected her bedroom to her night aide's bedroom. "Venera, I need coffee," she said. In her excitement, Bette had forgotten all about nature's earlier call.

A moment later, Venera's voice came through with a slight Croatian accent. "Mrs. Gartner, it's the middle of the night."

"I have a lot to do today and need to get an early start. First, go to my husband's study and bring me my cell phone. I need to call Rosie."

"Now? It's four o'clock."

"I know what time it is."

"I don't mean to be rude, but it's really early. Rosie wouldn't be up yet."

Bette paused, trying to decide if she wanted to chastise Venera for questioning her like that. *If and when I want to call my housekeeper is my business, not hers. But she's right*, Bette thought. *I can wait till seven to call her. In the meantime I can start getting everything organized in my head.*

It had been a long time since Bette had felt such an adrenaline rush.

"Just put the coffee on, then come help me out of bed," Bette told Venera. "And make sure to bring a broom and wear shoes. There's glass on the floor by my bed. Thank you. *Hallah yum.*"

"*Hvala vam*," Venera responded. "*H-va-la vam.*"

"*Challah vum*," Bette repeated, mangling the words yet again.

"*Hvala vam*," Venera repeated again.

"*Havala-vam*," Bette said. "Better?"

"Close."

TWO

The Old Lady's Night Aide

As SHE SLIPPED INTO HER CLOGS, VENERA THOUGHT ABOUT Mrs. Gartner's attempts to learn a few words in Croatian. It reminded her of the way her beloved grandmother botched the few words she knew in English when they watched old American movies together. Would that she could afford to mangle English that way, Venera thought, not that she would want to. She learned vocabulary and grammar in school, proper pronunciation and conversational English from the TV shows and movies she watched over and over and over. She was proud of how well she spoke English, without which she would never have gotten her job.

Venera decided to look in on Mrs. Gartner to see how she seemed before getting the coffee maker started. To her relief, when she opened the bedroom door, she heard light snoring. Mrs. Gartner must have dreamt that it was morning, Venera thought, even though she said she knew it was four.

Venera left the intercom on so she would hear if Mrs. Gartner woke up, then quietly closed the door. As she returned to her bedroom off the kitchen, Venera's mind returned to strokes and what could happen with old people, triggering her fear that her grandmother might have another stroke, could even die, before she returned to Jelsa. *I will never forgive myself if that happens,* she thought, overwhelmed with remorse about all the people she had let down when she came to America without saying goodbye.

Especially her fiancé.

Since then, despite calls, emails, texts, and postcards, she had not heard one word from him. Not one, which indicated just how hurt and angry he must have been. And who could blame him? Her family had cut her off as well, which she understood; she had shamed them before their small, tight community. However, she knew in her heart that when she returned, they would welcome her home back even if Jusef couldn't. Yet along with the remorse was the knowledge that if she hadn't come she would have spent the rest of her life regretting it. Jelsa: New York? Croatia: America? Little life: Big life. In Jelsa, she had a sense of belonging. Here in New York, even though she loved the excitement of city living, she was anonymous. How to decide? It was so confusing. Since her visa had expired, she knew if she were deported, the choice would be taken out of her hands.

Now that she was all worked up, there was no point in even trying to go back to sleep. Venera turned the volume high on the intercom in case Mrs. Gartner called out again, then opened the window and crawled onto the fire escape. The moon was hidden by clouds that left the night sky dark. A few lights were on in neighboring buildings, and the sound of the traffic could be heard. New York City, Venera mused, there was a reason it was called the city that never sleeps. At this hour in Jelsa, the only sound you might hear was the howl of mating cats.

She inhaled deeply, hoping to get a whiff of salt air from the nearby Hudson River. When she got off in the morning, Venera thought, unless the weather was really bad, she would go to the Boat Basin at 79th Street and watch the river traffic. Hopefully there would be some tugboats pushing huge cargo ships north.

For some reason, tugboats had always captured her imagination. She would love to meet a tugboat captain to find out what his life was like. She assumed they were all men. She would ask how he chose this job. Did he dream of being a tugboat captain as a kid? Was his dad a tugboat captain? What kind of training did he need? Did he find it romantic and adventuresome or boring? How often did he get to push an ocean liner?

Living in Manhattan with all its skyscrapers and being close to the Hudson River felt like a dream come true. Venera took a moment to thank the fates for landing this job two months ago. Before that, while living in a cramped apartment with her friend in a sketchy neighborhood, sometimes at night she would walk west to the river just to see the shimmering lights of the George Washington Bridge reflected on the water. She soaked up the view, her visual candy, storing it in her memory bank to access when in all probability she would wind up returning home to the life that awaited her.

There was a chill in the air, and Venera fleetingly considered going back in. *So what if I'm cold*, she thought. People the world over are cold and starving, living in refugee camps and war zones. Feeling like she might cry, she slapped her face. *Cut that out, you're just feeling sorry for yourself, not for them. And for what? You have a home; you can return anytime you want.*

A light was on across the air shaft in the bedroom of a potbellied, middle-aged man who often stood naked by the window. Venera figured he wanted an audience as some kind of a twisted turn on. She had seen him there at different times and wondered if he spent the whole night like that. "*Pokvarenjak*," she yelled into the night. Then, in English to make sure he got the message, "Pervert." Seeing him look up to see who had spoken, she ducked down, tucking her head between her knees. She had no intention of giving him the pleasure of thinking she was watching.

He reminded her of an old man who lived in her neighborhood back home who had wandered around exposing himself to people. Venera found him creepy, but her friends found him funny and used to toss rocks at him.

One day Venera's mother caught them doing it. "Stop, stop," she yelled, shooing them away with her hands. Then, walking over to the man, she said, "Close your pants and go home. Your sister is looking for you." After steering him in the right direction, Venera's mother approached the girls. "It's not right to be mean to someone who doesn't know what he's doing. He's a little . . ." She touched her head to indicate he was crazy. "He has never harmed anyone."

At the time, Venera had been confused by her mother's response. The old man may have been harmless, and yes, it was wrong to throw rocks, but Venera had also been taught that it was wrong to show your privates in public. Which was worse? Thinking about it now, Venera didn't understand why her mother hadn't warned him to stay away from them. Just as quickly, Venera chastised herself for mentally criticizing her mother. She was so kind; she only saw the good in people.

Her thoughts turned to Mrs. Gartner's early call, and she wondered if she should tell Mrs. Haight, Mrs. Gartner's daughter, about it. During her first week on the job, Mrs. Haight had told Venera to call her right away if she noticed anything at all wrong. She was very specific. "Call me, not Rosie." This was the first time since Venera had been working for Mrs. Gartner that she had been summoned in the middle of the night. And for what? Coffee! What could she possibly have to do before dawn? To her knowledge, Mrs. Gartner had never left the apartment in the time she had been working there and had nothing pressing to do during the day. It seemed out of character and worrisome. Maybe she had had one of those mini strokes—what was the name for them? Transient something or other? That might explain her being disoriented. Or the beginning of dementia? Although the old lady seemed totally sharp.

Rosie had warned her that Mrs. Gartner resented anything that anyone did that took away from her own authority, especially where her daughter was involved. And Venera got it. It infantilized her. But suppose something was wrong with her?

Venera climbed back inside, feeling weighed down by the responsibility for Mrs. Gartner's well-being. No matter what, though, even if she were to call Mrs. Haight, she would have to wait until morning.

THREE

The Old Lady's Daughter

FIFTY BLOCKS SOUTH, IN A NARROW TOWNHOUSE ON A SIDE street in the Chelsea district of Manhattan, Claire thrashed around in her sleep. She had a growing consciousness of hands on her shoulder and someone shouting at her to wake up.

"Get away," Claire screamed, flailing her arms at the person.

"Claire. Honey. Wake up!"

Slowly Claire roused out of her stupor and stared at a man, a man with a shock of faded reddish hair and a sad face who looked to be in his seventies.

"It's me, Jack. Your husband."

"Jack?" she mumbled, half-asleep.

"Yes, me. Jack. Your husband."

"Jack? Oh, Jack," Claire said with dawning recognition.

"It was so awful," she began, as if in a trance. "I sensed the presence of something next to my bed. I wasn't sure if it was an aura of some kind, or a ghost, or a person. Then I saw it was a child, a girl around six, so pretty, with long brown hair, wearing a long white nightgown. Reaching out her hand toward me. She had a halo streaming around her entire body. It was otherworldly, like she was a messenger letting me know I was about to die. I tried to get away, but I couldn't move."

"Claire, it was just a nightmare."

"My body froze," Claire interrupted, unable to take in what he said. "I kept trying and trying. I felt like a sitting duck. I knew there was no escaping my fate; my time was up."

"You were having a—"

"I thought Hope was reaching out for me to join her."

"Don't be ridiculous," Jack said. He got up and turned on a light. "See? No one is there."

"Oh my God, I must have had another night terror."

"That's what I've been trying to tell you."

"Don't be angry with me," Claire said, her voice small and scared as she eyed her husband blankly.

"My heart feels like it's about to jump out of my body. Feel it," Jack said, taking Claire's hand and putting it against his chest.

But Claire had drifted back to sleep. Dropping her hand, Jack shouted, "Claire!"

Claire roused, then turned her back away from him.

"Come on, wake up," Jack said. "We have to talk about your nightmares."

Claire slid out of bed and headed toward the windows.

"What are you doing?" Jack asked, getting out of bed and following her to the window.

"Opening the shades. You told me to wake up, right? What time is it, anyhow?"

"What difference does it make?"

"You're breathing down my neck," Claire said.

Jack took a few steps back as Claire opened the shades. Two pigeons were attempting to mate on the windowsill. Tapping on the window, Claire yelled, "Shoo! Go do your business elsewhere."

"Killjoy," Jack muttered under his breath as the pigeons' dance continued.

"Honest to God, our sill has become Chelsea's pigeon population's

13

public toilet. Mate. Poop. Mate. Poop. I cleaned off all the crap just last week."

"There has to be a solution—"

"Like what? Mace?"

"—to your nightmares."

"Night terrors. They are not nightmares. Night. Terrors." Claire opened the window and clapped.

As the pigeons took off, Jack said, "Night terrors. Nightmares. Whatever they are called, the impact on me is the same."

Shivering, Claire closed the window, then turned back to face her husband, her tone conciliatory. "I've told you. The sleep specialist I saw on television said the origin is neurological. It's not like I can get rewired."

Hoping that put an end to the conversation, Claire whirled past Jack and headed for the bathroom. She had no patience for discussing this this morning; she had a bigger problem on her hands. Her throat was on fire, and she feared she was coming down with something. She hadn't been to see her mother for three days and was feeling guilty about it. She planned to go there this morning, but suppose she had strep throat? She didn't want to expose her mother. Or worse still, Jack. If he got it, God help her. His man colds were epic.

"Where are you going now?" Jack asked.

"To get Airborne. My throat kills."

"No wonder," Jack replied, "the way you were screaming."

Claire stopped short, and Jack almost bumped into her. "I was? Seriously?"

"What do you think I've been talking about?"

"All I remember is being frightened."

"Well, trust me, you screamed."

"That's why my throat's sore," Claire said, immediately relieved. She turned back, but instead of getting back in bed she headed downstairs. Jack trailed Claire down the two flights of stairs, talking at her back. "You probably woke up half the neighborhood."

"Jack, come on," Claire said, trying not to laugh. "You don't really believe that."

"Any minute now, the police may show up at the door."

"It can't have been that bad."

"I don't think I'll be arrested, but one of these days I may die when you wake me up screaming in my ear."

When they got to the ground-floor foyer, Jack retrieved the *New York Times* that was on the floor beneath the mail slot in the front door as Claire went into the kitchen. A moment later, Jack joined Claire in the kitchen and sat down at the table for two by the window and opened up the paper. Claire felt a flash of relief—maybe he would move on.

No sooner had Claire turned on the coffeemaker than Jack put the paper down. "You have to stop telling me there's nothing that can be done and find a specialist who can cure you. You're being selfish."

"Selfish?" Claire repeated, totally annoyed.

"I've told you my doctor says this kind of stress can give me a heart attack."

"I'm sorry, but it's not like I do it on purpose. It's not exactly fun for me either, thinking I'm about to die. And speaking of selfish, what about you?"

"What about me?"

"Have you ever thought about how your inability to come to terms with your grief affects me, not to mention also strains your heart?"

"We were talking about your night terrors, not about me," Jack said. "Either fix it or sleep in Hope's old bedroom."

"Oh, no. No, no, no, no. No."

15

He had been lobbying for her to get help for years, but this was the first time he suggested separate bedrooms. And not just separate bedrooms, but Hope's old room. Claire paused, waiting for him to retract what he had just said.

All of the sudden, she ached for her father—not that he could have done anything about it, but he would have been furious at Jack for such a grossly insensitive suggestion. Furious. The door to Hope's room had rarely been opened in twenty-five years except by their once-a-week cleaning lady who occasionally dusted and vacuumed it. Jack hadn't stepped into it once since Hope's death.

Get a grip, Claire told herself. *Try a different tactic.*

"Jack. We've shared a bed for over fifty years. You're my security blanket. I don't want to sleep alone."

He reached for Claire's hand, but she pretended not to notice and instead brushed the sides of her hair back with both hands.

"I feel awful for you," he said. "Thinking you're about to die all the time. It can't be good for your heart, either."

"My heart's fine," Claire said.

She got up and went over to the bread box on the counter. "Want an English muffin? I bought some homemade strawberry jam at Chelsea Market to go with it."

"No thanks."

Jack picked up the newspaper and started reading. Claire removed a package of English muffins, then separated the muffin in half using her thumbs. After putting the muffin in the toaster, she went over to the coffeemaker and poured coffee into two mugs.

Placing Jack's mug in front of him, Claire said, "I thought maybe this weekend we could drive upstate and pick up some plants for the window boxes and garden. I was thinking pansies and ivy." She was hoping to change the subject and get the heat off her.

Jack plopped the paper down on the table and looked at Claire.

"What?" Claire asked, as if she didn't know. So much for changing the subject.

"We need to resolve this. What about Jia's room?"

"Are you serious? I thought we agreed to keep it in reserve for when Jia has children and they come for sleepovers. Now that she has a serious boyfriend, that day is coming soon."

"Even if she marries Kenny, it won't be for years. Young people these days are in no rush."

"Don't say anything to Jia," Claire said. "Knowing I have night terrors upsets her enough as it is."

"It upsets me too, Claire, but—"

"You don't want to have a heart attack. Got it. Enough with being selfish."

"Claire—"

"I'll think about seeing someone," Claire interrupted.

She needed to buy time, though she had no desire to go into therapy. Been there, done that, not that Jack ever knew it.

FOUR

The Old Lady's Great-Granddaughter

J IA WOKE UP AT THE EXACT MOMENT HER GRANDMOTHER
mentioned her name. Her grandfather Jack once said it was as if
grandmother and granddaughter were psychically connected, but in
this instance it was just a coincidence. Her face was being licked.

"Fuck!" Jia was really annoyed, having opted not to set her alarm
so she could get some desperately needed sleep. She had stayed up late
trying to finish an article whose deadline was fast approaching. She
jumped out bed and stepped on something hard and dry on the Tibetan
rug they had splurged on at ABC Carpet when she and Kenny moved
in together. She tried to jump over it and almost fell.

"Goddamnit!" she yelled as she struggled to keep her balance.
"Kenny! Arnold shat on the carpeting, and I stepped on it."

"Oh God," Kenny murmured, half asleep.

"You took him out of the crate!"

"Sorry. I'll clean it up."

"Honey, that's not the point. The trainer told us that if we weren't
consistent, the training wouldn't work."

"Tonight, I promise, Arnold will sleep all night in his crate,"
Kenny mumbled.

Jia grabbed a handful of tissues off her bedtable and carefully picked up the poop. *This better not be an omen*, Jia thought, as she headed for the bathroom to pee and wash the bottom of her foot—in that order. Nature couldn't wait. Nor could a discussion about what to do about the puppy.

She returned to the bedroom, scooped Arnold into her arms, took him to his crate in the kitchen, and then came back. She briefly glanced out the window to make sure their car hadn't been stolen. There had been a spate of car thefts recently in their area of the West Village. But their blue-and-white Mini Cooper was where they had parked it the previous night.

"This isn't working," Jia said as she sat on the edge of Kenny's side of the bed. The puppy was whining loudly, further cementing her determination.

"What this?" Kenny asked, suddenly alert.

"Arnold."

"On our first date, you told me your five-year plan included managing editor, marriage, two kids, and a dog."

"Yes, Kenny, but that was at the bottom of the list, not the top."

"But you always said you wanted a Jack Russell Terrier. Every time we see one on the street, you go nuts."

"I know but—"

"I thought I'd found the perfect birthday present."

"Kenny, getting a dog isn't a unilateral decision. We both work crazy hours, and dogs need time and attention, not to mention walking."

"I'll do all the walking. Or the dog walker. That was part of the deal."

"Yeah, but it isn't enough. He has accidents all the time. I know you were told he was housebroken, but that's a joke."

"Move over. I gotta pee," Kenny said. Jia stood up so Kenny could get out of bed. "There are studies on how dogs make humans better, happier people," Kenny said as he headed for the bathroom.

"Studies funded no doubt by Petco. Sweetie, Arnold is not making me a better, happier person. But wait, is that what you think? That I need to be a better—"

"No," Kenny responded, "though you might want to cook something other than Korean food."

"Shut up," Jia said, laughing. "Do you know how healthy it is?"

"So's Italian cuisine," Kenny yelled from the bathroom.

"Fine. You cook."

Jia heard the toilet flush. Moments later, he returned to bed and sat down next to Jia.

"So what's for dinner tonight?" Jia asked.

"Chef Boyardee," Kenny replied, drawing Jia into an embrace. "Time to kiss and make up?"

"Not until we figure out what to do." Pulling away, Jia sat back up. "It's true. Arnold is fast turning me into a tired, angry bitch. We'll get a dog, but let's wait until we're married and have kids and are tied down anyhow. Then we can have this conversation again."

Kenny didn't say anything, which Jia took as assent. He had to know she was right, she thought. He's a lawyer, a rational thinker.

"Okay," Kenny said. "Let's get married then. How long am I supposed to wait for you to say yes?"

That was definitely not the response Jia was looking for. "Don't change the subject," she said. "We are talking about the dog, not marriage."

"You said, and I quote, 'We'll get a dog, but let's wait until we're married and have kids and are tied down anyhow.' We've been together six years, we both have good jobs, we can afford—"

"You may be ready for marriage, but I'm not."

"Why?"

"I'm just not," she said, her voice filled with emotion. "Kenny, please don't push me on this."

She waited for him to say, "It's fine, we can wait, sorry to pressure you," but instead he said nothing, so Jia moved on as if he had agreed. "I'll take Arnold back to the breeder, okay? They'll understand. I won't even ask for the money back."

"Puppies are not like clothes you return to Bloomingdale's because they're the wrong size," Kenny said. "You can't go back to the pet store two months later and say you want to return a dog."

"Whoa. Wait, a pet store? You bought him from a pet store? Jesus, Kenny, that really sucks. How could a smart guy like you do something so stupid? You know those puppies come from puppy mills. You never get a dog from a pet store. No wonder he can't be trained."

Kenny jumped up and left the room, shouting, "Do what you have to do, but don't fucking lecture me."

Moments later, Kenny came out wearing jeans and a sweatshirt and headed toward the kitchen. Jia could hear him talking to Arnold. "Come on, Schwarzenegger, we're going out."

As soon as she heard the door close, Jia ran to the window to look out. A moment later, Kenny came down the brownstone steps with Arnold and started jogging east. Jia was scared. They had never had such an angry exchange. She knew she had come down hard on him, but taking off wasn't going to solve anything. *He'll cool down*, she reasoned. *I'll apologize, then we'll work something out. I guess we could move the crate into the bedroom, although Arnold might demand to sleep on the bed.*

Jia decided to take a hot bath. Hot water usually had a calming effect on her, but not today. As she lay soaking in the tub, her upset about the argument morphed into fear about her upcoming procedure scheduled for eleven that morning.

By the time she emerged from the bath that was intended to relax her, Jia felt like she would burst if she didn't tell someone about it. Even before their argument, she knew she wouldn't tell Kenny until she got the results; she couldn't deal with him peppering her with questions, nor with his anxiety. But she could confide in Rosie, her great-grandmother's housekeeper.

Jia had known Rosie ever since she was a kid. Rosie sometimes baby-sat for her when her grandparents went out. Now that she was an adult and the age gap had narrowed, Rosie felt more like an older sister.

Rosie was all common sense. She wouldn't panic, nor would she dismiss her fear. But she couldn't call her this early. Maybe at 7:00.

FIVE

The Old Lady's Housekeeper

THE BUZZING SOUND OF A MOSQUITO AWAKENED ROSIE. Half-asleep, she was about to swat at it when she realized it was the ringtone on her cellphone. Her ex was her only contact with that annoying ringtone—what the hell could he want at this hour? *What hour was it anyhow*, she wondered, *and where am I?* Nothing felt familiar.

Rosie checked her watch for the time: 5:25 a.m. As she groped around the bedsheets for her phone, which she usually put under her pillow, she wasn't worried, just pissed off. *What an asshole*, she thought, *so inconsiderate. Probably wants me to take Patty to the orthodontist so he doesn't have to take her, as if I can just leave work, which I can't, even though it's his week, and even though Patty, at fifteen, can get there on her own. He lobbied hard for joint custody just to punish me. Well, too bad. You asked for it, you got it. Deal with it.*

She became aware of someone next to her snoring.

Who?

Then she remembered.

Last night on the way home from work, Rosie had stopped at The Barking Dog Pub on Ninth Avenue to pick up an order of fish and chips to take home. As she waited, she sat at the bar to have a beer. A man on the stool next to her started a conversation—he was definitely not a regular. She assumed he was a businessman as he wore a suit and tie.

"Are you aware your ankles are swollen?"

Embarrassed, Rosie pulled her pants legs down over her sneakers and turned away from him. By the end of every workday, Rosie's ankles were swollen. She had had them checked, and she was okay. It was probably fat deposits, but she wasn't about to say that to the man. If his remark was meant as a pickup line, it was certainly an original approach.

"Look, I'm sorry if I offended you," the man said.

"Are you a doctor?"

"No. But I thought you might want to get that checked."

"Yeah, thanks," Rosie said. Anxious to get away, she shouted to the cook, "Luis, what's taking so long?"

"Hold your horses, Rosie. It's coming up any minute now," Luis shouted back.

"You are offended; I'm sorry. Can I at least buy you a drink while you wait?" the man asked.

What's with this guy, Rosie thought. *Is he attracted to me and my fat ankles?* She knew some guys preferred a woman with meat on their bones. Frank did. But she was more than pleasantly plump. Last time she stepped on a scale, she weighed 165, which for her 5'4" frame was a lot, even though she was large-boned and carried it well. She tried to watch her weight, but it was hard. She loved to eat, especially fried foods and sweets. Baklava was her biggest weakness—sugar, butter, nuts, and one thousand calories a bite—first introduced to Rosie and Mrs. G. by their downstairs neighbors.

It didn't help either that Jia always brought her a large box of Godiva chocolates when she visited Mrs. G. "Sweets for the sweet," Jia would say, then, "You are the best." Rosie wasn't sure if Jia meant the best person or the best housekeeper or the best fattie. Rosie would then chide herself for being cynical. Jia wasn't mean like that.

At least I'm attractive, she thought, *even if my hair is laced with white and the hard living I did in my twenties shows on my face.* "My little Irish Rose," her dad used to call her when she was a kid. She liked to think she resembled Sinéad Cusack—that is, if Sinéad had black hair—although not quite as pretty, nor with that husband. She sure wouldn't mind being married to Jeremy Irons, even though he was probably a rogue. Why was she always attracted to bad boys?

Her thoughts turned back to the man next to her. *Not a bad boy, but hey, if I'm his type, why not? It's been a very long time.*

"Sure. I'll have another beer," Rosie said.

They started talking. By the time Rosie's order was ready, they had moved to a table and shared the dinner. He was a widower, which she liked—they made good mates, not that she was looking to remarry, or at any rate, not until Patty graduated from high school and was, hopefully, in college.

Trying to recall what happened next, she realized that she must have had one too many beers because she had obviously gone home with him. One-night stands were not her thing, but then she thought, *I haven't been with a man for a year, not since Frank and I separated. It was time.*

Rosie tried to picture the man sleeping beside her—tallish, handsomish, mid-forties, a suit. Four-letter name starting with an *M*—Mike? Mark? Matt? Matt. Yeah, that was it. Matt. A nice guy.

She rolled out of bed, careful not to wake Matt, then fumbled in the dark for her pocketbook, guided by the buzzing sound. She removed the phone and saw Frank's photo with the "no" icon superimposed over it on the caller ID.

"Whatever it is, the answer is no," she hissed into the phone. "I work, too."

"Killer bit Patty, and we're at Roosevelt Hospital's emergency room."

"How bad?" Rosie responded, instantly awake. She glanced at Matt, hoping she hadn't woken him, but he remained fast asleep.

"Bad. Right between the thumb and index finger of her right hand. I think he may have hit an artery."

"Jesus, Frank," Rosie whispered. She started feeling around in the dark for her clothes, holding the phone to her ear with her right shoulder.

"Don't start."

"What're they gonna do?"

"We're waiting for the doctor. I'm pretty sure she'll need antibiotics and possibly stitches."

"You gotta put that fucking cat down."

Rosie hung up and, clothes in hand, tiptoed toward the door. It was open a crack, not enough for her to get out. She pushed it open with her foot. A crack of light spilled onto Matt.

"Wassgoingon?" a groggy male voice asked.

"Sorry, go back to sleep." She didn't dare mention his name just in case she had it wrong. Rosie went into the living room, quietly closing the bedroom door behind her. As she scrambled into her clothes, Rosie glanced around the room for her coat. "Holy shit," she uttered out loud, having spotted what she thought might be a Picasso, not that she knew all that much art, above the off-white, crushed-velvet sofa. Clearly Matt—yes, that was his name—or his deceased wife had both money and good taste, but where the hell was his apartment? She jotted a quick note to him before leaving—"Thanks for a lovely evening, Rosie"—and put her phone number below it. Just in case.

In the elevator, she examined herself in the mirror on the back wall to make sure she looked semi-presentable. She was still in her work clothes from the day before, which wouldn't give much away, but her hair was a mess. *It had been quite a night*, she thought, feeling sexy just thinking about it, as she removed a comb from her pocketbook.

When Rosie got to the street, she realized that Matt lived near the river in the trendy Meatpacking District. As she walked toward the subway at 14th and Eighth Avenue, she was overcome with guilt.

If she and Frank hadn't gotten divorced, Patty would not have had to split her time between two households and, more to the point, have to live with that damned feral cat Frank adopted, supposedly for Patty. Frank himself had been bitten twice by the animal. He thought the name Killer was funny. It wasn't. Cat bites were no joke.

Maybe now he would come to his senses. But maybe not. Frank was a macho man and didn't like being countered by her even when he knew she was right, which was part of why Rosie had left him. She couldn't take his controlling ways. The strain of the COVID-19 years just highlighted their differences, and Rosie worried about how their constant fighting affected Patty. She wanted to believe that Patty was better off, that the divorce was as much for Patty's good as it was for hers.

When she got down the stairs to the platform, the uptown train was just arriving. She found a seat across from a woman discreetly nursing her baby, seemingly oblivious to her surroundings. It was hard not to stare, it was such a beautiful tableau, but then a couple of teenage girls swinging around a pole noticed and started laughing. One of them shouted, "Got milk." The mother looked up and gave her the bird. *Good for you, Mom*, Rosie thought.

When the girls got off at the next stop. Rosie's thoughts shifted to Patty. She hoped her daughter would never be that obnoxious, but Patty was changing, and it worried Rosie. She had recently dyed her brown hair green, which Rosie knew was meant to shock her. It didn't, although Rosie pretended that it did. It wasn't like Patty was the first kid to dye her hair. *Let this be the worst of it*, she thought. *If Patty only knew what my parents had to put up with, dyed hair was nothing.*

Having blown her future by being a total fuckup in high school, Rosie was determined that her own daughter not go that route. She had high hopes for her only child.

Patty had shot up from 5'2" to 5'7" in a year and was now taller than her mother, creating a kind of power imbalance. Patty was a string bean, way too thin, and Rosie hoped that it was from the height gain and not an eating disorder. She feared Patty might be reacting to having an overweight mother.

Rosie wanted Patty to see a counselor, not that Patty was troubled per se, but her grades had slipped, and Rosie thought it was probably divorce-related. However, Frank would not agree. In his view, only crazy people went into therapy. Per their custody agreement, they had to make joint decisions on such matters.

A few days ago Rosie had called Frank to raise the issue again. "Frank, I'm really concerned about Patty. She's so smart; she can maybe get a scholarship to a good college, but she's not focused. She can't afford to screw up. Don't just rule it out. This is your week. Keep an eye on her."

"Last thing she needs is me hovering over her. I know what teenagers are like."

"You think having two sons with your ex qualifies you as an expert, even though you weren't living with them when they were in their teens?"

"Are you calling just to pick a fight?"

"No, sorry," she said, upset with herself for losing her temper.

"You make a drama out of every little thing."

"A drama? Jeopardizing her chance of a scholarship?" *The man is clueless*, she thought. *How did I stay with him so many years?* Willing herself to stay on track, she said, "I'm not being dramatic. All I'm suggesting is—"

"Maybe if you were home earlier. She gets home to an empty apartment and—"

"Don't you fucking dare! You want me to quit my job? What little child support I get doesn't begin to cover my—"

Frank hung up on her. Rosie was upset with herself for losing her cool, but he sure knew how to push her buttons. With what he made as an electrician, he had come out far better financially than she had in the divorce.

"This is 59th Street, Columbus Circle. Transfer is available . . ." came the voice over the speakers.

Rosie jumped out of her seat and headed for the door, steeling herself for what lay ahead.

When she got to the emergency room, she quickly scanned the crowded waiting area for Patty and Frank. Most of the people were staring vacantly at the blaring overhead TV; a baby was crying, and no wonder. Just being there was unnerving.

Not seeing Patty or Frank, she went to the reception desk where she was directed to a cubicle. Moving the curtain aside, Rosie saw Patty lying down, her eyes closed, as a nurse gave her an injection. Frank stood by holding her good hand; her other hand was all bandaged.

Rosie ran over to Patty and embraced her. "Honey, I'm here."

"Oh, Mom, it hurts so much," Patty said, her voice blurry. "And it bled; you can't imagine how much blood there was."

"Fucking cat," Rosie muttered under her breath.

"All set," the nurse said.

"Can we go?" Patty asked.

"Wait fifteen minutes to make sure the bleeding has stopped. Otherwise you'll need stitches."

"It's your left hand," Rosie said. "Now you can't even write."

"What's your point?"

"You have midterms coming up."

"I can probably still write. I'm ambidextrous."

"Since when? Since this morning?"

"Mom," Patty said, as if it were a three-syllable word. "You act like all that ever matters is my grades."

Rosie knew she needed to calm down, worried she would take her anger at Frank out on Patty. "I need coffee," Rosie said. "Can I get either of you anything?"

"Yeah, thanks. I'll have a cup. Black," Frank replied.

"Got it." Rosie turned to Patty. "Honey?"

"Maybe a donut, Mom."

As Rosie was walking away, her cellphone rang. She looked at the caller ID and saw that it was Jia. Rosie declined the call, messaging back that she couldn't talk now. No doubt it was nothing important and could wait. She was far too agitated to talk to anyone right now.

She sat down on a bench near the entrance to gather her thoughts. If the cat hit the artery at the base of Patty's thumb, stitches would be the least of her problems. She would have a hematoma for months that would hurt like hell. Rosie had a friend that that had happened to when she was a kid, and it made Rosie afraid of cats ever since with their germ-filled mouths. If Patty needed painkillers, there went her schoolwork. And if she stayed on them long enough, she could become addicted. *Fucking cat. If Frank doesn't get rid of it, I'll find a way to do it myself.*

She was so caught up in her anger she didn't notice Frank and Patty exit.

"Thanks for the coffee," Frank said, sounding annoyed.

"Sorry. I forgot."

"Your daughter was waiting for her donut."

"Dad," Patty said. "I wasn't hungry. Please don't pick a fight."

A cab pulled up, and a woman got out. Frank held the door open for Patty. "Come on, get in."

"I'll call you later to see how you're doing," Rosie said.

"You want me to drop you off?" Frank asked Rosie.

"I feel like walking," Rosie said, thinking he wanted to look good in front of Patty.

"You coming?" Frank asked Patty.

"Do I have to go to school today, Daddy? I barely slept."

When Frank hesitated, Rosie jumped in. "You've got midterms coming up, and more importantly, being busy keeps your mind off the pain."

"I didn't ask you; I asked Daddy. It's not your week," Patty replied.

"Don't be rude to your mother. I agree with her; you have to go to school," Frank said, not altogether convincingly.

"Call me if you need me," Rosie said as Frank and Patty got into the cab.

It took off too quickly for her to hear what address Frank had given the driver. Hopefully the address of Patty's school, even though it was a little early. But Patty could get breakfast at the nearby diner; she was probably hungry. And she could use something in her stomach, having been given antibiotics and pain meds. Pain meds . . . just what every teen does not need.

Then Rosie remembered Jia's call. Not feeling up to discussing what had happened with Patty, she would make it brief.

"Jia, everything okay?"

As Jia explained her situation to Rosie, Rosie felt her heart sink.

"Jia, honey," Rosie said, "you're far too young to get cancer. It's probably a false alarm." As soon as she said it, she felt like a jerk, dismissing what was a real concern just to get out of dealing with it. Even if Venera were available to cover for her for a few hours so she could accompany

Jia, Rosie worried that Patty might need her. Patty was her daughter, her priority.

"But if you need someone to hold your hand . . ." She knew she sounded hesitant, but she couldn't fake it.

"I just needed to get it off my chest; I already feel better," Jia said.

"But didn't you say you need someone to bring you home?"

"That's just bureaucratic bullshit to cover themselves if I fall. I can still walk," Jia said, with a little laugh.

"Call me the minute you know something, okay?"

After she hung up, Rosie wondered if Jia had picked up on her uncertainty. Rosie headed downtown, now doubly worried. That family did not need another tragedy.

SIX

The Old Lady's Night Aide

VENERA HAD THE KIND OF HEADACHE WHERE SHE FEARED she might throw up at any moment. She was on the way to the bathroom to get something for it when Mrs. Gartner's voice called out through the intercom in an urgent tone. "I need help."

Before Venera could respond, she heard, "Hurry." This time Mrs. Gartner sounded almost panicked.

Venera guessed what "hurry" meant. When she started the job, Rosie told her that Mrs. Gartner had had trouble holding back her bowels a couple of times lately, but this was the first time it had happened on her watch. Rosie said she had urged Mrs. Gartner to tell the doctor, but she refused, saying that everyone her age had digestive problems of one sort or another, which Venera thought was probably true but still no reason not to get medical advice. With what little she knew about Mrs. Gartner, Venera felt that she probably believed she could will the problem away.

Venera dashed out of the bedroom, through the kitchen, and down the hall to Mrs. Gartner's bedroom. The moment she opened the door, the smell of feces hit her.

"I had an accident. I'm so sorry," Mrs. Gartner repeated over and over as she lay in bed, covering her face with her hands.

I'm in trouble, Venera thought. *I can't vomit and make Mrs. Gartner feel even worse.* "It's okay, Mrs. Gartner, it's okay," Venera said as she ran past the bed on the way to the bathroom to get towels and wipes. While there, she opened the medicine cabinet to look for ibuprofen, but there was none. She noticed a plastic bin by the toilet and looked through the drawers. Sure enough, she found various over-the-counter medications as well as a prescription bottle for Ambien. She downed three Advil.

When she returned, Venera pulled back the sheets and placed a towel under Mrs. Gartner's buttocks before removing the soiled underwear and nightgown.

"I hate being old and helpless," Mrs. Gartner said, as Venera started wiping the feces off her bottom. "I'm just a burden. A useless burden."

"Don't say that. You are not a burden."

Venera had spoken more sharply than she had intended, but she meant what she said. It bothered her that, in America, old people were devalued. If they could afford it, the family paid others to care for them or shuffled them off to old people's homes to wait to die. In Jelsa, families took care of their own. Baka, her grandmother, had moved in with Venera's parents after her stroke and was also incontinent. Venera and her mother shared bedpan duties. It was not a burden; it was what was done. They understood that old age wasn't pretty. No wonder Mrs. Gartner felt the way she did. Why was she living alone? Why hadn't her daughter taken her in after her husband died, or if not then, when she broke her pelvis?

Venera wished she had a way to reassure Mrs. Gartner that she was not a burden, but the best she could do was treat her with dignity. One thing she was sure of, after only two months on this job, was that she liked working with old people. Whether in Croatia or America, she would get some kind of geriatric emergency training. If here, hopefully her immigration status—or lack thereof—would not be an issue.

As Venera gently cleaned her, Mrs. Gartner, her eyes closed, started talking to herself. "Imagine if George was alive and this happened? It would have been unbearable, not that George would have said anything to make me feel bad."

She paused.

"Can I tell you something you will keep between us?"

"Of course."

"I killed my husband."

"What?"

Venera wasn't sure she had heard right.

"I killed him. It was a cold, windy day in mid-February, and I was at my desk, and—"

Venera stopped listening. *What is she telling me, and why, why me, and what do I do about it if it's true?* Her attention returned to Mrs. Gartner when she yelled, "'No, Mr. G.,' Rosie said, 'No. You can't. Do you have any idea what it's like outside?' George shouted back, 'I don't care. I'm sick of being cooped up.' In all the years Rosie worked for us, she had never raised her voice at George. Or he at her. I ran into the foyer and found them having a tug of war with George struggling to put on his winter coat as Rosie tried to pull it off. Rosie yelled, 'Mrs. G., you have to stop him. He wants to go for a walk.' 'I'm going for a walk,' George snapped. He elbowed Rosie away and managed to get his coat on. I stood in front of the door to block him. 'George,' I said. 'Honey. You could fall. The sidewalks may be icy.' Rosie interrupted, saying, 'I almost fell a few times walking from the subway.' Glaring at us, George said, 'I'm almost one hundred years old, and you can't stop me, Rosie. You either, Foxy. Don't even try.'"

"Foxy—who's Foxy?" Venera asked.

"George sometimes called me Foxy."

"Why?"

"My maiden name was Fox."

"Oh," Venera said. "Sorry for interrupting."

"Poor George, he looked like he might cry, and I felt like his jail keeper. So I gave in, figuring we would be ten minutes at most. But once we got outside, George's adrenaline kicked in, and he wanted to walk down to the river. He was so happy. Every word out of his mouth was a superlative. Every child we passed was the most adorable child he'd ever seen, every dog the same; the sky was gorgeous, the buildings magnificent. I couldn't bring myself to spoil his adventure even though we were both freezing. We were out for close to an hour. The next day he came down with a cold. Then, oh God."

"Rosie told me," Venera interjected.

"She told you he got pneumonia and died three weeks later," Mrs. Gartner continued, her voice rising in anger. "From the day he entered the hospital until his death, the world changed. That awful COVID. He wasn't allowed to have visitors. Venera, I couldn't even visit my own husband. He died alone, and as if that wasn't bad enough, there were so many deaths, it was impossible to find a funeral home to take him. Bodies were being stored in refrigerated vans on Park Avenue. Oh my God, it was a nightmare. Thankfully Jia's boyfriend, Kenny, managed to pull strings and somehow get George into a funeral home. He then arranged for a burial, but we couldn't have a proper funeral. Can you imagine that?"

Even though Venera had finished the cleaning, she thought that if she stopped, Mrs. Gartner would clam up, so she began massaging Mrs. Gartner's arms and legs.

Mrs. Gartner let out a loud sigh. "If I had only listened to Rosie."

"You can't blame yourself."

"Everyone else did. My daughter, when she heard I had taken him out, yelled, 'Mother! How could you have done something that stupid!' Later she apologized, but—"

"That's terrible," Venera said. "Mrs. Gartner, the way I see it from what you said, you gave him a gift. It was a price he was willing to pay."

Poor woman, Venera thought, *what a weight she's been carrying. I don't like that daughter.*

"Do you think he has forgiven me?"

"Of course he has," Venera said, feeling as if she were a priest who had just heard confession, even though she worried that telling her she wasn't to blame implied that she had done something wrong.

"You are very kind."

"Do you want me to do your back?"

"Oh yes, thank you."

Venera gently turned Mrs. Gartner over, then started massaging her back.

"Everyone assumed I would be next," Mrs. Gartner said. "That's what often happens with long marriages. And I would've if I could've, but I couldn't."

"What do you mean?" *What a strange comment*, Venera thought. *Why does she think she can't die?*

Mrs. Gartner didn't answer the question. Instead she said, "You do know people can choose when to die."

"No, I don't."

"Then you're wrong. George chose to die on his birthday. March 19, 2020, a century to the day he was born."

"And you believe he willed it?"

But Mrs. Gartner had shut down, seemingly too exhausted for conversation. Venera was also drained. Not that her circumstances were anywhere near the same, but Venera knew what it was like to feel guilty.

When the massage was done, Venera helped Mrs. Gartner into clean underpants and a soft pink nightgown. Mrs. Gartner resumed talking, but her tone had shifted from sad to bitter. "I've outlived my siblings, my cousins, my friends, and worst of all, my husband. I never wanted to be the last one standing. Never, never, never."

"But, Mrs. Gartner," Venera said. "Your daughter, your great-granddaughter . . . you have people you love who love you and need you."

"That's the problem."

"Why?"

"Nothing, nothing. Ignore me, I'm just rambling."

Gathering up the soiled bedclothes, towels, and wipes, Venera couldn't help feeling that Mrs. Gartner had a lot more going on in her mind than anyone knew. As she tiptoed out of the room, she looked back and saw that Mrs. Gartner was either asleep or feigning sleep. She must have forgotten all about wanting to get up early, Venera thought, and all she said she had to do, whatever that might have been.

SEVEN

The Old Lady

BETTE PRETENDED TO BE SLEEPING UNTIL VENERA LEFT. She had dumped her guilt on the poor young woman and now felt foolish, but even more, she was angry at herself. She had only herself to blame for her inability to walk and the accompanying loss of independence. Had she given physical therapy more of a try after she broke her pelvis, she would still be able to walk, and she would not need a night aide, not that Venera wasn't a fine young woman. She hated having someone live in. She never had, even when Claire was young, except for babysitters.

Having been raised by nannies, Bette wanted her daughter's upbringing solely in her hands. Her father had been too preoccupied with business and life to know what went on, but Bette had a few really nutty nannies. One nanny, for example, used to terrify her with stories about dungeons where "wicked children who bite their nails" were sent. Another warned her that if she ever wandered off, she could be kidnapped like the Lindbergh baby. What Bette took from it was that you never knew what kind of nonsense a child might be told.

Occasionally, when Jia was a toddler, Bette and George would ask if she could stay with them for a few weeks. But even then, although she and George were well in their sixties and looking after a child day and night was a strain, Bette didn't want help. Aside from her concern about nannies in general, being responsible for Jia helped fill the awful void left by Hope's death.

Her mind wandered back to the night she fell, a little over a year ago.

She was going into the living room to get the large-print needle-point book Claire had brought her that afternoon when she tripped on the curled-up edge of a Persian rug and landed on the hardwood floor. When she tried to get up, she was immobilized with pain. Certain that her hip or pelvis was broken, afraid to move and make it worse, knowing that Rosie would find her in the morning when she came to work, Bette spent the night on the floor in a quandary.

If her self-diagnosis was right, she would have to be hospitalized. She knew all too well that at her age, being bedridden in the hospital often led to pneumonia, and pneumonia was the kiss of death. She was also afraid of what she might catch in the hospital. COVID-19 was no longer the threat it had been when George was dying, but even before then, Bette had heard stories of people who got some kind of fatal infection in the hospital.

No, there had to be another option. She remembered George telling her about one of his clients who had managed to get his hip x-rayed at home after a bad fall. She had no way to reach out to that person, but she would figure it out herself once she got off the floor. In the morning, she would get Rosie and Jimmy, the doorman, to put a blanket under her and gently carry her to bed. Then she would be back in charge.

As she lay there in pain, her daughter's often-repeated refrain echoed in her mind: "Mother, no one your age should live alone." Claire wanted her to get live-in help after George died, but Bette, valuing her privacy and independence, refused. The issue came to a head a few weeks after George's death. Bette had been going through condolence letters when Claire arrived with an agenda.

"Mother, you and I have a Zoom appointment with the woman who heads an employment agency. I brought my iPad."

"Are you trying to find me a job to keep me busy?"

"She can find you a home companion."

Bette was always amazed by her daughter's lack of sense of humor, less so by her wanting to take charge. A chip off the old block?

"I don't need a companion, a babysitter, or anyone else watching over me at night," Bette said. "I'm perfectly fine."

"Don't be so militantly independent. Do it for me so I don't have to worry about you."

"That's why I should hire someone? For your peace of mind? What about my peace of mind? I just lost my husband, and I don't need you pushing me. Back off, Claire."

"Mother," Claire said, her tone softer. "It would be company. Now that we all have to stay away from people, we can't even visit you without masks and COVID tests, if we can even get tested. If someone lived with you all the time—"

"And that person would never leave, never have days off . . ."

"Then come live with us."

"In a five-story townhouse with stairs? Where would I sleep?"

"Maybe we could convert the patio into a bedroom."

"So, every time I need to use the bathroom in the middle of the night, I'd have to climb two flights of stairs to your bedroom?"

"We could add a little bathroom next to the—"

"I appreciate the offer, but . . ."

"Okay, then maybe Jack and I should move in here with you."

"Claire, enough. Rosie comes every day, so it's not like I am always alone. She makes sure I have everything I need and wipes everything off, but when she's here, we both have to wear masks, so it's a relief when she leaves. And it's not like I don't know how to entertain myself."

That ended the conversation.

Claire then bought Bette an expensive Apple watch and showed her how to use it in case of a medical emergency. But it was metal and clunky and nowhere near as comfortable as the Fitbit Jia had given her. Its rubberlike band was comfortable to wear, and all she had to do was press a button on the side, and the device lit up with the time. She was told it had other functions, such as measuring her steps. *Maybe I'll go jogging along the Hudson River, all the way up to the bridge and back,* Bette thought with amusement. Mainly though Bette had no intention of having an emergency, and that was that.

But then she had one.

The minute she heard the key in the lock the following morning announcing Rosie's arrival, Bette called out, her voice weak from her all-nighter, "Rosie, is that you?"

"Oh my God, where are you, Mrs. G.?"

"In the living room."

Once she had been carried to her bed per her plan, Bette asked Rosie and Jimmy if they knew of an orthopedist in the area. As luck would have it, Jimmy knew a nurse who worked for one. He knew practically all the staff in the neighboring buildings. Bette instructed Rosie to go to the doctor's office and plead with the nurse to ask the doctor to check her out at home. Rosie was reluctant to leave Bette alone, but as Bette dryly remarked, it wasn't like she could get into a lot of trouble.

Getting the doctor to agree turned out to be easier than Bette had anticipated. He had elderly parents and understood that the last place an old person belonged was in a hospital unless absolutely necessary. An hour or so later, a technician came to the apartment and x-rayed Bette's hip. She had a hairline pelvic fracture and was told to remain off her feet for a few weeks, after which she would need physical therapy, which could also be done at home.

Once the technician left, Bette asked Rosie to bring her her phone so she could call Claire. She was anxious to take charge of the situation before Claire or Rosie had a chance to take over. She could already hear Claire saying, "I told you so."

If she had to have someone there during the night, she wanted it to be a young person who would be far more interested in living her own life than watching over an old lady It wasn't like she needed a nurse, just someone strong enough to help her in and out of the wheelchair and get things for her and smart enough to call for help if and when it was needed.

Despite the ordeal she had just been through, Bette willed herself to sound cheerful. "Good morning, dear. I just wanted to see how the chamber music concert was last night."

"As always, it was lovely—an all Chopin program," Claire said. "You would've loved it."

"You should have asked me. I'm sure Jack would have been happy to sacrifice his seat."

"No doubt. Next time I will."

"Did he manage to stay awake for the entire program?"

Lowering her voice, Claire said, "He nodded off briefly, but he will deny it if you ask him." Bette could hear Jack in the background asking Claire who she was talking to.

"Mother, can I call you back later? I'm late for a yoga class."

"Of course, dear. I just wanted to let you know that everything's fine—I'm okay—but I had a little fall."

"What?" Claire shouted. "Are you all right? Are you in the hospital?"

"Take it easy. I'm home and in bed. I arranged for someone to come to the apartment and x-ray my pelvis."

"You what?"

"I had it x-rayed, right in my own bed. It's just a hairline fracture, but I have to stay off my—"

"I'm coming over."

"No, you are not. I'm perfectly comfortable. I'm watching the *Today* show, and a needlepoint designer named Taylor Swift is about to come on to talk about her new book."

"Taylor Swift? I don't think so."

"Well, that's what they said."

"She's a singer."

"I guess she also does needlepoint."

"Somehow I doubt her designs would interest you."

"You don't know that."

"I'll be there shortly."

"Claire. No. Please. Go to your class. Rosie is here with me. I will need someone to stay over in the back bedroom at night until I'm back on my feet, but I'm on it."

"Meaning?"

"Between Rosie and Jimmy, I'm sure I'll find someone, and if I don't find someone by tonight, Rosie has offered to stay over until I do."

"What about her daughter? She can't leave her alone."

"She's fifteen, so she can, but Patty can also stay with her father."

"Mother, I'm calling a service."

"No, absolutely not! Please, Claire, you must listen to me. I don't want to make a big fuss about this. If I need something, I know how to reach you."

"How are you going to find someone? These days, most of the vetting is done electronically, and you are an absolute cyber-peasant."

"And proud of it. I promise, if I can't find someone, I'll let you know."

Claire was silent, and Bette thought she heard sniffling.

"Are you crying?" Bette asked.

"With Father gone, I don't what I would do if anything happened to you. You are my rock."

"Hardly, dear."

"Oh, but you are."

After hanging up, Bette asked Rosie to go downstairs and ask Jimmy if he knew someone who could help. She would offer him a finder's fee. According to Rosie, he always seemed to know someone looking for a job of one kind or another and got a nice little "unreported" income out of it.

Jimmy did know someone: Brigita. Brigita had worked for a family in the building as a nanny, but they had recently moved to Connecticut, and Brigita opted not to go with them. Now she was looking for work. Bette hired her on the spot.

But even after her bone healed, afraid of another fall after the trauma of that long night, Bette lost the nerve to walk. The longer she remained off her feet, the more her muscles atrophied, so in time walking was no longer a choice.

Now here she was a year later, wedded to a wheelchair, wedded to Rosie, and wedded to Venera, to whom she had unburdened herself. She would never have trusted Brigita with such a secret. Bette found Brigita cold, which was why her decision to follow her boyfriend to Chicago was a relief. Venera, her replacement, seemed simpatico. Still, it was humiliating.

Even more humiliating, Bette thought, was Venera cleaning her up, as well as the job that lay ahead washing the filthy sheets and clothes. What did she do with them anyhow? Every floor in the building had a laundry room near the incinerator. Bette hoped that Venera wouldn't put them in the washing machine as is. Not only would that add to her own humiliation, but their neighbor across the hall, Gertrude Sidenstriker, might smell the odor and know where it came from.

With everything such a hassle, Bette's bucket list was down to one item: letting go. But how could she? Claire's words—"You are my rock"—had played in her mind ever since she heard them. *How could she say such a thing to me?* Bette thought. *I'm not immortal. What does it mean anyhow? How am I her rock? Was it just an outburst at such an emotional time, her way of saying she loves me? Even Jia says things to me like, 'When you go, I'm going with you.' I know she doesn't mean it, but she should think about how that makes me feel. Not good. I hate feeling that needed, and it's silly anyhow. Claire is needed far more than I am, by Jack, by Jia.*

It was all very perplexing and left Bette wondering what "work" she had left to do.

EIGHT

The Old Lady's Night Aide

AFTER LEAVING MRS. GARTNER, VENERA WENT DIRECTLY to the bathroom off the kitchen and tossed everything but the wipes on the shower floor, then dumped the papers into the trash and tied the top.

She brought a bottle of liquid detergent with her into the shower, then turned on the water and stripped. After pouring detergent over the dirty linens, Venera mushed them with her feet until there was no more fecal matter visible. She turned off the tap, then stamped on the linens to get the water out before wringing them out by hand. She scooped them up and dumped them in the sink, then took a long, hot shower.

After she got out, Venera put her head down and back-brushed her long hair one hundred strokes. She thought her hair was her best feature and took good care of it. She eyed herself in the bathroom mirror. Jusef used to tell her she looked just like Billie Eilish, which Venera loved. After all, Billie was a star. She wasn't a great beauty. She was rather plain—not ugly, just plain, short, with a boyish, unsexy body, gray eyes, and long brown hair that she used to hide her face under.

Even though Venera, too, was short and a little plain, with similar coloring, she thought she was better looking than Billie. In fact, the owner of the restaurant in Jelsa where she waitressed put a picture of her holding a platter on the cover of the menu, so she figured she was definitely closer to pretty than plain.

When I go back, Venera mused, *maybe I'll surprise Jusef by cutting my hair shoulder length to look more sophisticated, like, "Hey, no one my age in New York has a braid." Bet he'd like it. I might too. Actually, he wouldn't. Jusef loves catching hold of my braid when I walk too fast. I mean, he used to love catching it. Past tense. But in New York it's a little dangerous. More than once some jerk has grabbed it and tried to stop me. Which is why I now have a bun and take karate lessons at a studio near the apartment. Soon I'll be ready for Bruce Lee!*

Venera took a final glimpse in the mirror and noticed that she looked sad. *Too much thinking will do that. But who wants to look at a sad face? Mrs. Gartner does not need any more negativity right now.* Venera practiced smiling but felt foolish.

She went into the kitchen to take the linens to the laundry room and the trash to the incinerator. They were heavy, and she had to use both arms to carry them. She pushed the back door open with her foot and tried to slip out without letting it slam, knowing that the cranky neighbor across the hall might be lying in wait. She had reason to be concerned.

One day, shortly after she started the job, she was taking out the garbage when the neighbor came tearing out of her apartment to reprimand her. Venera had no idea how the woman even knew she was there unless she made a habit of spying through the peephole in the kitchen door for God knows what. A small green bird was perched on her shoulder and had crapped on the front of her robe, but the woman didn't seem to notice. The bird started screeching, then flew at Venera and tried to bite her.

Venera swatted at the bird, screaming, "Stop it! Stop it."

The woman swatted back at Venera as the bird continued the attack. The battle ended with Venera retreating in fear back into the apartment. Ever since then, she was careful to not alert the neighbor.

However, the bundles she was carrying were awkward and, despite her care, the door slammed behind her. Startled, Venera dropped them. The contents spilled all over the tile floor in front of the incinerator closet. A stink arose, and Venera started gagging. She ran back into the apartment to get another bag and a pair of rubber gloves, then returned to clean up the mess, praying all the while that, by some miracle, the nosy, nasty neighbor Miss Sidenstriker, nocturnal creature that she was, had not woken up.

NINE

The Old Lady's
Across-the-Hall Neighbor

Miss Sidenstriker heard the back door slam and bolted out of bed, ready for battle. Even though the noise rarely woke her, in Miss Sidenstriker's mind it had become a daily occurrence ever since old lady Gartner's previous night aide, Brigita—such a pretty name for such an unattractive person, inside and out, though who was she to talk—moved to Chicago and was replaced by another Eastern European no-doubt-undocumented immigrant—who, for unknown reasons, seemed to think the trash needed to be taken to the incinerator at dawn, even though it meant letting the back door slam behind her, even though she told her repeatedly that it woke her since her bedroom wall was adjacent to the incinerator room, and even though Miss Sidenstriker knew that the Slav bitch Venereal (her pet name for her) didn't get off duty until ten when the Irish housekeeper, Rosie, arrived, which meant Venereal had plenty of time to do it later.

This morning, the noise was so loud that Miss Sidenstriker wondered for a brief moment if there might have been an explosion in the building. She considered calling down to the doorman Jimmy to see if anyone else had heard the noise, but then she remembered that he wasn't on duty until eight and the night doorman barely spoke English.

What a city, she thought, *overrun with immigrants who didn't speak English.* She could never understand why, if they wanted to come to America so badly, they didn't bother to learn English. *I miss the days before Mrs. Gartner's fall, before the invasion of the Slav night aides,* she thought. *Come to think of it, I miss George Gartner, too. And Mom and Dad. And the pandemic, when everyone wore masks and the sidewalks were empty and people stayed home.*

Miss Sidenstriker rolled out of bed, a task that seemed to get harder with every passing year. She walked as fast as her body allowed to the back door, ready to confront Venereal, but she had forgotten that the door was locked. She fiddled with the lock, then yanked the door open, worried she would be too late.

But there she was on all fours, her long hair pinned atop her head, her scrawny little jean-clad butt facing Miss Sidenstriker, scrambling to clean up trash that covered the floor. The can must have fallen out of her hands, hence the racket. And the stench.

Covering her face with her hands, Miss Sidenstriker screamed, "Clumsy fool! How many times do I have to tell you not to slam the door? Every morning, every morning you do the same thing."

Ignoring her, Venera finished what she was doing.

"Hey! You! I'm talking to you," Miss Sidenstriker said, grabbing Venera's arm and squeezing it. "Do you even speak English?"

Venera stood up and glared at Miss Sidenstriker, then pulled up her sleeve to look at the red marks left by Miss Sidenstriker's fingers. *"Jebena kučka,"* Venera muttered menacingly in Croatian. *"Prijavit ću vas policiji."*

What was that last word? Police? Miss Sidenstriker wondered. *Great. Now the Slav bitch will accuse me of assaulting her. They may not speak English, but they sure know how to use the law against you.*

"Venereal," Miss Sidenstriker said in what she considered her sweetest tone of voice. "Can we start the morning over? Please try to be more considerate. I have a heart condition." With that, she put her hand over her heart to drive the point home. "It's not good for me to be startled."

"Is Venera," Venera hissed in Miss Sidenstriker's face. "Ven. Era." With that, she left. Fuming, Miss Sidenstriker went back to bed. Closing her eyes, she fantasized about how she would like to strangle Venereal. *I'll put my fingers around her neck and press my thumbs into the soft spot in the middle until her eyes pop out like the rubber face toy that when squeezed makes the eyes bulge out.* She pictured the look of helplessness on Venereal's round face. The image coupled with her nickname for the woman made her laugh. She so rarely laughed that what came out sounded more like a cough.

Short of living out her fantasy, she decided she needed an ally. Maybe Mrs. Gartner's housekeeper would rein Venereal in. She would speak to Rosie when she came to work at ten. She also considered lodging a complaint against her with the super. When she took a walk later on, she could tell the doorman she needed to speak to him. But then she dismissed the idea as a waste of time. *The help always stick together,* she thought, *viewing tenants as if they were the enemy.*

For the first time since the death of her parents a decade ago—first her father, then her mother—Miss Sidenstriker considered moving into their bedroom. Having idealized them, their bedroom with the dark velvet drapes and heavy mahogany furniture seemed sacrosanct in her mind, especially their bed. She rarely even went into the room; she had no need to. Even though her bedroom was small, it was sufficient for her needs—just not the quiet needed for a good night's rest thanks to Venereal's selfish, uncaring, unkind predawn wake-up calls.

At times, she felt like she had a target on her back that read "Kick Me." Were her parents still alive, Venereal would not have dared to be so discourteous. Her mother knew how dangerous the world was, how mean people could be. Only at home did Miss Sidenstriker ever feel safe.

Awash in self-pity, she revisited the memory that affected her to this day. It was school recess, and she was sitting in her usual spot on a bench reading a book. Her nose was runny because her allergies were bad, and she was in the middle of a sneezing fit when Bitsy Bingham, the most popular girl in her private school class, approached, followed by her coterie of followers.

"Ya sick? Gotta cold, Trudy?" Bitsy asked. Miss Sidenstriker was so unused to being addressed by her peers that she looked around to see who Bitsy was talking to, which Bitsy's groupies seemed to find funny. No one ever called her Trudy except her parents.

"Yeah, Trudy. That is your name, isn't it? I'm talking to you."

"Just allergies."

"Whatcha reading?"

Miss Sidenstriker turned the book around to look at the title in order to buy time before speaking, not sure if it was a trick question.

"Ah . . . *Anne of Green Gables*?" She was so nervous that it came out as a question.

"Any good?"

"It's really wonderful. It's all about—"

"We have a question for you," Bitsy interrupted. She turned around to her groupies and winked, then turned back to Miss Sidenstriker. "Was your mother a strawberry?"

Miss Sidenstriker froze, knowing that when she blew her nose, she must have accidentally wiped off the makeup her mother used to hide the blotchy red birthmark that covered most of her left cheek.

Everyone around her laughed. Another girl started chanting, "Strawberry Sidenstriker," over and over as the others shrieked with laughter.

Then Bitsy started singing the song from the movie *Chitty Chitty Bang Bang*, mangling the lyrics. "Trudy Scrumptious, though we may sound presumptuous, never go away because we love you, Trudy. Honest we do."

"Trudy Scrumptious," Peggy, one of Bitsy's cohorts, screamed. "Trudy Scrumptious, Trudy Scrumptious—Gertrude Sidenstriker, I dub thee forever after Trudy Scrumptious."

"No," Bitsy said. "That's too long. T. Scrum." Thereafter, everyone in the class called her T. Scrum.

Miss Sidenstriker understood then and there that her mother was right. People were basically mean. She had her parents, who were loving, undemanding, nonjudgmental. *What more could anyone need?* she thought.

Except, of course, Captain Flint before . . .

She stopped. It was too painful to go there.

Just then, she heard a man's voice screaming, "Nah, nah, nah, not Hamid-khan. Those bastards," so loudly that it filtered up through the thick floor.

Damn those ill-mannered Iranians, Miss Sidenstriker thought, referring to the family who lived beneath her. *The Iranians*—that was how she referred to them in her mind—*they act like they are the only people in the world*. Over the years, she had had the misfortune of sharing an elevator with the Iranians a few times.

Usually the parents would enter the elevator jabbering away in a bastardized mix of English and Farsi as if she were invisible, as their teenage son talked loudly on his phone. One time she covered her ears in protest. The mother noticed and said, "Dariush, lower your voice." *Dariush*, Miss Sidenstriker thought. *They named their kid Dariush after a king? No wonder he acts entitled.*

But she hadn't seen the parents in years. Maybe they returned to

Iran, good riddance, but then why would they keep the apartment, surely not just for the son, who by now must be in his mid-twenties. Maybe they were one of those super-rich oil families and maintaining a six-room apartment was peanuts to them. But then why would the young man live in the maid's room—unless he wasn't related but was their driver or manservant? That seemed unlikely. And what was happening to him anyhow that was making him howl? Was he being robbed? Or murdered? Or was it some perverse form of sex play? Whatever it was, it had to stop.

She got an umbrella out of the closet and banged on the floor. She continued banging long after the noise stopped. But then she panicked. Suppose he was being attacked by an intruder who had gotten in through the fire escape and now might escape through the window and climb up to her floor? Even though her window had shutters covering it and a padlocked gate as well, she felt uneasy.

Miss Sidenstriker fumbled between her mattress and box springs for the can of Mace she kept there for just such an emergency. Her adrenaline pumped just thinking about such an encounter.

She moved her desk chair to the side of the window, a foot away from the shutters, then sat down, ready and waiting.

TEN

The Old Lady's
Downstairs Neighbor

DARIUSH HEARD THUMPING ON THE CEILING AND WAS startled. He hadn't realized that he was shouting, but apparently Miss Sidenstriker had.

The news he had just seen on Al Jazeera was deeply upsetting. Hamid Amiri, a former colleague of his father who worked for the *Washington Post*, had gone to Iran with his children to introduce them to his homeland and was arrested and charged with being a CIA operative. A patent lie.

Dariush felt sick, fearing that Hamid-khan would be questioned. Not simply questioned but tortured. No doubt his real "crime" was that of belonging to Bahá'í, a religion banned in Iran—Dariush's religion. Hamid-khan was way too savvy to have put his real religion in his passport. More likely it was because he had written about Dariush's father's arrest when he returned to Iran close to seven years ago, hoping to help get him out of prison. Alas, with no success.

Closing his laptop, Dariush eyed the framed postcard-sized photo of Bahá'u'lláh, the founder of the Bahá'í religion, that sat on the desk in his "office." It was so hard to understand why a faith based on tolerance and respect for all religions was so threatening to the mullahs that its followers were persecuted and even murdered, but it was.

Shaken by the news, Dariush was filled with a sense of foreboding. He needed to call his mother to make sure she was alright. He normally called on Fridays, the day of rest in Iran, but he couldn't wait. He punched in the fifteen-digit number to Tehran on his cell phone. As a rule he used WhatsApp so he could see her, but not today when he was upset and scared. She would take one look at him and know, and it would make it hard for both of them.

He waited for his mother to pick up, knowing she would answer. It was afternoon in Tehran, and he assumed she was in his grandmother's kitchen drinking tea. With his free hand, he felt his undershirt. It was soaked in sweat. He yanked it over his head and let it drop on the floor.

"*Salaam Dariush Jan. Chetore?*" his mother responded, her voice calm, interrupting his thoughts. "Hello, dear Dariush, how are you?"

Dariush breathed a sigh of relief. If there was a problem, he would have detected it the moment she said *salaam*.

"Just calling to say hello, Maman."

"Is everything alright? It's only Tuesday."

"I just missed you, that's all."

"I thank God every day you are safe in America."

"Maman . . . the phones." *They* listened to all U. S. calls; he knew *they* did.

"*Chashm,*" she said. "Okay. How did you do in the backgammon competition?" Dariush had competed in the 18th New York Metro Open.

"I did well."

"You won?"

"No, but I played well."

"That's great. Your dad, may he rest in peace, would have been so proud of you. George Gartner too. How George loved taking you on."

Anxious to change the subject, Dariush said, "Maman, I heard the news about . . ."—he searched for a way to ask in code—"Habib. Is it true he is . . ." again he paused, "engaged?"

"Habib," she repeated, letting Dariush know she had gotten the message. "Yes. Habib is very happy." *So*, Dariush thought, *he must have been released. He sure got lucky. What a dumb risk he took going back to Iran, not just for himself but his family.*

"Any news of Baba?" he asked.

"Not really."

Dariush didn't know why he even bothered asking about his father. Whenever he thought about his father living in the torture chamber known as Evin, he got depressed. It was so hard not knowing how his father really was. *How long could he take it? God knows what they may have done to him.*

"Okay, talk to you soon. Send my love to Mamanjan. *Khoda hafez.*" Dariush spoke quickly before hanging up, afraid his mother would put his grandmother on the phone. He didn't feel up to talking to her.

That damn news story, Dariush mused. Even though Hamid-khan had been released, every Bahá'í in Iran lived under the threat of arrest. His mother was at high risk. A journalist, she wrote articles about the plight of the Bahá'ís under a pseudonym and leaked them to colleagues in America. Dariush desperately wanted her to stop, but there was no way to say it directly, assuming their calls and emails were monitored. Not that she would have listened.

Thoroughly agitated, he forgot all about the upstairs neighbor signaling him to be quiet and roared in frustration at the top of his lungs.

It didn't take long for the thumping to resume.

Dariush went to his bedroom to try to sleep, but no sooner did he lie down than an uninvited and unwelcome image of George Gartner lying on the living room floor in a pool of blood rushed at him. He hadn't thought about him in a long time, but his mother mentioning his name and his overall state of disquiet must have triggered the image.

Dariush leapt out of bed. He did not want to go there; it was an image that flashed in front of him when he was stressed, as he was now. He had to do something to relieve his nerves. Perhaps a shower, then a run alongside the river path next to the West Side Highway before heading to work at the New York Historical Society? Yes, that's what he would do. Then, at the end of the day, he would go to Zabars. He needed some Gruyère and white cheddar cheese so he could make a three-layer grilled cheese sandwich for dinner with the peasant bread he had baked the previous night.

ELEVEN

The Old Lady's Daughter

B EFORE LEAVING FOR WORK, JACK MADE CLAIRE PROMISE TO call a therapist. "Got the message," she said, implying that she would without actually lying.

Claire walked up the stairs to Hope's old bedroom and stood in front of the door, frozen. Putting her hand on the doorknob, Claire waited for the urge to enter to pass. Instead, she felt compelled to go in. She needed to know if her reaction to sleeping in Hope's room was a knee jerk response or perhaps worth considering.

As she entered, she felt as if she had fallen back into the 1980s. The walls were covered with floral Laura Ashley wallpaper that matched the bedspread on the white canopy bed. All of Hope's stuffed animals had been given to Jia, but the needlepoint pillow Claire's mother had made, with the quote "Where There's a Will, There's a Way" in the center, remained on the bed. One entire wall was devoted to a collage of posters, photographs, stickers, and notes tacked to a corkboard. Claire had almost forgotten her daughter's Michael Jackson phase, but there MJ was, his poster tacked to the wall along with Michael J. Fox and the *Top Gun* movie poster with Tom Cruise.

Sprinkled between photos of Hope with her friends were some photos that Claire still remembered taking. Hope at seven sitting up in bed, holding her arms out for a good night hug. Hope at twelve lying on the floor in her "be happy" T-shirt with her friend Stacy, motioning to the camera/Claire that they needed privacy. Hope at fifteen in her pajamas, hugging a stuffed animal. Hope at eighteen packing for college, wearing a Boston University sweatshirt.

Claire walked over to the white desk and pushed the play button on the tape recorder. Stevie Wonder's voice rang out, "I Just Called to Say I Love You." Claire lay down on the bed and folded her arms across her face, caught up in memories of the past.

Hope going off to college was the start of the next chapter of Claire's life, the end of the hands-on parenting that had been her primary focus. Not that Hope didn't return home for vacations, but in her freshman year she met an MIT student, Daeshim Kahng, and after that, nothing was the same.

"Mom, a guy I know, he goes to MIT," Hope's call home had begun. "He lives in Seoul and has nowhere to go over the holidays. Mind if he stays with us over Christmas break?" That was how Hope had phrased it—a friend—which her parents thought meant someone who could stay in the top-floor bedroom Claire used as a studio that doubled as a guest room.

Hope arrived home with Daeshim a few days before Christmas. "Mom and Dad, this is my friend Daeshim, but everyone calls him Dae," Hope said as the four of them stood in the entrance hall.

Claire's first impression of Daeshim was positive. Tall, good-looking, impeccable manners, classy, mature for his age—but that may have been because there was a formality about him.

"Welcome," Claire said, noting that Hope seemed a little flushed. She nudged Jack, who seemed fixated on the fact that Hope was clutching Daeshim's arm.

"Thank you so much for your hospitality," Dae said with a slight accent. "I can't tell you how nice it is to meet you. You have a lovely daughter."

When Jack didn't respond, Hope jumped in to cover up for her father's silence. "I can't wait to show Dae the Christmas windows on Fifth Avenue," she told Claire. "He's never been to New York."

"I'm really looking forward to it," Dae said, equally enthused.

Again Jack had nothing to add to the conversation, which Claire found awkward. "Why don't you start by showing Dae our tree?" Claire suggested.

"I'd love to see it," Dae said.

The minute Hope and Dae had gone upstairs to the living room on the second floor, Claire lit into Jack. "What's your problem?"

"He's more than a friend."

"So?" If he was more than "just a guy I know," Claire was glad. As far as she knew, Hope had never had a serious boyfriend.

"Is your issue that he's Korean?"

"Of course not, although being from such different cultures creates all sorts of problems in relationships."

"You already have them married?"

"Do you think they're sleeping together?"

"Possibly."

"Better not happen under my roof."

"Seriously?" Claire asked Jack as he were from another planet. *Why do so many men have double standards when it comes to their daughters?* Claire thought. Were Hope a boy, Jack wouldn't have batted an eyelash.

"Does Hope know anything about contraception?"

"Yes. I mean, I'm sure she does."

"Jesus Christ, Claire. You haven't spoken to her about it?"

"Of course I have. Jack, what is going on with you? Your daughter is growing up. It's okay."

"Not okay if she winds up pregnant with her first boyfriend ever."

Claire knew that Jack was right; she should have had a frank talk with Hope about sex. *Coulda, woulda, shoulda.* How could she admit that to Jack? She wasn't even sure she knew why she hadn't, probably because she didn't want to have to explain what had happened to her.

But, of course, Hope must have guessed; it was so silly to keep up the pretense. Claire could envision Hope's response to the discussion. "Mom, you're awfully invested in my not getting pregnant. Does this have anything to do with you having me seven months after you and Dad got married and me weighing eight pounds?"

Besides which, Hope and her friends had seemed so well informed, even when they were barely in their teens. Once, when Hope was in seventh grade, Claire overheard her on the phone with a friend. "Hear what happened at the party?" Hope had said, then started laughing. "Yeah, two BJs . . . in the girls bathroom. . . . Lynn was in another stall and heard everything."

Claire wasn't sure which shocked her more, her daughter's casual mention of blow jobs or the fact that kids her age were already sexually active. Before she hung up, Claire heard Hope say, "No, no, it's gross. I wouldn't," which was reassuring. To Claire's knowledge, Hope didn't get into trouble of any kind, and now that she had a nice boyfriend, who may or may not be the first, at least it didn't have to be a secret any longer.

After graduation, Hope and Daeshim moved into an apartment together in Brooklyn, and while Claire and Jack saw them frequently, their home/this bedroom was no longer Hope's home/Hope's bedroom. Two years later they got married.

A year later their daughter was born. They named her Bette Jia Kahng, but called her Jia, which meant beautiful in Korean. And that she was, inside and out. Everyone doted on her.

When Jia was four, Hope and Dae took Jia to Seoul to meet her other grandparents. While there, Hope was hit by a car while riding a bike in heavy traffic and died of head injuries.

Claire tried unsuccessfully to turn off the memory of that awful day when Dae called to say that Hope had been killed. She kept asking him to repeat himself, not wanting to believe it was real. The minute she hung up, she called Jack, then her parents, but she was crying so hard that she couldn't get the words out.

Her parents got there first, and when she was finally able to relay the news, her father collapsed. Hope was his adored and adoring namesake. By the time Jack got home, her father had recovered. For Claire, that day became the dividing line between Before and After, as if she had lived two different lives.

Overcome with grief that felt as fresh as the day it happened, Claire stumbled toward the door. She needed to get out of the room that held so many memories, determined to never put herself through that again. No, she could not, would not, be able to sleep in it. End of story.

But then she stopped. While she couldn't imagine sleeping in the room, at least she could clear it out, give the clothes away. It wasn't as if holding on to them kept Hope alive somehow. But to whom should she give the clothes? Jia was the most likely choice, but she was petite, maybe a size two or four, and Hope had been a size eight. Her mother's night aide Venera looked about the same size—maybe she might like something. And the rest she would donate.

TWELVE

The Old Lady

A<small>T THE SAME TIME</small> C<small>LAIRE WAS RELIVING THE WORST</small> trauma of her life, her mother was waking up.

As Bette got her bearings, she recalled with dismay that she had soiled herself and then let her guard down with Venera. But then she chided herself. *Focus on your decision, old girl. Forget your humiliation. Time to reboot your early morning excitement.*

She reached over to the Echo Dot on her nightstand that Jia had gifted her the previous Christmas. What a gift it was, possibly the best gift of her life, certainly of her old age. She was sorry George never got to have such a toy, knowing he would have loved to have had Ella Fitzgerald or Dinah Shore or Helen O'Connell at his fingertips, metaphorically speaking.

Bette tapped the Echo Dot and said, "Some Enchanted Evening." She loved hearing Ezio Pinza's rich Italian bass crooning close to her ear. As was often the case, but especially this morning, Bette was awash in memories of George, and the lyrics swept her back in time to her third date with him.

They had gone dancing at the Palladium on Broadway and 53rd Street, even though Bette had told him she was a terrible dancer, in part because of her limp.

"I don't care if you're a good dancer or a bad dancer. I just want an excuse to hold you," he had said.

She didn't know if it was a line or not, but she didn't care. She was aching for him to hold her. He had never so much as kissed her on the cheek.

As he led her onto the dance floor, George walked over to the bandleader and whispered in his ear, then handed him a folded bill. A moment later, the band started playing one of the most popular songs of the day: "Some Enchanted Evening." Holding Bette close in his arms, George sang along with the male singer of the big band. The lyrics were all about how when you find someone you truly love, you should never let them go.

To say that Bette was surprised would be an understatement. Even though she was already falling in love, she had no idea that it was mutual.

"Mrs. Gartner, are you ready to get out of bed?" Venera called from behind the door.

Startled, Bette called back, "No!" She didn't feel ready to face Venera.

"Everything okay?"

"Yes."

Bette tried to get out of bed and into her wheelchair by herself. *I'm not totally helpless*, she reasoned. *Once I'm in my wheelchair, I can easily wheel myself into the bathroom, wash my face, and brush my teeth.*

Bette grunted and groaned as she struggled to hoist herself off the bed and into her wheelchair. The door opened, and Venera ran in. "Sorry, but I was waiting outside the door and could hear you," Venera said, rushing to her side. "Don't do that. You could fall."

Bette dropped back onto the bed, tired by the effort and grateful to have been rescued. *What was I thinking?* she wondered. *This is no day to take chances.*

"Help me into the chair," Bette demanded, her frustration coming out as anger.

"Do you need a moment to rest?"

"No, there isn't time."

"Mrs. Gartner, you have all the time you need," Venera said. She put her arms under Bette's arms and lifted her in the wheelchair.

"No, not today, I don't."

"Why?"

Ignoring the question, Bette snapped, "I want to get dressed."

"Now, before breakfast?"

"Yes, now. Bring me the pale blue shirtdress that's in the closet."

"You aways wear a pantsuit. Why a dress?" Venera asked.

"Don't question me, Venera. I know what I want." Bette knew she was being curt with Venera because of her earlier embarrassment and shame. She was acting like it was Venera's fault, and the sweet girl had been really kind, but she couldn't help herself.

"Which closet is it in?"

"The one closer to the bathroom. The other one holds my evening clothes," Bette said.

Venera found the dress and brought it over to Bette just as "Some Enchanted Evening" was ending.

"That song is so beautiful," Venera said.

"It's from a show called *South Pacific*," Bette said, being chatty to make up for her earlier sharpness. "My husband sometimes sang it to me. He would put the album on his beloved Capehart record player, then hold out his hand, and I would go to him, and we would dance around the living room."

"Mrs. Gartner, that is the most romantic thing I've ever heard in my life. My fiancé would never do such a thing," Venera said as she straightened the bed sheets.

"I didn't know you were engaged."

"I was," Venera said, then quickly added, "I mean, I am."

"Someone you met him here?"

"No, he's from my hometown. Jelsa."

"Then what are you doing here?"

"Is this okay?" Venera asked, holding up dress for Bette to see.

"It's fine," Bette said, wondering why Venera hadn't answered her question. *Perhaps one of them had a change of heart? I'm sure there's a story here, but I won't pry. Maybe she, too, is a private person. I can respect that.*

"How did you know your husband was the right person for you?" Venera asked.

"I'm not sure you ever really know. We were just lucky."

"How did you meet?"

"It was such a long time ago. Do you really want to know?"

"I really do, Mrs. Gartner."

"I don't have much time, so I'll make it short. I had gone to B. Altman—that was a department store on 34th and Fifth Avenue that closed many years ago—to buy a book on needlepoint designs. Afterward I was standing in front of one of their windows admiring the Christmas display when a passerby slipped on the ice and crashed into me, and we both fell down."

"Were you hurt?"

"More startled than hurt, though my knees were bruised and bleeding."

"What about the man?"

"George was okay, but he was so embarrassed—"

"Your future husband," Venera said, clapping her hands.

"Don't get ahead of me," Bette said, amused by Venera's enthusiasm. "He was also concerned about my knees."

"He should have been. It was his fault."

"Venera, it was an accident. A happy accident, as it turned out. Now that you know how we met, help me into the dress."

It was about two sizes too big.

"Do you want me to get you a belt?"

"No, I'd rather be comfortable. No one's going to see me except the medium."

"What's a medium?"

"Someone who tries to help you make contact with the dead."

"Mrs. Gartner, do you believe in that?"

"I do. It just doesn't always work."

"Rosie didn't mention the appointment to me."

"I don't have an appointment," Bette said in a firm voice, sending the message that they had talked enough. "But I need my phone. I think I left it in the study, and bring me the printout of Jia's latest article. Rosie left it on the coffee table in the living room for me to read."

Once Venera was out of the room, Bette returned to the memory of that fateful day. George had been so flustered and adorable, she fell for him almost on the spot. He insisted that she come with him to Polk's Hobbies on 33rd Street, where she could get her knees cleaned up.

"I go there all the time," he had said. "They know me, and they have a bathroom you can use. By the way," he said, "my name is George Gartner."

"Bette Fox."

"Not Foxy?"

"Not yet," Bette said, laughing.

George held his arm for her, and she took it—not that she needed it.

"You're limping," George said. "I'm really sorry."

"I have a slight limp because one of my legs is a little shorter than the other. I had polio as a child."

"Oh," George muttered, "that's terrible." He seemed embarrassed.

"Not really. It was when I was a kid. Ancient history." Bette knew she was glossing over what had been a challenging period in her childhood, but she didn't feel up to going into detail. Besides, as she had told him, it was a long time ago. At the moment, her focus was on her stinging knee and the man at her side.

At Polk's Hobbies, then subsequently at lunch, she found out that he was a junior partner at a patent law firm and, like her, born and raised in the city. He performed card tricks as a hobby at children's parties, and most importantly, he was single.

At the time, Bette, a junior at Wellesley, had little experience dating, especially someone ten years her senior. If George had asked her to spend the night with him, she might have been tempted—that's how smitten she was—but he didn't. George was a gentleman. And she knew she wouldn't have dared to go anyhow.

When Venera returned with the phone, Bette immediately called Rosie. It went to voice mail, so she left a message:

"Rosie, I need you to come as soon as you get this and plan to stay late. Tonight, I am giving a dinner party."

"You are?" Venera asked, her voice unable to mask her surprise.

"Yes. And I will need you to help Rosie. Needless to say, I will compensate you for your time. Now, bring me the Chloe perfume bottle on top of my dresser."

As soon as Venera brought the bottle over, Bette put her finger over the top and turned the bottle upside down. "Oh no, it's empty." She dabbed what little perfume there was on her neck. "I'm ready for my breakfast."

Venera headed for the door.

"Wait!" Bette said.

"Yes, Mrs. Gartner?"

"What I said earlier . . . about killing my husband. Keep that between us."

"Of course."

THIRTEEN

The Old Lady's
Great-Granddaughter

Afer her bath and phone call with Rosie, Jia went back to bed, hoping to fall back asleep.

"I have good news," Kenny shouted from the kitchen, waking Jia up. She glanced at the digital clock on her bedtable and was shocked to see that it was almost eight.

"I'm in the bedroom," she called.

Arnold bounded in ahead of Kenny.

"Did I wake you?" Kenny asked.

"It's fine. I have to get my piece written anyhow. So, what's the good news?"

"This guy in my office, he told me he and his wife are thinking of getting a dog, so I texted him to see if he wants Arnie."

"You what?" Jia said, as Arnold jumped on the bed. Jia grabbed him and held him against her chest.

"What're you doing? I'm confused."

"You keep making decisions on your own that involve me."

"Damnit, Jia, you all but said you didn't want to keep Arnold. I give up."

Kenny walked out of the bedroom.

"Hey, Kenny!" Jia called. "Come back. We need to talk."

"I have to shower and get ready for work."

Pissed, Jia got out of bed and headed for the bathroom to confront Kenny, but she was too late—the shower was already running. For a moment, Jia had almost forgotten about her fear. Almost. But now it came back.

Figuring out what to do about Arnold or Kenny's tendency to walk away from an argument were not today's top priority. She had more urgent concerns, the first of which was to figure out who could pick her up after the procedure. She hated to push Rosie, who seemed reluctant, but her options were limited. Certainly not Nana or Papa. The last thing she would ever want to do would be to worry them if it turned out to be nothing. Nor did she want to alarm any of her friends or coworkers, who would forever after monitor her health even if she was A-OK. That left Kenny, but the idea of even saying the word *cancer* out loud stopped her.

Just then, the laxatives she had taken to flush out her intestines kicked in, and she was desperate to get into the bathroom. She banged on the door.

"Let me in," she shouted.

When Kenny didn't respond, she figured he couldn't hear through the sound of the water. She tried the door, but it was locked. Locked! Furious, she pounded on the door.

"Damnit, open up! I have to use the toilet." By now she was doubled over in pain. "Kenny, open the goddamn door. I'm having a colonoscopy. I may have cancer."

When again there was no response, Jia raced to the tiny guest bathroom off the foyer. As she sat on the toilet, she was relieved Kenny hadn't heard. Being a lawyer, he would have a lot of questions and would insist on meeting the doctor first, which would increase her anxiety. No, her best bet was to ask the receptionist to put her in an Uber after the procedure. And if that wasn't okay, then she would sleep off whatever they had given her to put her out in the waiting room.

Her appointment wasn't until eleven, and she really needed to get that article finished. Jia sat down at her desk, opened her laptop, and started typing. "The queen-sized bed has an antique, semicircular, inlaid wood headboard in the same period and style as the dresser," Jia read aloud from a Word file on her laptop. "(Note to self: Confirm the period.) Above the dresser is a large mirror with an intricately carved gold wood frame. In the center of one wall is a marble fireplace with a still life of neutral-colored assorted jars and a vase holding pink and white peonies above it. Two rose velvet armchairs face the fireplace, each with a needlepoint pillow designed and made by Bette Gartner. (Note to self: Okay to use Granny's name but don't mention that it's her bedroom.) One reads 'Old Age Isn't for Sissies,' the other 'Laugh and the World Laughs with You. Cry and You Cry Alone.' There is a small glass table between the chairs that holds a collection of Limoges boxes, giving the room a homey feeling despite its elegance."

"This sucks," Jia shouted, deleting the passage she had just written. She hated the assignment, hated style pieces in general. *Who cares about "Some of Manhattan's Most Beautiful Rooms"?* She knew that if her Nana or Granny knew that one of the rooms she was using was Granny's, they would be upset, but too late now to do anything about it.

She started over.

"As I entered the bedroom, I felt like I had stepped into the past. Light poured into the spacious ash-paneled bedroom through two large windows flanked by floor-to-ceiling pale-green silk drapes, with rose, pink, and white-tasseled fringes bordering the edges. A rather delicate antique desk [Note to self: check the period] stood between the windows. Beneath each window was a stand that held orchid plants, a few in bloom but most of them cut back awaiting a second life. Between the wallpaper covered with birds and leafy vines [Note to self: find out wallpaper company] and the plush, pale-green carpeting, there's a sense of being in a garden."

Just as she felt that she was on a roll, she heard the ping of an arriving email. She checked, and it was from her dad saying that he hoped to come to New York on business in June. *Appa,* Jia thought, *oh Appa.* If she did have cancer, just the thought of telling him put her back in full anxiety mode. She would have to find a way to put off his visit. She wouldn't be able to manage his pain along with everyone else's. *Nana and Papa and Granny—it will kill them. Kenny, too, will be heartbroken.*

As much as she missed her great-granddad, for the first time in the years since his death, she was glad he was gone. One less person to share the pain. How she had loved him! What other child had a great-grandfather who would bring her to Korean lessons every Saturday, sit in on them, and then take her to Rumpelmayer's for tea and pastry followed by a walk across the park? What other kid had a great-grandfather who performed card tricks at their birthday parties?

She placed her fingers over the keyboard, willing herself to finish the article, but try as she might, she was unable to come up with one more word of fluff. Finally she gave up. *Fuck work,* she thought. *What do I care about my job, I could be dead in a year.*

Closing the laptop, she lay her head on it. Her back ached, a sure sign that the cancer had spread to her bones. Her head ached, too, and she blanked on the name of her doctor. *Could the cancer have spread to my brain that quickly?* she wondered.

Kenny passed by her desk, heading for the door. Jia knew that he had to see her, but he seemed to be deliberately ignoring her. After he left, Jia had a sudden urge to fill him in. She rushed to the door and opened it.

"Kenny! Wait!"

But she was too late. *He probably ran down the stairs*, she thought, *his preferred method of exercise.* She considered calling him, but the impulse to tell him was gone.

Arnold started whining, and Jia realized that Kenny must have put him in his crate before going to work. She went into the kitchen to free him. As she knelt down to unlatch the crate, Arnold's tail started wagging. The second she opened the door, he jumped on her and covered her with wet dog kisses.

Plopping down on the floor next to the crate, Jia scooped Arnold into her arms and nuzzled him. "My own little service pup," she said, then burst into tears. Arnold kept licking her face, which made Jia cry even harder. It was like the floodgates had opened, and it took a few minutes before Jia managed to get control of herself. "Okay, enough," she said, half laughing as she wiped her face against her shoulder. "What have you done to me, Arnie?" She put the puppy down, stood up and stretched, then picked Arnold back up. "I wish I could take you with me to the doctor. I'm going to need you."

Still holding the dog, Jia went back to her bedroom and sat down on her side of the bed. "Five minutes, that's all. Then I have to leave." She slid under the covers and tucked Arnold in beside her. "Good thing Kenny can't see us. I'm breaking every rule." Absentmindedly stroking the dog's head, Jia said, "What do you think, Buddy? Was I wrong not to tell Kenny? Don't answer. I'm like you; I prefer to lick my own wounds. You understand."

Jia closed her eyes. Within seconds she fell asleep.

FOURTEEN

The Old Lady's Housekeeper

WHEN ROSIE OPENED THE KITCHEN DOOR TO APT 14B, Venera was waiting for her.

"You won't believe this," Venera said, her tone matching her disbelief. "Mrs. Gartner is giving a dinner party. Tonight."

"Are you sure you understood what she said?" Rosie asked, taken aback. She was not in the mood for additional surprises.

"Yes. She's been anxiously waiting for you so she can tell you what you need to make. Didn't you listen to her phone message?"

"No, it's been a rather . . ." Rosie paused, searching for the right word, ". . . hectic morning." She wasn't sure why she hadn't just told Venera about Patty's cat bite, but she didn't have the patience to go into it at that moment, especially given that she had just been informed about a dinner party for that same night.

"I better see what Mrs. G. has in mind. I'm out of practice. She hasn't had a party since long before Mr. G. passed."

"That's not all," Venera said. "She asked me to get her into a dress instead of what she usually wears and is waiting for you to take her somewhere."

"Take her out?"

"I think so."

"Did she say where?"

"She mentioned a medium."

"Jesus, Mary, Mother of God."

As Rosie was about to go to Mrs. G.'s bedroom, Venera stopped her to tell her about the ugly confrontation she had had with Miss Sidenstriker.

"I dread running into her," Venera said. "I pretend not to hear or understand. Don't ever tell her my English is good, Rosie. I fake it with her to avoid conversation. I even put on more of an accent."

Rosie laughed. "Good one, Venera."

"I need to take a walk by the river to clear my head. Mrs. Gartner was up at four and then again an hour later when she had an accident."

"What do you mean?"

"She poo'd in her pants."

"I told you that could happen."

"It's okay. I cleaned it up. But I could use some fresh air. When I get back, I can help you."

When Venera left, she let the door slam behind her. *The girl's got spunk, that's for sure*, Rosie thought, amused.

A moment or so later, she heard Miss Sidenstriker shout, "You! Venereal!"

Rosie opened the door to see what was going on. Venera was pushing the down elevator button over and over as if that would hasten its arrival as Miss Sidenstriker jabbed her right index finger in Venera's face.

"Do you speak English?" Miss Sidenstriker asked in the kind of loud, slow voice people often used when speaking to a foreigner as if the person were deaf. When the elevator arrived, Venera rushed in without answering. As the doors closed, Miss Sidenstriker angrily wagged her finger at Venera in a warning gesture.

"What was that all about?" Rosie asked.

Miss Sidenstriker spun around, her eyes sending daggers at Rosie. "Are you spying on me?"

"What?" Rosie asked. "No. I heard voices and wanted to make sure—"

"I didn't take you to be a busybody. My mistake."

"I'm not. But I heard you yelling at Venera."

"Next time mind your own goddamn business."

"That wasn't necessary, Miss Sidenstriker," Rosie said, using all her discipline not to say something really rude she knew she would regret. *That woman has changed in the last couple of months*, Rosie thought. *Not that she wasn't always a lonely, pathetic woman, but she didn't used to be this nasty. God rest his soul, I think Mr. G. actually enjoyed her company. He had the patience of a saint.*

Rosie waited for Miss Sidenstriker to return to her apartment, but the woman was looking over Rosie's shoulder, riveted by something she saw in the living room. Rosie turned to see what had caught her attention. It was the mother-daughter portrait above the mantelpiece. She was about to tell Miss Sidenstriker who was in it when she changed her mind, thinking it was none of her business.

"Excuse me," Rosie said. She was about to close the door in Miss Sidenstriker's face when Miss Sidenstriker put her hand out to stop her.

"I'm sorry if I was sharp with you," she said, her face contorted into what looked like an attempt to smile. "It was just . . ." Clutching her heart, Miss Sidenstriker continued. "My heart was racing and . . ."

Here we go. Who does she think she's fooling with that act? Rosie thought. *She's probably going to live to be 120 or older, like the cockroach that she is.*

Miss Sidenstriker's face tightened as she began again. "It is not good for me to get upset. Maybe you can say something to Venereal. She's very thoughtless. Someone needs to teach her how to close the door without letting it slam."

"Miss Sidenstriker, you know perfectly well her name is not Venereal. It's Venera. Venera."

"What do you care?" Miss Sidenstriker said.

"I care about Venera. Name-calling is beneath you." Rosie was shocked at her own rudeness, but she didn't work for the woman; she could say whatever she wanted to say, and her resolve to not react to her meanness was gone.

"Bet she's undocumented," Miss Sidenstriker stammered as her birthmark turned purple. "I am going to call ICE."

"You wouldn't!" Rosie said, her voice filled with shock.

Miss Sidenstriker smirked, which Rosie wasn't sure how to interpret. *Is she just trying to get a reaction out of me?* Rosie wondered. *On the other hand, she is just mean enough to do it. I'd better turn this around fast.*

"Miss Sidenstriker, please. Mrs. Gartner is very old and doesn't adjust well to changes in her care. She has never done anything to you."

Miss Sidenstriker turned around and was almost at her apartment door when Rosie came up with an idea. "Wait," Rosie said, speaking at Miss Sidenstriker's back. "I think we have some leftover mud pie from yesterday. Let me bring you some." Rosie knew that Miss Sidenstriker loved sweets because at night she often left a paper plate of extra dessert by her kitchen door that would be gone in the morning. Miss Sidenstriker paused a moment, then opened her apartment door and hurried inside. *Oh well, I tried*, Rosie thought, as she went back inside Mrs. G.'s apartment.

A moment later she heard footsteps cross the hallway between the two apartments, and then Miss Sidenstriker yelled outside the door, "I am seventy-one years old with a serious heart condition, and I cannot afford to be startled awake every morning."

What a piece of work she is, Rosie thought. *Not even a dog could love such a person.*

FIFTEEN

The Old Lady's Across-the-Hall Neighbor

MISS SIDENSTRIKER FELT SALIVA GATHERING IN HER mouth as she returned to her apartment. Mud pie, her absolute favorite, but a trap. If she accepted Rosie's peace offering, it would be as if she were willing to overlook the fact that the Irish bitch had chastised her. Then tried to give her a guilt trip. The nerve of her.

If Miss Piggy had an ounce of decency in her, when she said she had a heart condition, she would have said something along the lines of "I am so, so sorry, Miss Sidenstriker. I will reprimand Venereal, and please know to call on me anytime you need anything," but did that happen? No. Peace? Not likely.

It wasn't always like that. During the final years of George Gartner's life, she and Rosie had been allies of a sort. Miss Sidenstriker would on occasion hear shuffling footsteps in the hallway. When she looked out the peephole, she would see George—that's what old man Gartner asked her to call him—wandering around.

The first time it happened, he was in his pajamas, which seemed strange for such a dignified man. But by then, he was really old and at times a little senile. She was familiar with dementia. In her father's final year, he had declined and had to be closely watched. One time, for example, he slipped out of the apartment and took the elevator to the basement. She and her mother were frantic with worry, searching all over until they found him.

Miss Sidenstriker decided to ask George if he needed help finding the door to his apartment on the hunch that he felt lost. To her great surprise, he asked if he could come in. She thought he must be bored and needed to see a fresh face, not that her face was fresh. She considered inviting him in. She was also a little bored, and it was so out of the ordinary for her that it almost seemed like an adventure. It wasn't like he was going to attack her or anything. But then it occurred to her that his wife would worry he was missing.

"First, let me tell Rosie you're here," Miss Sidenstriker said.

"No, I don't want them to know," he said with a chuckle. "They'll make me come back." *Let them stew*, she thought, as she opened the door.

The first thing he did as he sat down in her kitchen was ask if she had any whiskey. *So that's what he wants*, she thought. *Why not?* She was not much of a drinker, but her parents had a fairly well-stocked bar. Since their passing, she occasionally helped herself to a drink when stressed. She didn't care what it was, she hated all of it, but she wasn't going for taste—just the effect.

The first visit was brief. After he had a shot of whiskey, energized, he thanked her and left. Thereafter, he would occasionally come begging for another nip. It was usually after five. As he told her, in the old days it was the time when he would have had a pre-dinner drink or two. But his wife wouldn't let him drink anymore; she said it interfered with his medications. She had even locked their liquor cabinet. But Miss Sidenstriker wasn't his wife, and she didn't like denying him what must be one of his few remaining pleasures.

Miss Sidenstriker soon realized that Rosie knew where he was. Otherwise, she would have been up and down the hallways calling for him. On subsequent visits, after half an hour or so, Rosie would ring the doorbell, two short rings. It became their signal to send him home. Shortly afterward, Miss Sidenstriker would walk him to his back door, and Rosie would let him in. It was as if she and Rosie had a secret pact.

In the beginning, he talked, and she listened. He told her all about his long career as an attorney, about how once a week he did pro bono work for young inventors who couldn't afford legal fees, and about the terrible tragedy of his granddaughter Hope's death. One time, when he was older and closer to death—and had had more than a sip of whiskey—he spoke about being a soldier in World War II. Clearly the trauma had never left him, and Miss Sidenstriker had the feeling that he had kept it bottled up inside all these decades.

"When I came back, Trudy (by now they were both on a first name basis, and George used her nickname, which she didn't mind coming from him), I was not the same person. At the time no one knew what post-traumatic stress disorder was, but I was a mess."

"In what way?"

"I was jumpy. Every time a truck backfired or a siren went by, my whole body would shake. Bette would have to hold me until I calmed down."

"Well, George," Miss Sidenstriker had said, "I don't know how any decent person could come back whole after the constant fear of being injured or killed."

George picked up the thread. "It was against everything I've ever believed in. Seeing your friends blown up, you can never erase those images. But almost as bad, having to kill people. It was—" He stopped there and never talked about it again.

She came to welcome his visits. It was the only relationship she had ever had in her life where she felt she served a purpose. She had never felt that before, not even with her parents, who had each other. *How ironic was that? Me, in a therapeutic role.*

Amazed that anyone would share such personal information with others, Miss Sidenstriker was satisfied to let him do all the talking. But then, he seemed to run out of steam and switched his focus to her.

He seemed genuinely interested, so she relented. Their conversations became the most intimate ones she had ever had before or since. Just as he had needed to pour out his life story, so did she. It was relatively easy doing it with an old man at the end of his life. Even if he remembered what she had said, who was he going to tell?

She started with her work; that seemed safe enough. She confessed that after graduating from Barnard, she had trouble finding a job to her liking because her people skills were so limited. She finally got a job as a bookkeeper through an employment agency, but it was far below her education and abilities, and it didn't last. Same story over the next two years when she found most of the people she had to work with were lazy or incompetent, and she wasn't shy about saying so. As a result, she was fired twice and quit once.

One day, by chance she bumped into a fellow Barnard classmate at the Neue Gallery who mentioned a job opening as a copy editor at a publishing company in Boston, and she jumped at it, even though it meant leaving Manhattan and her parents. Her parents begged her not to go, worried about her being alone in a big city where God knows what could happen to her. But her belief that an educated woman should be self-supporting was greater than her fear of the unknown.

Her salary afforded her a sunny, if small, one-bedroom apartment in a charming old brownstone on Newbury Street that had been converted into apartments. To her relief, she liked the city of Boston with all its history and culture.

On one of his visits, George surprised her by asking why she had never married. No one had ever asked her that before, and it was no one's goddamn business, but she decided to tell him the truth and keep it short.

"In college I had to read and write a paper about *Lady Chatterley's Lover*. I almost dropped out of the course, not that I didn't know there was smut, but why read it? The idea of having to share a bed, much less what goes on under the sheets . . . well, no thank you."

George had a good laugh over that, saying, "Too bad. You missed out on a lot of pleasure." She recalled feeling mortified by his response and resolved to stay clear of anything that he might find suggestive of physical intimacy again in their conversations.

Another time, when he seemed quite alert, she spoke of her fear of people. "I could happily read all day, especially early nineteenth-century literature. I far prefer the Bennets, the Bateses, the Bertrams, the Churchills, the Morlands, and the other families in Jane Austen's fictional world to my contemporaries."

"You know, the social pressures of that period were intense. I suspect you would not have been happy to live with those constraints."

"Perhaps, but that doesn't stop me from enjoying entering their fictional world."

As his ability to focus became increasingly limited, she tried to think of ways to entertain him other than sharing life experiences. Usually at the time of day he would visit, she was would be working on the *New York Times* crossword, so she tried to see if he could help. She knew, from what he had told her, that in the old days, he was a whiz at it. However, she soon realized that it was too complicated a task, and it frustrated him. A couple of times, he got really angry. His face turned red, and he started cursing, which scared her—not for her safety, but she was afraid he might have a heart attack.

After that, she got some fully illustrated children's classics out of the library to read to him, hoping he would remember and enjoy the stories and the pictures. They were wonderfully written books that could be enjoyed by all ages. And that's exactly what happened during their final visits.

A few weeks before his death, he stopped coming, and Miss Sidenstriker was not sure why. It really bothered her. Had she done something to alienate him? Was he unwell? She finally decided to ask Rosie and was told that he had had a bad cold he couldn't seem to shake, and his wife had him on bed rest.

The news made Miss Sidenstriker sad, and she wondered if she should send over the books they had read together. She asked Rosie about it, and Rosie discouraged her, saying he spent much of his time sleeping or watching television. That was her last friendly conversation with Rosie.

No more. Rosie had crossed a line.

Miss Sidenstriker felt really tired, and the day had barely begun. She had lied about having a heart condition, but she did have high blood pressure that was controlled with medication. She sensed that it was higher than it should be at the moment, and why wouldn't it be with such an emotional start to the day? If she checked it now with her home monitor and it was high, it would go even higher because the number would scare her. So she opted not to check.

Her mind went back to the painting she had seen over Rosie's shoulder in the Gartners' living room. While she had glimpsed it before, it was the first time she had gotten such a long look. From a distance, it resembled the painting of a mother holding a conch shell to her daughter's ear to listen to the ocean by the nineteenth-century French artist William-Adolphe Bouguereau. She was almost sure she had seen the same painting when passing through a gallery at the Metropolitan Museum when she was a child. In her memory, she had been struck by the perfection of the child's face, but her mother pulled her away, anxious to get to the cafeteria ahead of the crowds.

During her years in Boston, she had been briefly tempted to buy a poster of it she had seen in some catalog but decided it was too sentimental for her taste. But what a coincidence, and how odd that her neighbor would put a poster above her mantle and not an original. Very odd, indeed. Could Mrs. Gartner be hard up?

What with all the tumult of the morning, Miss Sidenstriker almost forgot that she had an 11:30 a.m. appointment with her lawyer to change her will. Based on her genetic history, she didn't expect to live long past seventy-five, so time was of the essence. Now that her last remaining cousin, Norman, was gone, she needed to change the beneficiary from him to the Gardner Museum and Smile Train. On her last visit to her lawyer, he had suggested that she might want to leave something to Elsa, the cleaning woman who had worked for years for her parents and still came in once a week to vacuum and do other heavy work for her. But Miss Sidenstriker considered Elsa sloppy and only kept her because she didn't want some stranger coming into the apartment. She had worked hard and saved for her old age; how she disbursed her money was up to her.

Just thinking about the suggestion angered her. What did her lawyer know about pain? Those children's faces on Smile Train ads, doomed at birth to a life of derision, and to think that her hard-earned money could change their lives, whereas Elsa would probably buy cell phones for her spoiled grandchildren. As if children didn't already spend enough time on one electronic screen or another.

She decided to cancel the appointment. She had no patience for Mr. Gladden or Goldberg or whatever his name was, and it wasn't like she was going to die tomorrow. She would go instead to the Riverside Library and return some books that were due and see if *Great Expectations* was in. Time for a return to Dickens.

SIXTEEN

The Old Lady

Bette was waiting in her wheelchair when Rosie came into the bedroom.

"Rosemary, what took you so long? It's ten past ten," Bette said, her tone impatient.

"I'm sorry, Mrs. G., but your not-very-pleasant neighbor waylaid me with complaints about—"

"I don't care about that right now. I have an urgent errand I need to do in the neighborhood, and I need to get moving."

"What could possibly be so urgent? It's really windy out. You could catch cold."

"So what if I get a cold?" Bette said, wheeling herself toward the bedroom door.

"Seriously, Mrs. G.?"

"Something's going to get me sooner or later."

Trailing behind her, Rosie said, "You do not want to get sick. If you recall—"

My God, Bette thought, *is she trying to give me a guilt trip about George?* She swiveled around to face Rosie. "Who is in charge here? You or me?"

"All I meant was—"

"Let's just drop it."

"Mrs. G., on a different note, how can I leave? Venera told me you need me to cook dinner for a party tonight, and I need to order groceries and get organized."

"She overheard me when I left you a phone message. I did not say I need you to cook. I simply said I'm having a party. I think it might be better to order in the food, as I have other things I need you to do. Now let's go; the morning is half over. We can talk on the way."

Bette wheeled herself past Rosie to the front door. After her fall, her doctor had suggested a motorized wheelchair, but Bette countered with, "For getting around my apartment? Ridiculous. My upper body needs the exercise." She was right: after a year of being in a wheelchair, her arm muscles were strong.

"Where are we going?" Rosie asked, blocking the door. "Venera said you mentioned seeing a medium."

"I have errands. Move out of the way."

"Does Mrs. Haight know you are going out?"

"Rosie, what has come over you, talking to me like I'm a disobedient child?"

"I'm sorry, Mrs. G., but you haven't been outdoors in ages, and today is really windy, and you haven't even said where you're going. Whatever errands you need done, Venera or I can do them for you."

"It's something I have to do myself. Now, for the last time, let's go."

"If Mr. G. were alive, he would have me fired."

Bette turned her head around and glared at Rosie. "Don't bring George into this."

"Oh . . . kay," Rosie said, drawing out the word. "Just let me get you a blanket and a mask, if we still have any on hand."

"I am not wearing a mask."

"It will protect you from the wind, if nothing else."

"N period. O period."

Rosie tucked a blanket over Bette's legs before leaving on the "mystery" errand. When they got down to the ground floor, Jimmy rushed forward to greet them.

"Mrs. Gartner, I haven't seen you in ages. How are you?"

"Alive," Bette said.

"Oh, I can see that," Jimmy said with a smile. "You are alive, all right. Say, Rosie, if you hear of anyone looking for a job—"

"Who died?" Bette asked. "Old man Williamson?"

"Mrs. G.!" Rosie said, laughing.

"No one died, Mrs. Gartner. The Posners are moving to London soon, and their housekeeper needs a job."

"When the time comes, Jimmy, you will look out for Rosie, won't you?"

"I hate that kind of talk, Mrs. G.," Rosie said.

"It's called taking care of business. Right, Jimmy?"

"I'm afraid it is," Jimmy said.

"So that's settled."

When they got to the street, Rosie asked Bette for directions. "I believe it's on 64th Street between Broadway and Columbus."

"What's 'it'?"

"'It' is where I want to go. I'll know when I see it. Even if it means winding up and down a few blocks." Bette paused, then added, "The exercise will do you good."

"Was that necessary, Mrs. G.?"

This time it was Bette who didn't respond. She knew it was uncalled for, but she didn't have patience for so much back-and-forth, with Rosie asking if Claire knew she was going out and even bringing George into it. *I can't stand overprotectiveness. Just because I can't walk doesn't mean I can't think for myself.*

When they got to 69th Street and Broadway, they started weaving across every block in the 60s from Broadway to Columbus. Bette barked instructions at Rosie for the dinner party, from the foods to order from Citarella to the flowers for the table and how she wanted the dining room table set up. When she came up for air, Bette asked Rosie if she had gotten all that.

"I'm trying, Mrs. G. I'm trying. You haven't said how many people."

"That's because I am not yet sure. As soon as we get back, I'll make a list and then write invitations to be hand-delivered."

"I'm supposed to go all over town delivering invitations and leave you alone?"

"Well, maybe Venera can deliver them. There won't be many."

"Just give me a ballpark figure. Five? Ten? Twenty? Thirty? A hundred?"

"Don't be absurd. More like ten. All my friends are dead."

When they reached Columbus Circle with no success, Rosie said, "Maybe whatever the place is that you're looking for has moved."

"Could be," Bette responded, sounding discouraged.

They started back north in silence. Then Bette remembered. "67th between Columbus and Central Park West. Next to a little tailor shop."

Adjacent to the tailor shop was a small bodega with a poster in the window that read *Mavis Jane Robbins, Psychic Medium, trained with world renowned TV spiritualist Amber Whitefeather.* In the center of the poster was a photo of a rather ordinary-looking woman wearing a simple print dress. She could be thirty; she could be fifty. She could be a housewife. She could be an investment banker. An arrow pointed to a narrow alleyway next to the shop.

"This is it," Bette said, pointing to the sign.

"So it was a medium. Not errands," Rosie said. "Mrs. G., these people are phonies. You want your fortune told, I can do it for you. When I was a kid, I once read palms at a church fair and—"

"Are you going to wheel me there, or do I need to do it myself?" Bette had about had it with Rosie challenging her authority.

"You're the boss."

"Yes, I am. Now, come face me." Rosie braked the wheelchair, then walked in front of it. Bette patted her neck, motioning Rosie to come closer.

"Smell anything?" she asked.

Rosie sniffed her chest. "Dove soap?"

"No," Bette said, pushing Rosie's head up to her throat. "What about here?"

"Perfume?"

Satisfied, Bette instructed Rosie to continue on their way.

"Do you need perfume in order to be allowed to enter like some kind of a code?" Rosie asked.

"I am going to pretend I didn't hear that," Bette said, relieved that Rosie hadn't been hurt by her pulling rank. They usually enjoyed a kind of camaraderie that lessened the employer/employee gap. Bette rarely acted bossy with Rosie, and she liked that Rosie didn't kowtow to her, but today everything was imbued with a sense of urgency. There was no time to waste with interference of any kind, even though Bette understood that Rosie, with her big heart, was just looking out for her.

The studio at the end of the alley had a large picture window, the perimeters of which were framed with delicate, leafy floral decals. Rosie and Bette looked into the room, which had white walls, two black chairs, and a glass-topped desk. It seemed stark in contract to the floral decals. Mavis Jane Robbins was nowhere in sight.

Bette would have called ahead for an appointment if she had remembered the woman's name from the one time they had met after George died, but she didn't until she saw the poster.

"Knock on the door," Bette said.

Rosie did, but no one came. "Are you sure this is the right place?"

"Pretty sure."

"Maybe she had to shut down during the pandemic."

"Let's just wait."

"Maybe she saw Whoopi Goldberg in the movie *Ghost* and is in back piling on necklaces and—"

"Rosie!"

Just then the inside door in the studio opened, and Mavis Jane Robbins entered the room wearing a white shirt and black pants—and no jewelry.

"Knock again," Bette commanded, all excited. "Hurry before someone else comes."

"Yeah," Rosie said, in full sarcastic mode, "I'm sure."

The door opened.

"Welcome," Mavis Jane Robbins said with a smile.

"Is this a good time?" Bette asked. "Do you have time to see me?"

"I just had a cancellation, so yes, it is."

"Such luck," Rosie muttered under her breath as she wheeled Bette into the studio.

"You look familiar," Mavis Jane Robbins said, addressing Bette.

"I was here a few years ago with my daughter after my—" Bette stopped, suddenly remembering that Rosie was still there. She had no intention of telling Rosie or anyone else what her purpose was, so she dismissed Rosie with "Go work on the to-do list and come back in half an hour."

Bette waited for Rosie to leave before telling the medium the reason for her visit.

SEVENTEEN

The Old Lady's
Across-the-Hall Neighbor

M ISS SIDENSTRIKER LOOKED OUT THE PEEPHOLE OF HER
front door to make sure no one was in the hallway before leaving
for her walk to the library. Seeing that the coast was clear, she opened
the door and eyed the floor, anxious to see if the super had told the
handyman to wash it after Venereal's trash spill since she had called
to report it. Shockingly, he had. The black-and-white one-inch-square
checkerboard tiles were cleaner than usual, and she would know since
she checked them daily. Perhaps he had added Clorox or something
new to the mix? Unlikely. The black tiles didn't really show dirt, but
the white ones often looked almost gray from a combination of dirty
water being sloshed over them—which constituted cleaning to the
handyman—plus the dirt left by foot traffic.

As she waited for the elevator, she prayed—well, not prayed (she was
an atheist), more like wished—that no one was in it. She had little interest in trying to make small talk with a fellow tenant. "How are you?"
"Nice day, isn't it?" "Going for a walk?" Like they or she cared.

When it arrived at her floor, her wish had been answered—it was
empty. Now all she had to worry about was if it stopped on a lower
floor, especially the floor below. She had no desire to see the Iranian.

The elevator stopped one floor down, and Dariush got on, iPhone in hand. He briefly nodded at her, then went back to whoever he was speaking to, partly in English, partly in Farsi. At one point he said, "I spoke to Mom," at which point Miss Sidenstriker recalled that Dariush had older sisters.

As soon as they got to the ground floor and Dariush got off, Miss Sidenstriker took a moment to examine her reflection in a mirrored panel facing the door, unaware that there was a ceiling spy cam linked to the front desk. She tugged a few wisps of hair back into the bun of her dull gray hair, then, removing her wire-rimmed glasses, came closer to make sure there wasn't anything stuck between her teeth. There was, so she removed a toothpick from the bottom of her Le Sportsac tote bag and flicked it off. It landed on the mirror, which gave Miss Sidenstriker a moment's pleasure. Seeing that her "good" cheek might still be somewhat flushed after the morning's encounter with Venereal, she dug back into her tote for her cover-up. She applied an extra coat to her birthmark as well, although it was all but impossible to totally conceal.

She stepped back to see if she had missed anything. One of the buttons of her olive-green shirt had opened, so she buttoned it. The last thing she wanted was for some construction worker to catch a glimpse of her ample bosoms and make a comment, not that anyone ever had, but you could never be too careful. Lastly, she yanked down her brown skirt.

Exiting the elevator, she hid behind the large column that was by the elevator and peered down the lobby corridor to see if anyone was near the entrance, but she saw no one. *Where was Jimmy?* she wondered. *Maybe getting someone a cab? Or lurking outside smoking a cigarette or marijuana?* In that case, she would detect the smell and notify the super. Building employees were not allowed to smoke within a block of the premises—at least that's what she believed. She would have to check to see if she was right. Or maybe he was rendezvousing in the basement with his male lover. One time, she had seen him leave work with another man and was pretty sure he was a homosexual, or gay, or queer, or cis something, whatever the "in" word was these days. He did have a slightly effeminate walk.

As she walked toward the entrance, Miss Sidenstriker made a mental note to let the super know that Jimmy had left the desk unattended. However, when she got close to the entrance, to her dismay, Jimmy was there, deep in conversation with Venereal, of all people. *How did I miss seeing them?* she wondered, before remembering that her glasses were in her hand, and she was, as the saying went, blind as a bat without them.

How do they communicate when Venereal's English is so limited? Or is it? Maybe she just fakes not understanding when she's with me. But she's not that clever. Miss Sidenstriker was sure they had been spying on her by the way they turned quickly away when she approached. Venereal was probably telling him her one-sided version of their incident. She used to think Jimmy was nice enough, even though you never knew with service people if they were just being nice for a better tip. But now she despised him.

They stopped talking as she approached, then Venereal fled toward the door. Another dead giveaway. *Damn them.* Why were people always talking about her behind her back? Miss Sidenstriker watched Venereal dash down the stairs to the street, almost knocking the Iranian over. He grabbed the banister to retain his balance as Venereal quickly muttered, "Sorry," but kept going. *Such a rude, rude person*, Miss Sidenstriker thought. She almost felt sorry for the Iranian.

"Good morning, Miss Sidenstriker," Jimmy said, forcing her attention back to him. He sounded like he was acting cheerful for her benefit, yet another clue that they had been talking about her.

"What's good about it?" Miss Sidenstriker snapped angrily, but then she realized that if she was going to report Venereal to ICE, she needed to know her last name. Maybe Jimmy knew. Better make nice.

Smiling a tight smile, almost a grimace, she began again. "How are you today?"

"How nice of you to ask," Jimmy said, sounding surprised. "I'm okay."

That worked, she thought. *Maybe take it a step further.*

"And how is your—" She paused, not sure how to phrase it. "Friend?"

"My friend?"

Now she was stuck. How to answer that? Did he think she meant his maybe boyfriend or Venereal?

"You mean Venera?" Jimmy asked, inadvertently coming to her rescue.

"Yes, yes. Her," she spit out. "Such a pretty name. Is her last name as unusual?"

"Chayka? Not really."

"How do you spell it?"

Jimmy appeared uncomfortable. "I'm not sure."

"C-h-a-y-k-a?"

"That doesn't sound right," he said. "Maybe C-h-a-i-k-h-e-a? or something along those lines."

He's lying, Miss Sidenstriker thought, but there was no use confronting him. It was clear he wasn't going to answer. He had his loyalties, and they weren't to her.

As she headed out, Jimmy called after her, "Enjoy the day, Miss Sidenstriker."

Much as she wanted to call back, "Up yours," she didn't—that would be undignified.

When she got outside, she realized she had forgotten to check the weather. It was colder than she had anticipated, but she didn't want to go back in for a sweater. She didn't feel like facing Jimmy again.

Miss Sidenstriker started walking south at a fast clip to warm up, her head filled with thoughts of how else she might find out Venereal's last name. She could ask Rosie, but it was doubtful she would tell her since she would know why she wanted it. But then it occurred to her that it shouldn't be that hard to find now that she knew what it sounded like. As soon as she got back, she would Google Croatian surnames starting with *Ch*.

EIGHTEEN

The Old Lady's Night Aide

H AVING BOLTED OUT THE DOOR IN THE MIDST OF TALKING with her new friend Jimmy, Venera felt bad about almost knocking over the attractive man going down the stairs, but thankfully he didn't fall. She decided that if she saw him again, she would apologize properly.

She started running south, then west toward the pathway along the Hudson River up to 86th Street. She then turned back south and ran to the dog park at 72nd, brushing away the tears brought on by the wind whipping her face. She was preoccupied and, as a result, unable to enjoy the river the way she usually did.

She stopped briefly to look at the dogs; that usually calmed her down. Alas, the park was surprisingly empty, so no doggie fix today. Venera reversed direction and headed north toward Mrs. Gartner's building, almost bumping into, but not even seeing, Miss Sidenstriker.

When she got back to the apartment, she had planned to see if Rosie needed any help. Instead, when she got to her bedroom, she pulled her suitcase out from beneath the bed and removed her treasured postcard of the building. She had found it while browsing in a small tourist shop that sold souvenirs of old New York. On the front was an exterior photo, and on the reverse was written, "Designed by Clifford Watkins, a protégé of Stanford White, The Stevens is an eighteen-story Beaux Arts gem completed in 1910. Most units feature architectural details of the period with eleven-foot ceilings covered with plasterwork designs, wall moldings, some wood-paneled rooms with fireplaces, all with parquet floors."

She read the copy for about the hundredth time, then dropped the card, feeling numb and a bit sad. In all likelihood, she would go back to Croatia and settle down, with or without Jusef, and all this would be a distant memory. If she showed this card to her friends, no one would believe that she had ever lived there, especially if she told them about the apartment she lived in. She might not even believe it herself; it was so far outside the realm of her life there.

Mrs. Gartner's apartment seemed to Venera right out of *Lifestyles of the Rich and Famous*. Her parents' entire home could probably fit into Mrs. Gartner's living room. Aside from the living room, there was a dining room, a wood-paneled study, a kitchen with a separate pantry, three bedrooms, and four bathrooms! Imagine that! Four bathrooms!

Every room contained books and paintings and photographs, even the bathrooms. Some nights after Mrs. Gartner fell asleep, Venera would study the photos for clues about who everyone was, filling in what she didn't know with her own stories about their lives. They were all so good-looking and well-dressed.

She especially loved the wedding pictures. There was one that Venera assumed had to be Mrs. Gartner and her husband based on the date inscribed on the silver frame: April 26, 1948. Mrs. Gartner looked radiant in a long white gown as she clutched the arm of her tuxedo-clad husband. So elegant. Venera dubbed them Princess Di, if she'd had brown hair, and Prince Charles, but with a happier ending.

Another photo was of Mrs. Gartner's daughter, Claire, and her husband. Venera had met Claire a couple of times, and while she was probably in her early seventies, she was easily recognizable: brunette, like her mother once was; pretty like her mother but taller, as tall as her husband, who was tall with bright red hair. The Princess of Wales and Prince Harry, even though they weren't married to one another in reality. They were casually dressed, hardly a typical wedding photo, but it was housed in a frame inscribed with the date June 1, 1972. Maybe they eloped?

A third photo was of pretty brunette woman and an attractive Asian man. Julia Roberts and Bruce Lee. Sure. But who were they? There were many pictures of a little redheaded girl with slightly Asian features at different ages, often with Claire and her husband. Was she Mrs. Gartner's great-granddaughter, whom she had yet to meet since she only visited during the day when Venera was off? She looked a lot like the child in the portrait in the living room, and the mother resembled the woman in the photo standing with the Asian man. Venera thought it could be a family portrait if it were not for the fact that it was obviously painted a century or so ago.

Venera stared at the portrait, wanting to soak up the gentleness of the woman who knelt next to the child, holding a shell to her ear. The longer she looked at the painting, the more Venera felt like she could almost hear the ocean. The woman wore a long, teal-blue jumper-style dress with white lace sleeves and a bib. Her head was cocked toward the girl, who looked straight ahead. The child, dressed in a white dress, wore old-fashioned lace-up boots and had a snail shell in her hand.

There were so many questions she wanted to ask Mrs. Gartner, but she rarely had an opportunity like the conversation they had had that morning. For whatever reason, Mrs. Gartner had been accessible. Venera now knew how she met her husband, but there was so much more she wanted to know. Did she go to college? Ever have a job? A career?

Venera guessed probably not. She was not of that generation. Had she always had a housekeeper? Rosie had worked for her for over twenty years, but what about before that? Was her daughter raised by a nanny? If she didn't work, how did she spend her days? Did she take carriage rides through Central Park and visit museums and have lunch with friends and go to the Broadway musicals and the ballet and the opera and shop in fancy stores for beautiful dresses to wear at night when she went out to dine at fine restaurants with her husband?

Yes, of course that's what she did, Venera thought, recalling the closets she had seen this morning that were filled with gorgeous clothes. One closet for cocktail dresses and ballgowns, another packed with suits and day dresses. In Venera's eyes, Mrs. Gartner had a perfect life.

She was especially curious to know why the family was so small. In her mind the women must have been really forward-thinking to plan such small families, to still be a parent but be less tied down emotionally, physically, and financially. She hoped Jusef, if he welcomed her back, would consider the same.

Jusef. Always back to Jusef, the boy she had loved through adolescence and into manhood. Jusef, the fiancé she stood up two days before their wedding. She thought about the night that was the catalyst for what she did.

She was lying with her head on Jusef's lap in the back seat of his car, their only place for privacy, discussing where to go on their honeymoon.

"Let's take a real trip with the money people will give us," Venera said.

"Like where?" Jusef responded.

"Like . . ." Venera paused as if she were thinking, but she knew exactly where she wanted to go. "Like New York."

"New York? No. I don't want to be killed by some gun-crazy lunatic." Jusef's cousin's cousin's cousin, or some such relative, had gone to Las Vegas in 2017 and was injured, though not killed, in a mass shooting, which left Jusef with a bad taste for America with all the random shootings.

"That's so dumb. People go there all the time and don't get killed. Anika has been there for two years, and she says New York is the most exciting place on—"

"Anika," Jusef replied. "I should have guessed. I'm supposed to trust my life to your crazy friend."

"Hey, she's not crazy. She just wants more than Jelsa has to offer."

After a few minutes of silence, Jusef got up and climbed through the divide to the front seat. Venera remained in back with her eyes closed. As Jusef started the car, he said, "I was going to surprise you. I booked us a room with a balcony at the Splendida Palace in Split."

Venera bolted upright. "Split? You want to honeymoon in *Split*?"

Jusef didn't say anything, which Venera knew said volumes. He was angry.

"Look," Venera said, "I'm sure the hotel is amazing, but Jusef, this may be our only chance for a real adventure before we get bogged down by life."

Suddenly parking the car on a side street, Jusef turned the engine off and looked back at Venera. "What does that mean, 'bogged down'? You mean with kids?"

"When you have kids, you are never really free," Venera said. As the oldest of six, she knew what she was talking about.

"I don't understand you. That's what life's about. Children. I want as many as God can give us."

She got out of the back seat and went around to the front, giving herself a little time to regroup.

Once seated, she said, "Jusef, I'm only twenty-two, and I spent two of those years in lockdown when I could have been having fun, a lot of that time spent babysitting my siblings. I know nothing of life. I wait tables at the restaurant all day, I come home to my parents' house; the next day, the same thing. You go to work at the garage fixing cars, come home to your parents. Day in, day out. Weekends we go out dancing, drink too much beer, have sex in the woods or on the beach or in the back seat of your car. If I get pregnant, which I could since we sometimes get careless, then it's over; I will never see the world."

"You can see the world in books, on TV, in movies—"

"I've done that all my life. That's not what I'm talking about. I want to see the places I dream about. I want to know what it's like to be in a city filled with people from all over the world who don't know you and don't know your business, where you have some space, some breathing room."

"What do you mean, breathing room?" He took a deep breath. "See? I can breathe just fine."

"Okay, forget it."

"Anika totally brainwashed you. What's wrong with Jelsa?"

Neither one spoke on the ride back to Venera's parents' home. When Jusef stopped the car, Venera tried a new approach.

"I have an idea," she said, trying to make light of it even though she was dead serious. "How about I go to New York for a visit by myself to get it out of my system, then come back and we get married and honeymoon in Split and then make a baby. How's that for a plan?"

"I hate it. I'm ready to start a family now. I want to be a young father like my own dad."

Clearly, Jusef wasn't about to budge. It was a stalemate.

The closer she got to the wedding date, the more Venera panicked. No doubt she would be with child within a few months, and her fate would be sealed.

So she fled to New York.

She figured she would stay until her visitor visa expired. That would also give Jusef time to get past his anger and miss her, or so she hoped.

She hadn't really thought through the consequences. Her visa had already expired; she was living in New York on borrowed time. So, why hadn't she returned? She had seen as many of the touristy attractions that brought her to New York as she could afford in the first place, and now that she was working, she didn't have the time or money to do the kind of the things rich people did. She needed to stop watching shows like *The Kardashians*—all they did was make her realize what she could never have.

She knew that if Jusef welcomed her back, he would have no interest in limiting their family, not after saying he wanted as many children "as God can give us," as if the size of a family was only up to God.

Whether as Jusef's wife or not, when she returned home, it would be to a life similar to her mother's and those of the other women in her village. It was a good life; it really was. So then, why did it not seem like enough? Was she the kind of person who would always want more, always be dissatisfied?

Venera went back to her bedroom and eyed the suitcase. Should she pack? She could be ready to leave the next day. Should she reach out to Jusef and push for a response?

She put the postcard back in the suitcase, closed it, and got out her phone. Sitting on the edge of the narrow bed, she stared at the gadget a long time before finally punching in the password. She pressed the green message icon, then the video camera, turning it on herself.

"Jusuf, I'm sorry," she said, then burst into tears.

Venera stopped recording and brushed the tears away, then began again with the same result. She hesitated, wondering if perhaps Jusef would be sympathetic if he saw her crying. But then he might feel she was trying to be manipulative, and it would backfire. That is, if he even looked at the message.

She decided to send a text message instead. "Jusef. Let me know where I stand."

She reread what she had written, then pressed send. Lying on the bed, she felt a mix of emotions: miserable, confused, and upset with herself for putting her future entirely in Jusef's hands again.

NINETEEN

The Old Lady's Housekeeper

WOULD THAT I WERE A FLY ON THE WALL INSIDE MAVIS *Jane Robbins's studio*, Rosie thought, as she waited for Mrs. G. on an old wooden bench covered with pigeon droppings at the end of the alleyway. *Maybe a séance, with Mrs. G. hoping to communicate with Mr. G. That's about as likely as snow in July. Even unlikelier. But if it makes Mrs. G. feel a connection to him, what's the harm?*

God knows Rosie missed him, too. He was a real gentleman. No matter what she did for him, no matter how small, "Please, Rosemary," or "Thank you, Rosemary." Always Rosemary, never Rosie, which she took as a sign of, in his view, respect. On St. Patrick's Day, he would march into the kitchen in the morning to make sure she noticed his green tie. That night he would bring home green carnations for her. And on holidays, always a thoughtful bonus, even on Mother's Day. They maintained their boundaries—she knew her position—but she couldn't help it, she loved him like a father.

Rosie was curious why now, why today, Mrs. G. wanted to contact him. Whatever the reason, Rosie resolved not to be a spoiler. She needed to shut her big trap and play along.

Rosie saw the door open, and Mavis Jane Robbins wheeled out Mrs.

G. *Wonder what that half hour cost*, Rosie thought. *A hundred bucks? More? Does she give guarantees?*

"I can't thank you enough," Mrs. G. told the medium. "Nine-thirty, then. Don't be late. I don't want to risk falling asleep before you get there."

"I'll be there, but remember, no guarantees."

Man, that woman is savvy, Rosie thought, *covering herself like that. And I bet she gets paid again—twice in one day.*

After the medium went back inside, Mrs. G. told Rosie to add Mavis Jane Robbins to the list.

"She's coming to the party? Will the guests be getting their fortunes told or commune with the dead?" Rosie asked, trying her best not to sound snarky.

"Never you mind."

"That sounds like a yes."

Despite her skepticism, Rosie was genuinely interested in experiencing what it might be like. Maybe she could ask to have her future told after all the guests were done. *Who knows, maybe she will say she sees a Matt in my future. Or if not Matt, a nice man—with no cats—and with money. Wouldn't that be a hoot.*

"Now, do we still have any champagne at home?"

"Champagne? Is this going to be that kind of celebration?"

"I guess you could say that."

"But you're not going to tell me what it is."

"You got that right."

"I'll check when we get back."

Just then they passed the Bloomingdale's outlet at Broadway and 72nd Street. "Stop. I need to go in."

Rosie wheeled Mrs. G. into the store, then waited to be told which department to go to.

"Stay here. I can manage on my own." With that, Mrs. G. wheeled herself off in the direction of the perfume counter. *Perfume*, Rosie mused. *First she asks me to smell her neck before seeing the medium; now she wants to buy some.*

Today, out of the blue, she's like a woman possessed, and so uncharacteristically bossy. I should be glad she wants to do something other than sit around watching television, but why a dinner party? Is she inviting some secret admirer, some old geezer from her past? Wouldn't that be something? You always read about people who were in love as teenagers and then reconnect fifty years later. In this case, seventy-five years later. Her daughter might die of shock. And jealousy. Laughing, Rosie thought, *Better position myself behind Mrs. Haight to catch her if a stranger appears.*

Rosie saw a salesperson reach across the counter and hand Mrs. G. a bag. A moment later Mrs. G. returned, clutching a small Bloomie's bag in her lap, smiling enigmatically. As Rosie wheeled her back home, she looked down and saw Mrs. G.'s head bent over in the wheelchair. *No wonder she fell asleep*, Rosie thought. *She hasn't done this much in years, and it's not even lunchtime. But knowing her, if I tap her shoulder she will wake up and quickly deny that she was sleeping.*

As soon as they got back to the apartment, Mrs. G. came back to life and began barking instructions at Rosie. "After you check to see if we have champagne, call Citarella to get their catering menu."

Rosie parked the wheelchair in the kitchen as she went to check the pantry. "I'll need to know how many people are invited before I order," Rosie called out. "And before I set the table."

"I'll get to that."

Mrs. G. wheeled herself to a counter to retrieve a pad and paper as Rosie returned carrying a few bottles of Dom Pérignon. She put them in the refrigerator to chill.

"Three enough?" Rosie asked.

"If that's all we have, it will have to be," Mrs. G. answered, then handed Rosie the pad and pencil. "Write this down. Call the florist— you know which one I use—and order an arrangement of pink peonies and white hydrangeas for the dining room table."

"How much do you want to spend?"

"Whatever it costs; I don't care."

"Seriously?"

"Yes. As long as it's beautiful and you can see the face of whoever is across the table."

"You used to like ivy dangling from it."

"Yes. Order ivy, too. Hopefully Stuart is still there and will remember what I always ordered for dinner parties. Then call Marceline and see if she can come here this afternoon and do my hair."

"Mrs. G., did you forget? Marceline retired."

"Then maybe she can recommend someone."

"I don't have her number," Rosie said. "And the salon probably closed during the pandemic."

"Well, try them anyhow and see if they have someone else. I have to do something about my hair. Worst case scenario, you or Venera can give it a try."

"That's scary, Mrs. G. I'm not good with hair. Patty is, but that doesn't help. This is her week with her dad."

It went on like that for a while, with Mrs. G. repeating the same instructions she had given Rosie earlier when they were out regarding the linens, flatware, glassware, and china she wanted used.

"So, just to be clear," Rosie interrupted. "You want to use only your best linens, although last time you used the Belgian lace tablecloth and napkins and we sent them to be cleaned and you saw what they charged, you swore never again."

"Do I need your permission to use my own linens?"

"Of course not! I was just reminding you—"

"The cost be damned. Now, get started with the phone calls. And I need to decide what to wear when you're done."

"But you still haven't told me who's coming."

"Oh, yes. The guest list. And I want the invitations hand-delivered."

"What invitations?" Rosie asked, trying to keep up with all the instructions.

"I'll write them by hand. If they look too much like chicken scrawl, then you can redo them. Venera can deliver them."

"Before I call Citarella, I need to know how many people to order dinner for."

Mrs. G. paused, then, spreading out her fingers, slowly ticked off names, tapping a finger for each person.

"You—"

"Me?"

"You—"

"As a guest?" Rosie said, sounding as astonished as she felt.

"Yes, I want you and Venera and—"

"Venera, too?"

"Can I go on?"

"Wait. No, Mrs. G. I can't sit with your guests. It would be very awkward for them and for me."

"You have to trust that I know what I'm doing. All my friends are dead, and there is no one you don't know. It'll be fine."

"But who is going to serve and clean up?"

"It will be a buffet. Self-service."

"And a genie will come afterward and clear the table and do the dishes?"

"Yes," Mrs. G. said, sounding impish, then continued the head count. "Claire and, of course, Jack. Jia and her wonderful young man."

"Kenny," Rosie said.

"I know his name. Kenny. And Gertrude Sidenstriker—"

"Mrs. G., do you know how difficult she has become?"

"Gertrude," Mrs. G. repeated in a firm voice. "And last, the young man George used to play backgammon with and who brings me that delicious pastry from his country."

"Do you want me to remind you of his name? It starts with D."

"No. It will come to me. So that's . . ." and again Mrs. G. counted off her fingers, "Me, you, Venera, Claire, Jack, Jia, Kenny, Miss Sidenstriker, and Dariush, that's his name. That's nine."

"You forgot the medium."

"She's coming at 9:30. Dinner's at 8:00."

Rosie's head was spinning. She got that Mrs. G. wanted her family, but her and Venera and Miss Sourpuss and Dariush? It was all too weird. And what about Patty? She was planning to ask Frank if she could have dinner with her tonight or just stop by to see how she was. But Mrs. G. would need help, if not her presence at the table.

Mrs. G. clapped her hands in front of Rosie's face. "What are you waiting for? And where's Venera? I need her to deliver the invites."

"She went for a walk, but she may be back."

"Wheel me to my bedroom so I can get started on the invitations, and then see if Venera is back."

As they headed toward the bedroom, Rosie started laughing. "Am I getting an invitation, too?"

"What's so funny?" Mrs. G. said. "Of course you are."

If only she knew, Rosie thought. In her first year on the job, when Mr. and Mrs. G. were not home, Rosie would sometimes sit at one end of the table and pretend Frank was at the other end, and they were hosting a party for their friends and neighbors. The wine would be flowing, and everyone would be talking and laughing, their voices louder as the evening wore on. The fantasy never lasted long; it was too far-fetched, and besides which, she was nervous that one of the Gartners might return home and catch her in the act.

But now it would no longer be make-believe, even though she would not be the hostess. Despite being nervous, Rosie was starting to become excited about being a guest at that table. God knows what Mrs. G. was up to, but it would surely be an experience of a lifetime. She just hoped Patty was okay.

TWENTY

The Old Lady's
Across-the-Hall Neighbor

B<small>Y SOME MIRACLE—CERTAINLY</small> G<small>OD-WHO-DIDN'T-EXIST</small>
wasn't looking out for her—Miss Sidenstriker had managed to
keep her balance when Venereal whipped by her earlier that morning.
Was she in tears? Miss Sidenstriker wondered. *I sure hope so. Maybe the
inconsiderate little immigrant is afraid I'll call ICE, as well she should be,
and she'll be on the next flight back to Croatia or, better yet, Transylvania
or Siberia.*

After pausing to catch her breath after what had been a bad scare,
she decided to skip the library and take a walk instead in Central Park.
It would be good for her plumbing, which had become a problem of late
despite eating kiwis like they were M&M's. The last thing she wanted
to do was discuss her bowel habits with her doctor. If walking and eating foods meant to aid digestion didn't work, she would have to buy
something for constipation at a drugstore. Certainly not her regular
one where they all knew her. Her constipation was none of anyone's
goddamn business.

She turned around and headed north toward 77th Street, then east to
Columbus Avenue. Many years ago, there used to be a restaurant called

Isabella's on the southeast corner. Miss Sidenstriker had read somewhere that the owner was Ingrid Bergman's daughter. Probably just a rumor to make it seem glamorous. While she had never dined there when it was still open, from the outside looking in, it looked inviting—that is, if you had people you wanted to be with. She couldn't imagine why it had closed; it always looked full, but then there were always changes on Columbus Avenue, what with such high rents. You never knew what unnecessary store would pop up next, and conversely, which absolutely essential store would be gone overnight.

Her mother had told her that in the old days there were barber shops and hardware stores and meat markets and all the stores that really mattered. But that was then. Thank God her parents had rented the apartment she lived in now when there was still rent control, or she wouldn't be able to afford to remain there. She fully expected to eventually leave feet first, and then the rent would probably quadruple. Or worse. Not her problem.

Heading along the lovely tree-lined street that faced the southern side of the Museum of Natural History, she glanced into townhouse windows at living rooms and dens and kitchens, judging the people who lived there based on the clutter or the absence of it. When she got to Storico, the New York Historical Society's restaurant, she paused to peer inside. It looked chic, but it lacked the warmth of Isabella's. She had googled their brunch menu online and knew they served Challah French Toast. Her stomach churned. It hurt just thinking about it, but she never ate out. Dining alone in a restaurant made her look as if she had no one to be with, which, although true, was no one's goddamn business. *Damn that Venereal,* Miss Sidenstriker thought. *She had me too agitated to finish my breakfast.*

Miss Sidenstriker hurried on to the corner of 77th Street and Central Park West. She accidentally brushed past a couple who had just turned onto the street. They were deep in conversation, and she thought she heard the woman say, "Strawberry," even though they had seemed oblivious to her. She knew intellectually that she often imagined snubs, but as much as she thought that she was probably projecting on them, why would someone say the word *strawberry* unless it was about her?

She had to know. Forgetting all about going to the park, she turned around to follow them. As she did, the woman looked back at her with a "fuck off" glare in her eyes. *Does she know I'm following them?* Miss Sidenstriker wondered, *or was the bitch eyeing the pigeon that just flew by? Am I too close? But if I move back I won't be able to hear what they are saying.*

Miss Sidenstriker saw past them to a dog walker who had stopped mid-block to let one of the pack of large unruly dogs relieve itself. To her disgust, he didn't pick up the pile but kept going. *He should be fined*, she thought, but then it occurred to her that maybe the woman was so engaged in their conversation that she might unknowingly step in it with her expensive-looking designer heels. *If only I believed in prayer.*

Miss Sidenstriker inched closer. "Everything there is so fresh," she heard the man say. "Let's see if they have swordfish." Did he somehow sense that she was listening and made it sound like they were food shopping to throw her off? Just then Miss Sidenstriker stepped on a penny and started to slip. She caught her balance, then stooped to pick it up. By then the couple was too far away to catch up to.

She examined the penny, then removed her glasses from her bag for a closer look. 1967. Good old Abe. Could it be valuable? George would have known. He had told her that he had collected coins in his youth, but she would have to research it. Or was its value merely in having found it, signifying in some mystical way good luck? She could sorely use some.

Penny in hand, she resumed her walk. She saw that the woman had stopped by a fenced-in tree and was using a tissue to wipe something off her shoe, the bottom of which was red with some brown gunk attached to it. *Oh my,* Miss Sidenstriker thought, *miracles can happen.*

She hastened her step to make sure she was right, that it was dog shit and not a wad of gum, which was a nuisance but not nearly as bad, when she saw the woman resume walking. A moment later the couple entered a townhouse, one with the living room lined with bookshelves. There were books everywhere, in piles by chairs, on tables, even the floor. *How can people live like that?* she wondered, *so sloppy and disorganized,* even though, had she not thought that they were talking about her, she would have been impressed that they were readers like herself. She was so preoccupied that just as she reached the side entrance of the Historical Society, she failed to see a crack in the sidewalk. She tripped and fell forward, landing hard on her right knee. She wasn't sure if the pain was greater or the mortification.

She poked her head up to see if anyone had noticed, horrified by the thought that anyone following behind her would have a bird's eye view of her undergarments given that her legs were splayed out. She drew them together, and with her good hand, reached back and pushed her skirt down.

To her relief, no one was behind her, but two hooded teenagers were running toward her. Panicked, she tried to get to her feet to avoid being mugged, but they were faster. Each boy got on one side, put an arm under her armpits, and hoisted her up. Her heart pounded as they asked her if she was hurt. Instead of answering, she looked down at the sidewalk at the contents of her Le Sportsac.

"Don't worry, we don't want your money," the taller of the boys said, as he reached down and picked up her wallet and keys.

"Hey, whatcha got on your face? Blood?" the other one chimed in. He reached to touch Miss Sidenstriker's cheek, but she slapped it away.

"Shut up," the tall boy said. "It's a birthmark."

"Sorry," the other boy said, then laughing, took off across the street. The taller of the two handed Miss Sidenstriker her wallet and keys, then ran after his friend. Miss Sidenstriker covered her birthmark with her hand, practically hyperventilating. She could hear them laughing as they entered the park. It made her miss the days of wearing a mask during COVID-19, the only time she had ever felt safe outside her home.

When the adrenaline from the fall and the incident had worn off, she tried to walk but the pain in her knee was unbearable. Could her kneecap be broken? That would be tragic. How would she ever manage?

Just then a woman in a white uniform got out of a cab right in front of her. Miss Sidenstriker decided to try to talk to her, assuming that she was a doctor or nurse.

"Miss, excuse me," she said. "I just had a bad fall, and I think my kneecap may be broken." The woman gave Miss Sidenstriker a once-over, which Miss Sidenstriker understood. She would have done the same, suspecting some kind of trick.

"Can you put any weight on it?" the woman said, apparently satisfied that she wasn't being scammed.

Miss Sidenstriker tried to do as she was told, but it was too painful.

"Mind if I feel it?" the nurse/doctor person asked.

"If you must."

As the nurse gently probed Miss Sidenstriker's knee, nosy passersby looked on. To her horror, she saw her Iranian downstairs neighbor approach. Miss Sidenstriker closed her eyes and tried to imagine herself somewhere far away.

"I don't think it's broken, but you need to get it checked right away," the nurse said. "No matter what, you'll get a hematoma, and it will be very painful. Your knee needs to be iced and your leg elevated."

Miss Sidenstriker mumbled thank you, afraid that if she tried to say anything more she would further embarrass herself by crying.

The Iranian stepped forward and tried to take her arm, but she elbowed him away.

"I live in her building," he told the nurse. "I can go with her to the hospital. I just need to let my assistant at the museum know."

Miss Sidenstriker didn't protest further. She felt utterly helpless at that moment. The nurse waited with her until Dariush returned.

He hailed a cab. This time Miss Sidenstriker allowed him to take her arm.

TWENTY-ONE

The Old Lady's Daughter

CLAIRE, IN HER BEDROOM, BURROWED THROUGH HER desk drawers for the slip of paper with the name of a psychiatrist who specialized in hypnotherapy, Dr. Anabeth Parker. Her internist had given her the referral many years ago during her annual checkup when Claire mentioned the night terrors. "Try it—what do you have to lose?" her doctor had said, not realizing the extent of Claire's resistance to therapy of any kind. *Maybe Dr. Parker has retired*, Claire thought. After all, during the pandemic, would hypnosis have worked via Zoom?

Claire eyed the card, but the words had become a blur. Hypnosis would involve a trip into her unconscious mind and back, and she had zero interest in examining her dormant feelings about anything—not her marriage, not Hope's death, not the career that never had a chance to get off the ground—ever again. With anyone. Talking about things just made them worse. Better to let sleeping dogs lie.

The first time she had seen a therapist was a few years into her marriage. Claire was unhappy and knew that if she told her parents or her friends, they would be full of unwanted advice. What she wanted was an impartial sounding board.

The initial visit was a double session to allow Dr. Weiland, the therapist, time to get as much history as possible about Claire and her marriage, starting with when and how she and Jack met.

As Claire relayed to Dr. Weiland, she met Jack in her junior year at RISD at a comedy club in Boston. She had gone there with her roommate Jessie, and by the time they got there, they were both pretty high. The place was super crowded, and Claire and Jessie wound up sitting at a table with a bunch of wannabe actors. Jessie took one look at the guy seated across from Claire, then nudged her. "That hair can't possibly be real."

"What hair?" Claire asked.

"The guy sitting across from you. What do you bet he dyes it that color—no one can have hair that orange."

"Hey, Carrot Top," Claire said loudly to the guy, as people around them shushed her. "My friend here says your hair is dyed."

"I was kidding," Jessie said, laughing, as the guy pulled a wool cap out of his jacket pocket and pulled it over his head, then playfully stuck his tongue out at her.

"Don't hide it," Claire said. "I think it's cute."

"No, you don't."

"Yes, I do. My father's brother has red hair, too."

"And you think your uncle is cute?" he said provocatively.

Claire stood up, reached over, and yanked the cap off his head as people shouted for her to sit down, they couldn't see the show. The guy tried to grab it back, but Claire tore away from the table. He chased after her.

She wove around tables heading for the exit and finally out onto the sidewalk, where she stood, waving the cap at him as if she were a matador flagging a bull. When he finally got close, he grabbed at her waist to stop her. "Gotcha, String Bean," he said, alluding to her 5'10" height.

"Oh yeah, Carrot Top," she said, pulling away.

The next time he caught her, it ended with them kissing. Had she been alone, she probably would have wound up in his apartment, but Jessie was with her, and they had to get back to Providence.

In no time they were a couple. His name was Jack Haight, and he was a senior at the Berklee College of Music, majoring in musical theater. Their friends all called them Carrot Top and String Bean. As graduation approached, Claire and Jack talked about a future together, although at the same time, each was planning their next logical career step. Claire, an artist, hoped to continue studying while beginning to show her work; Jack needed to find an agent and start auditioning, whichever came first. Although his parents didn't stop him from pursuing his dream, they made it clear that once school ended, he was on his own financially. They left the door open for him to enter the family insurance business.

Then Claire got pregnant. She knew right away when her period was a week late, as she was always regular. She was stunned. She thought she had been careful, but then she remembered she had forgotten to take the pill one weekend when Jack was staying over.

There was no way she could tell her parents, not that they would ever turn their backs on her, but it would disappoint and embarrass them. She especially hated disappointing her father. She considered her options:

Tell Jack, who would probably want to get married, even though she didn't want to pressure him into marriage, nor did she feel ready.

Get an abortion, a terrifying prospect. She had heard a few horror stories about them from friends.

Go to Italy to "study art," have the baby, and give it up for adoption there.

Go to Italy, come home with the baby and a story about an impulsive, brief marriage that didn't work out.

In short, lousy options. The only thing she felt clear about was that this was her problem, not Jack's. It wasn't fair to burden him when it had been her carelessness. He wanted to be an actor and would have enough trouble supporting himself. As much as she loved him—because she loved him—she needed to break it off with him ASAP.

Not sure she could do it in person, she wrote him a "Dear John" letter. Two days later, when he received it, he borrowed a friend's car and drove to Providence, arriving around 9:00 p.m. He found Claire curled up on the sofa in the living room of her suite, the door unlocked.

"What the fuck is going on?" he yelled, startling her.

Claire yelled back, "Shut the door!"

As Jack closed the door, Claire turned over to face away from him. He stormed over to the sofa.

"Well?" he demanded.

"Jack, it was time," Claire said, her voice nasal from crying. "We both need to go in our own direction and not be saddled with a commitment to each other."

"I won't talk to your back." Jack waited for Claire to turn around, but when she didn't, he continued. "I thought you loved me—or were you lying?"

"Don't make this harder than it has to be. I feel sick about it, too."

"You feel sick about dumping me, but you're doing it anyhow? That's not like you, Claire. There has to be more to this."

He paused, expecting a response that didn't come. "Did you meet someone, is that it?"

"Please leave," Claire screamed. "Just leave."

Jack kicked the side of the sofa, then took off. Claire waited five minutes, then turned around to make sure she was alone. Her eyes were bloodshot, her hair uncombed. She looked like the mess she felt inside. She rolled off the sofa and walked over to the door and was about to lock it when Jack burst back in, limping.

"You're pregnant," he said—a statement, not a question.

Determined to stick to the plan, Claire told him she had it all worked out. It was not his problem. But that was not how he saw it.

"What about having an abortion?" he asked.

"Jack, no, I can't. I'll have the baby and give it up to a couple who wants to adopt."

"Are you serious? Give away our own kid?"

"Our own kid," he said. She couldn't believe his words. While she was too scared to have an abortion, she thought she could give the baby up, even though it would be hard. But if he was on board, well, then she would have the baby and keep the baby—and somehow make it work.

"Just to be clear. You're okay if I get an abortion but not with giving a baby away?"

"Right now, it's just cells, but a baby, that's a whole different ball game. It's real."

"Jack, I'm giving you a pass. You can walk away."

"Promise me you won't do anything till I get back to you. I need to sleep on it." With that, Jack left.

Three days later, he called and proposed, and soon after they got married in a civil ceremony in Boston. Choosing to basically elope had been Claire's decision. She had two reasons. One, she didn't want either of them to have enough time to think about what they were doing and how it would impact them and their families. *Just get married*, she thought, *then figure out the rest*. Two, if she told her parents she was engaged, her mother would take over and want to plan a big wedding, something that would take months of preparation, at which time there would be no hiding her pregnancy.

Claire adored her parents, especially her father. She was daddy's little girl. She hated that she would be hurting them and dreaded making the call. When she finally got up the nerve, the first words out of her mother's mouth were "You're pregnant." Her mother was too smart for

Claire to even try to deny it, so she didn't. Then her mother called out to her father, "George, you're going to be a grandfather."

In the end, despite their shock, her parents took it well and were thrilled about their impending grandparenthood. They also agreed that what Claire and Jack had done was best under the circumstances.

When Jack told his parents, they were equally sanguine about it. They offered to give them their Chelsea brownstone since they were moving to Arizona and agreed to pay a year's worth of the expenses, which were not insignificant. If during that time Jack wasn't able to make a living as an actor, then he could work in the family insurance business or find something else, but he would be on his own.

A year later, Jack, now with a wife and daughter to support, reluctantly became an insurance agent, and the playful guy Claire fell for changed. As did their happy relationship.

"If you hadn't gotten pregnant and forced me into marriage," Jack began one night when he had had too much to drink, "I wouldn't be stuck in a job—"

"Forced you? I told you—"

"You knew I had no choice. You could've gotten an abortion, and I'd have never even known."

"I can't believe you're saying that. I tried to break it off; you never would've known if you hadn't shown up, so don't blame me. I'm not sure which is worse—saying I could've gotten an abortion on some butcher's kitchen table and possibly died or wishing Hope was never born."

"You know that's not what I'm saying."

"Then what are you saying?"

"Forget it," Jack said, heading out of the room and toward the stairs. A moment later she heard the front door slam.

He apologized profusely the next day, saying he didn't mean it, but Claire knew he did.

A couple of years later, Claire wanted to have another child; Jack did not, saying they couldn't afford it. Claire recounted the conversation, still fresh in her mind.

"Yes, we can," she had argued. "Your dad can give you a raise."

"Claire, I hope to God I don't have to spend the rest of my life selling insurance."

"You mean you're still auditioning?"

"I haven't hidden it from you."

"Yes, you have."

"It's more that I didn't mention it. I didn't lie."

"Oh, Jack. How long do we have to wait for your break?"

"As long as it takes."

"My parents can help," Claire had said, trying a different tack. "I'm sure Dad would say yes in a nanosecond."

"No. It's my responsibility to support my family."

"But it's okay when it's your parents?"

"It's different."

"Even if it means we can't have more children?"

"Claire, try to understand. As much as my job is sucking my soul dry, I can't live off your parents. I'd lose all respect for myself, and you would, too."

As she told Dr. Weiland, she really tried to understand, but she badly wanted Hope to have at least one sibling.

"So what do I do? If I push Jack until he gives in, he'll resent me and the child."

"Making it as an actor is a long shot at best. Let him go pursue his dream. You're still in your twenties; you could have more children— and a better marriage—with another man. You'd both be happier."

His suggestion ended the therapy and scared Claire back into her marriage. *It had to be hard to be stuck in a business you hate*, she thought.

It wasn't that Jack didn't adore Hope. He was a wonderful father, and as he told Claire, he would be a better husband if he were happier doing what he loved—and she agreed.

Eventually, Jack realized he was unlikely to make it as an actor, at least professionally. He joined a neighborhood acting group that met monthly in different members' apartments to read through plays and musicals, which not only gave him an outlet for his talent but also provided him and Claire with a fun social life. By then, Hope was in grade school, and Claire was deeply involved with classes at the Art Students League. So, even if they could have afforded to expand the family, it simply was no longer a priority.

Claire's second experience with therapy, a year or so after Hope's death, was more successful. Her gynecologist had given her a referral to a grief therapist, an older woman who had also lost a child. Almost from the first session, Claire felt less alone.

Over the course of a few sessions, Claire told Dr. Altman that before her daughter's tragedy she had been happy. She loved being a grand-mother and had growing confidence in her work. Her portraits had been gaining recognition, and she was getting paid for commissions. One had been for ten thousand dollars, which covered a two-week trip to Europe with Jack and Jia.

The work she was proudest of was the portrait she had painted of Hope holding Jia. It had taken her a long time to decide how to approach it. Hope was such a natural mother, and the bond between the two of them was beautiful. Unlike her other portraits, which had a contemporary feel to them, Claire wanted this one to have a sense of timelessness.

Not wanting to make it overtly sentimental, she chose not to have them looking at each other but rather to have Jia looking outward as Hope held a shell to her ear. The scene came to her one day when the three of them were at the beach together on the Jersey Shore. Finding a conch shell, Hope had held it to Jia's ear so she could hear the ocean. It reminded Claire of a painting she had seen in a museum many years ago. She whipped out her camera and captured the moment, then transplanted them onto canvas. She titled it *Mother Love*.

However, the tragedy changed all that. Her motivation dried up overnight as both she and Jack withdrew into their own misery. Isolating from each other, unable to give each other comfort, Claire wasn't sure how she could face spending the rest of her life this sad and lonely. She needed to know if her feelings were a normal by-product of her devastating loss or more about her crumbling marriage.

Claire filled Dr. Altman in on the background of her marriage, saying that she thought that she had made peace with Jack's unwillingness to have more children, but when Hope died, her anger resurfaced. While she couldn't know if losing their only child would have been any less painful if they had had more children, the hole in their lives would have been less. She assumed that Jack probably thought about it as well, knowing that as traumatic as Hope's death had been for her, at least her grief was not complicated by guilt about refusing to have more children. But she could only guess what Jack was feeling since he never talked about it. He had shut down—he even dropped out of the acting group. But at least, Claire said, he had work to keep him busy, even if he didn't love it.

Dr. Altman encouraged Claire to apply to the Yale School of Art. New Haven wasn't that far a commute, and Claire had told her that her favorite teacher at RISD was now at Yale. But just when Claire was about to start the Yale program, the company Dae worked for called him back to Korea. Aside from his own deep sorrow, Dae told Claire and Jack that he felt out of his element being a single parent to a child who was also grieving. He worried that she had never met his family, didn't speak Korean, and had had little exposure to such a different culture. While he didn't ask outright, Claire sensed he wanted them to offer to have Jia live with them.

Such an offer was a no-brainer for both her and Jack. If Jia moved to Korea, it would compound their already unbearable loss. They needed their granddaughter as much as she needed them. They worked out an arrangement with Dae whereby Jia lived with them during the school year and studied Korean. Summers she spent a month with her dad in Seoul.

When Dae left, even though her mother had offered to stay with Jia on the days she had classes, Claire didn't have the emotional strength to raise a young child and commute to New Haven or nurture a career. She dropped out; raising Jia was her main and only priority. She also ended therapy, foregoing any thought of leaving Jack. There was little evidence that she had been an artist other than the portrait she had given her mother of Hope and Jia before Hope's death—and the Yale School of Art's periodic mailings.

Still holding Dr. Parker's card, Claire couldn't believe she had allowed herself to open the Pandora's box of her life for the second time in one morning. All because of Jack's insistence that she seek therapy or sleep in Hope's room.

Claire ripped the card into confetti-sized pieces and tossed them into the wastebasket. *Time to do half an hour of yoga, a therapy of sorts,* she thought, *then head uptown to see Mother.*

TWENTY-TWO

The Old Lady's Great-Granddaughter

A S SHE WAS GETTING DRESSED TO GO TO HER APPOINTMENT, Jia thought about how ironic it was that a dog brought Kenny and her together and now was putting them at odds. Her mind wandered to the day they met.

At the time, she was living with Macy, her best friend and former roommate at Cornell, in a tiny one-bedroom apartment on the Lower East Side. It was a bitterly cold Saturday in January with several inches of snow in the forecast. Jia figured it was the perfect day to hunker down in bed and binge-watch *Friends* or some other series about young people whose problems she could identify with. She had recently broken up with her musician boyfriend and was newly and happily single.

"Get out of bed," Macy yelled as she came into Jia's bedroom, dressed in snow gear. "We're going to the Meadowlands to look at puppies."

"You're crazy," Jia said.

"Get up. Come on, it'll be fun."

"We can't get a puppy. And besides, it's about to snow."

"There will be hundreds of dogs from shelters all over the Northeast, many of them hurricane survivors."

"So?"

"So, I want to see what kind of a dog I want when I have kids."

"But you don't want kids . . . or to get married."

Macy and Jia knew just about everything there was to know about each other.

"That's now. Maybe I'll change my mind in ten years. Now get up!"

"And how exactly do you plan to get there?"

"They have buses that leave from the Port Authority."

"If the snow keeps on like this, we could get stranded."

"What snow?" Macy teased. "At home, this would be akin to a rain shower." This was the first time it had snowed since Macy had moved to New York from Milwaukee in September.

"Well, this is New York, not Wisconsin. Everything grinds to a halt with a few inches of snow. Take pictures of the dogs for me."

But as soon as Macy left the room, Jia worried what would happen if there were a blizzard and Macy got stuck in New Jersey by herself. She would feel like shit. Besides, maybe it would be an adventure.

"Mace, give me five minutes," Jia called out. "And check the bus schedules."

By the time they got to the Meadowlands, there were two inches of snow on the ground. But that didn't seem to faze potential dog owners. The place was packed with aisles of about six hundred cages of barking dogs and screaming (mostly with joy) kids and adults. Anyone who already had a dog at home had brought their dog along to make sure their pet got along with the adoptee. Folding tables lined the perimeters, manned by personnel from the various rescue sites. As if the place wasn't noisy enough, every time someone adopted a dog, bells would ring. It was, in a word, chaotic.

As Macy ran up and down the aisles, Jia sat down on a folding chair near one of the tables and Googled the weather. It wasn't that she didn't adore dogs—she did. That was just the problem. She didn't want to be tempted to get a puppy. All she needed was to see a little Jack Russell pup eyeing her, his tail wagging away, and she would be in trouble.

After half an hour or so, Macy found her. "Come with me right away. You have to see this puppy."

When they got to the cage, "Macy's puppy," a Wheaton mix, was out of the cage and being petted by a man about their age as another man spoke to a woman holding a clipboard.

"Hey," Macy said, sounding annoyed. "I was here first. I just went to get my friend."

"Sorry, but we've been here a while, and I didn't see anyone," the man who was speaking to the woman with the clipboard said. Based on their conversation, it was obvious the man planned to adopt the dog.

"This place is ginormous. It took time to find—"

"Macy," Jia whispered. "What're you doing? We can't possibly—"

The other man interrupted. "Maybe it was a different dog in another aisle?"

"Absolutely not."

"There's a dog that's almost identical two aisles over. Can I show you?" the other man asked. "It might be the one you saw."

"I'll look," Macy said reluctantly, "but if it's not . . ."

Macy followed the man, who turned out to be Kenny. When they came back, Macy somewhat sheepishly confessed that she wasn't ready to adopt.

Kenny's friend Adam adopted the dog, and the five of them cabbed it back to Manhattan in a semi-blizzard. By the time Kenny and Adam dropped Jia and Macy back at their apartment, Kenny had already asked Jia out—and Macy knew what kind of dog she wanted if and when the day came.

Even though they had a dinner date for the following Friday, the next day Kenny asked Jia to go sledding with him in Central Park. She quickly said yes. She loved that he had a kid side to him, but then she remembered that she didn't have a sled.

"Worry not," he told her, "we can use trays." They arranged to meet at the Hippo Playground on Riverside Drive and 91st Street.

When she got there, the playground was packed, and Jia worried that they might not recognize each other in their snow gear. She tried to picture him. Short, sandy brown hair, but he probably would be wearing a hat. Maybe six feet, which helped. Handsome despite the fact that his nose was a little crooked, possibly broken as a kid but not fixed, which showed a lack of vanity. *It shouldn't be that hard*, she thought, *but how would be recognize me?* She was bundled up from head to toe and wearing sunglasses. She removed the glasses so he could see her face.

When it was half an hour past the time they were supposed to meet, Jia was really pissed off at him *and* at herself. How could she have so mistaken his interest and his character? *What an asshole*, she thought, *arranging to meet on the coldest day of the year and then not showing up.*

She headed toward Riverside Drive and hailed a cab. She was so into her head that she didn't notice the man inside the cab paying with a credit card.

"Jia, I am so, so sorry," Kenny said as he got out. Jia stared at him a moment before registering who it was. "I was almost out the door when my mother called."

"I have to warm up. I'm freezing. I've been waiting all this time," Jia said, unable to mask her irritation.

Kenny took her arm and helped her inside the cab, then got in after her.

"Rumpelmayer's," he told the driver. Putting his arms around Jia, Kenny held her close, trying to warm her up. "Forgive me?"

"I thought you stood me up," Jia said, her teeth still chattering.

"I knew you'd think that, but I was stuck on the call. My mother was all upset. My parents fight all the time, and no matter how much I tell them I don't want to be put in the middle, they both want me to hear their side."

"Why do they stay together if they're that unhappy?" Jia asked.

"I'm not sure they're unhappy."

"That's funny. Maybe they like to make up?"

"Oh yeah. That's part of it. Anyhow, that was the delay."

As she started to warm up, she noticed Kenny's attire. "That's how you wanted to go sledding? In jeans?"

"Hey, I'm no wimp," Kenny said.

By the time the cab arrived at Rumpelmayer's, Jia was already half in love with Kenny. He was kind and smart, and he loved Rumpelmayer's as much as she did. Coincidentally, his grandparents often brought him there on weekends as a child. In fact they might have even been there at the same time. She could tell that he really loved his parents, and for her, family was everything.

The more she thought about Kenny, the more Jia regretted not telling him about her appointment. But as she thought about what she could have said, the idea of even articulating her fear stopped her cold. She couldn't tolerate his sympathy; it would scare her, make it seem more real. She needed to do it alone. When it was over, when she knew the results, then . . . no, she couldn't go there either.

But she had to consider the possibilities so she wouldn't be caught off guard. She decided that if the colonoscopy found anything suspicious, and a biopsy confirmed it, and it was stage four—although she knew that if that were the case, she would probably have more symptoms—she would tell no one. She had no interest in horrible treatments to buy a limited amount of time. Instead she would find a painless way to die once the symptoms affected the quality of her life but before anyone suspected she had cancer.

Jia felt strangely calm knowing she had a plan. She looked out the window to see what the weather was like. It looked nice, so Jia decided to walk to her appointment with Dr. Cunningham. She loved April when everything started to come alive after winter. Since his office was on First Avenue and 36th Street, and her apartment was on West 12th Street, she could brisk-weave a diagonal path north and east, hopefully not having to stop for many lights, thus making it exercise.

Before leaving, she checked the temperature on her iPhone: sixty degrees. It was funny how sixty degrees in the spring could feel almost hot, whereas sixty degrees in the fall seemed positively cold.

She tossed a few toys into Arnold's crate before shutting him in and left the light on for him, then quickly left. She hoped against hope that the most recent training had had some benefit and Arnold wouldn't spend the day whining.

When she exited the building, she felt chilled, which took her by surprise. *Is it the outside temperature or am I so nervous that it feels colder than it is?* She walked quickly, wrapping her arms around her body for warmth. Still not sure if it was her fear or the outside air, she eyed approaching pedestrians to see what they were wearing or if they also appeared cold.

Seeing an elderly woman approach, Jia slowed her pace and smiled at the woman. When the woman smiled back, Jia said, "A bit nippy today, isn't it?"

The woman replied, "You ask me, it's warmer than I like."

Warmer. That threw Jia. She decided to ask another stranger, a man holding hands with a little girl, probably taking her home from some class. The kid was wearing a sweater, the man a suit. "A bit nippy, isn't it?"

"Excuse me?" the man said in a tone that was not friendly. "I had to force Casey to wear a sweater. She didn't think she needed it."

As he passed, Jia realized that maybe he thought she was being critical of his parenting. She turned around to look at the pair. Casey turned back at the same time and stuck her tongue out at her. Jia had to laugh. Kids were so honest. *Game on*, Jia thought. She put her fingers in her ears and wiggled them at Casey. But then someone bumped into her, saying, "Do you mind?" in an annoyed voice. By the time Jia had apologized, she looked back for Casey, but she and her dad were out of sight.

She was starting to warm up, although she wasn't sure if it was because she was walking at a fast clip or distracted by her interactions. She glanced at a large digital thermometer in a store window and saw it was now sixty-five. She released her arms, feeling instantly warmer. "I will be fine, I am far too young to have cancer, I do not have cancer, I cannot have cancer," a mantra she kept repeating over and over.

But then she remembered Emma.

The previous night, after she and Kenny had made love, Kenny got up to go to the bathroom. She clicked on the television. The film *Terms of Endearment* was about to come on.

"Kenny," Jia called. "Feel up to a movie?"

"No." Then, "What is it?"

"*Terms of Endearment*. It says it's a comedy with Shirley MacLaine and Jack Nicholson and Debra Winger—should be fun."

"Who's Debra Winger?" he asked.

"I don't know."

"Enjoy," he said, suggesting he probably preferred sleep.

"I'll watch in the living room."

Jia was blindsided when midway through, Emma, Debra Winger's character, a young mother with young kids, got breast cancer. "Fuck you!" she yelled at the TV. "You call this a comedy?"

She knew she should turn it off, but she couldn't—she had to know, even though she was sure she knew what would happen. She considered waking Kenny to watch with her, but he would probably say something along the lines of "Are you nuts?" He hated depressing shows. She *was* nuts. Who wants to see a "comedy" about a young woman dying the night before you have a procedure to see if you have cancer? It was masochistic to continue watching, but she was riveted, identifying both with Emma, dead of cancer before she was forty, and Emma's daughter, Melanie, who lost her mom.

For the first time in years, Jia missed her mother, or rather, missed not having had her in her life. She had so few memories of her that in her mind, she was almost an abstraction: the beautiful woman in the portrait of the two of them. Jia remembered—was it a memory or what others had told her?—that she had loved to traipse around in her mother's high heels, wearing her mother's pale-blue cashmere bathrobe. It swam on her, so when she walked in it, it would make her mother laugh. For several years after her mother died, Jia couldn't fall asleep unless she was holding the robe—her way of trying to hold on to her mother.

At least in the movie, Melanie's dad didn't leave, although he was too absorbed in his own pain to be there for her. Her dad was the same. Then, a year later, he returned to Korea for work, and she lost him as a primary parental figure. Once Jia went down that rabbit hole, memories she thought were lost came to the surface.

As a child, she wasn't aware of missing her father. It wasn't like he had disappeared. He called and wrote and sent presents, and she saw him every summer for a few weeks. And it wasn't like she didn't have a family. Nana and Papa were always there for her, not to mention Granny and Granddad, who doted on her.

But the movie put her in touch with feelings she chose not to dwell on. It wasn't like she could fix the fact that she was, in effect, an orphan.

It was funny how her looks identified her as part of a culture she knew so little about, and she felt a sudden urge to move to Seoul for a year to get to know her father and her Korean family better. But when? Not if she had cancer and not if Kenny wanted to make partner. And how could she just pick up and leave New York with Granny so old? Jia couldn't imagine not being there for Granny as long as she was alive. No, it was just a fantasy.

Her thoughts turned back to Emma. *How awful to know you won't live to see your children grow up. How do you prepare your children for your death? How do you say goodbye? At least my mother never knew what hit her.*

By the time she got to the doctor's office, Jia was a total mess. The receptionist was not happy when she saw that Jia had come alone.

"I thought I told you you needed someone with you," the receptionist said.

"I'm sure you did," Jia lied. "I was so frazzled I didn't take in."

"Is there someone you can call now? You should be good to go by around one."

"I can't take an Uber?" Jia asked.

The nurse shook her head no. "After you make arrangements, we can get you started."

Jia sat in the waiting area and pretended to make a call. If she really couldn't Uber it, Rosie was her backup.

But then she thought, *I really need Kenny right now. If I had told him, he would have come.* She considered calling him, then changed her mind. No matter what the result, she would tell him tonight. No need to get him worked up if it turned out to be nothing.

TWENTY-THREE

The Old Lady's Downstairs Neighbor

Across town, Dariush and Miss Sidenstriker had just arrived at Roosevelt Hospital's emergency room. Holding her arm, Dariush helped Miss Sidenstriker find a seat in the crowded waiting area, then went to the reception desk. Several people were ahead of him. As he waited in line, he looked back at Miss Sidenstriker, whose face had turned to stone.

When his turn came, he leaned over the desk to whisper to the receptionist, "See the old woman in the green shirt sitting in the front row on the left?"

The receptionist didn't bother to look up but instead handed him a clipboard with forms on it.

"Fill these out and return them to me."

"Her kneecap may be broken and she's in great pain. Can't that wait?"

"No, sir, it can't."

He had only been to an emergency room once before when Mr. Gartner fell in his apartment, and at that time, Dariush had arrived after the ambulance that brought Mr. Gartner there, so he didn't know emergency room protocol.

Unhinged by that memory as well as infuriated by the receptionist's indifference, Dariush grabbed the clipboard. As he looked around for two seats together, Miss Sidenstriker waved him over.

"You can leave now," she said, taking the clipboard out of his hands.

So much for gratitude, Dariush thought. It was tempting to do what she asked, but then Dariush thought about the Bahá'í teachings his father had drilled into him as a child. "Service to others is for the love of God, not for praise, not for reward in the next world. Let your heart burn with loving-kindness for all those who may cross your path."

"I'll be here to take you home when you're ready to leave," Dariush told Miss Sidenstriker, then hurried outside. She had no idea how hard it was for him to even be there, what a sacrifice he was making. No idea. He felt himself drifting back in time to that awful November day five years ago.

Dariush had just opened the front door to his apartment to retrieve the newspaper when he heard shuffling footsteps coming down the back stairway of the building. He assumed that it was Mr. Gartner, who periodically slipped out of his apartment to roam the hallways. Sometimes he would come down a flight and knock on Dariush's door to see if Dariush's father wanted to play backgammon, forgetting or unaware that his parents had gone to Iran a couple of years prior.

When Dariush would open the door, Mr. Gartner would say, "Arya! Ready to be beaten?" or words to that effect. Dariush wouldn't correct him but rather would invite him in to play. Some days he seemed sharp, others foggy, and Dariush learned to meet him where he was mentally. It became a lesson in dealing with dementia.

On the day in question, no sooner had Dariush opened the door to let Mr. Gartner in than he heard Mrs. Gartner call out, "George! Come back up."

"*Shh*. Don't say I'm here," he whispered as he held up a pretend card. "I found my Get Out of Jail card."

Dariush walked over to the stairwell and called up. "Mrs. Gartner, is it okay if I borrow your husband to play backgammon? I'll bring him back up when we're done."

"All right, Dariush, but use the elevator, not the stairs," she called back.

Once the door was closed, Mr. Gartner headed straight for the kitchen and opened the lid of a pot that was on the stove. "What's for dinner?" he called out.

"A Persian stew with celery, parsley, and lamb. I'll give you some before you go."

Then Mr. Gartner took his place at the backgammon table that was positioned in front of one of the living room windows. Behind him was a tall standing radiator, the kind only found in old buildings. Dariush sat across from him.

"Tan or brown?" Dariush asked.

"Arya, you know I always choose tan."

"Right, George, sorry." Dariush had to push himself to call the old man by his first name. It felt disrespectful, but, as Arya, he had no choice.

After arranging the pieces on the board, Dariush handed Mr. Gartner one of the dice. Each man tossed a die to see who went first. Dariush got three, Mr. Gartner four, and the game was on.

It was one of Mr. Gartner's on days, and the game was spirited. Every time he took one of Dariush's pieces, he pumped his fists and shouted, "Yes," as if he were a teenager. Dariush always tried to let him win, but on that day he didn't have to throw the game. Mr. Gartner held his own and was about to win when Dariush tossed the dice and got double sixes, which put him in the lead.

"Arya, you cheated," Mr. Gartner yelled. "You switched the dice. Just like you always do." Mr. Gartner excitedly got up and, leaning across the table, grabbed the lapels of Dariush's shirt and shook him, all the time yelling, "You cheater. Cheater."

"Mr. Gartner . . . George . . . please, sit down. There's a misunderstanding," Dariush said. He stood up with the intention of going over to Mr. Gartner and holding him until he calmed down. But in so doing, Mr. Gartner let go of the lapels of Dariush's shirt and lost his balance. Dariush watched as if in slow motion as Mr. Gartner fell backward, whacking the back of his head against the radiator on the way down. Blood gushed out of the wound as he lay slumped on the floor. Dariush was horrified. Ever since he was a child, he had fainted at the sight of blood, stemming from when he had to have blood drawn prior to a tonsillectomy at the age of six. He remembered how a nurse tried to prick his finger to get his blood type, but he had freaked out and had to be held down. As he kept fighting the nurse off, another nurse came, and together they held him down, while a third nurse inserted a needle in the crook of his arm to get the blood. By then he was soaked in sweat and too exhausted to fight. Even as an adult, he was fearful of having his blood drawn or even seeing blood. It was embarrassing, but he had no control over it. But now he had to act.

Dariush grabbed his phone and called 9-1-1, then ran to Mr. Gartner's side. "Are you alright? Can you hear me?" When he got no response, Dariush felt Mr. Gartner's carotid neck artery for a pulse and got one.

Thank God, Dariush thought. Blood was pooling on the floor under Mr. Gartner's head, and Dariush could feel it seeping into his pants legs. In a panic, he was about to do mouth-to-mouth when he heard, in a whisper, "Arya, my brains are falling out."

"No, no, they're not. It's just a gash; it can be stitched up. I've called for an ambulance," Dariush said in a rush, trying to sound reassuring.

"But, George, I need to let your wife know you fell. What's your home number?"

"I'm not sure."

Now what? I can't leave him to run upstairs and tell her. Hearing the wail of an approaching siren brought him to his senses. As soon as the paramedics arrived, he contacted Jimmy, the doorman, and told him to notify Mrs. Gartner.

As the paramedics were lifting Mr. Gartner onto a stretcher, his wife came flying into the apartment saying, "Oh no, oh no, George, no," as she ran to her husband's side. Mr. Gartner's eyes were closed as she took his hand.

"Bette?" he said in a weak voice. "Is that you, my sweet?"

"Excuse us, ma'am, you need to move back," one of the paramedics said as he hoisted up the stretcher.

As they headed for the door, Mrs. Gartner said, "Wait for me—I need to get my coat and pocketbook."

"No," one of the EMTs said. "He's lost a lot of blood. We have to get to the hospital before he goes into shock. Now please, move back."

Dariush barely had time to ask which hospital they were going to before they loaded the stretcher into the service elevator and were gone. Dariush told Mrs. Gartner he would take her to the hospital as soon as she was ready.

When they got to the reception area of the emergency room at Roosevelt Hospital, Dariush and Mrs. Gartner were told they needed information about the patient's medical history right away. Mrs. Gartner asked Dariush to go in ahead of her so her husband could see a familiar face as she did the paperwork.

Dariush passed through double doors into a spacious room. Monitors beeped and the hospital staff moved quietly and purposefully in and out of the curtained cubicles lining the perimeters of the room. No one seemed aware of his presence.

Clog-clad feet moved behind the curtains around the cubicles, but he had no way of knowing which one Mr. Gartner was in. He couldn't just peer inside, and he was loath to interrupt any of the nurses who seemed so busy. He considered sitting on one of the folding chairs by the entrance and waiting for Mrs. Gartner, but she wanted him to be with her husband.

Just then a curtain was pushed aside at the far end of the room, and a nurse exited, leaving the curtain open. Dariush saw a medical team working on Mr. Gartner, who was sitting shirtless upright in bed with monitors attached to his chest. Dariush walked hesitantly forward and stood at the end of the bed, hoping Mr. Gartner would notice him.

He watched as a nurse held Mr. Gartner's arms down. A doctor who looked even younger than Dariush injected Lidocaine on the site of the wound. A couple of minutes later, he poured some kind of liquid into the wound, then started probing inside the back of Mr. Gartner's scalp to remove tissue. Mr. Gartner kept groaning, and Dariush was shocked by what seemed to him the callousness of the doctor. Dariush prayed that the ordeal would be over before Mrs. Gartner got there—and also before he passed out.

Suddenly Dariush saw Mr. Gartner's eyeballs roll upward and his head fall back. The monitor started beeping—he had flatlined. Code Blue was announced over the loudspeakers. A moment later, Dariush was pushed aside as a team of doctors descended into the cubicle and closed the curtain.

Dariush was beside himself, sure Mr. Gartner had died and wondering how to tell his wife. Before he had a chance to figure out what to say to Mrs. Gartner, the curtain was again pushed aside, and the emergency team left. Dariush gathered his courage and looked inside. To his immense relief, Mr. Gartner was looking right at him as the surgeon began stitching the wound.

"George, it's—" Dariush was about to say his name, but caught himself. "It's Arya, your friend and neighbor. I'm here, and your wife will be here shortly. Okay?"

Groaning, Mr. Gartner tried to reach his hands back to touch the wound, but the nurse held them down. "They took out my brain," he said in a small, scared voice.

"No, they're just trying to help you," Dariush said. "Remember, we were playing backgammon when—" Dariush froze, not sure whether to remind Mr. Gartner that he thought he was cheating.

But then the doctor spoke. "Sir, you had a bad fall. I had to clean out the wound, so it won't get infected. Now I'm stitching it up." He continued talking through what he was doing. "Just a few more stitches. There. Now it needs to be bandaged."

Mr. Gartner calmed down.

Dariush saw Mrs. Gartner enter the emergency room. He rushed to her side and led her to one of the folding chairs. "They just finished stitching up the wound," he told her, trying to sound reassuring.

A moment later, the doctor approached them. Dariush jumped up to intercept him. "Does his wife need to know he flatlined?"

"Are you related?"

"No, but—"

"I'm sorry," the doctor said, walking past Dariush to Mrs. Gartner. He explained that her husband had passed out from the pain and had to be resuscitated but was now resting. However, as a precaution they wanted to admit him for observation and further tests. He said that they were free to go in the cubicle but that it might take some time to find a bed.

When the doctor left, Mrs. Gartner asked Dariush what had happened.

"He thought I was cheating, I don't know why. He yelled, 'Arya, you're cheating.' I tried to calm him down, but he got up too quickly and fell backward. If only I hadn't tried to approach him."

"Lately, he gets agitated at times. It's not your fault, but playing backgammon may not be good for him. He becomes competitive and then gets frustrated by his limitations."

"But he was doing well until I got double sixes. That had nothing to do with his limitations; it was just bad luck."

"He may not see the difference."

"I feel awful."

"Go home and change, Dariush," Mrs. Gartner said. "I'm staying with him."

Dariush escorted Mrs. Gartner to her husband's side before leaving, saying he would come back for her when she was ready to return home. He had to get out of there fast. The whole experience had been harrowing, first thinking Mr. Gartner was dead back in the apartment, then again just a few minutes ago. The blood on the legs of his pants had dried and stiffened, and he desperately wanted to get home, shower, and change. Then he would mop up the bloody mess on the floor, a task he dreaded.

Just then a child's screams brought Dariush out of the memory. He looked up and saw a young woman running toward the entrance to the emergency room holding a child, whose arm hung limply by her side. A young man accompanied them.

As they disappeared inside, his mind switched to Miss Sidenstriker. What was taking so long?

TWENTY-FOUR

The Old Lady

B ETTE WAS TIRED AFTER HER OUTING, NOT SO MUCH physically as emotionally. She told Rosie she wanted to rest for half an hour before writing the invitations, instructing her to wake her if she fell asleep.

But tired as she was, ever since the moment she had decided to have a dinner party, her mind had been drifting to random memories of the past. Just now, she thought about her father, poor man, having to raise a daughter by himself in his fifties after losing his wife. *What had that been like?* It was a thought that had never occurred to her before. He must have been grief stricken and overwhelmed. She regretted that she had never once asked him what it was like, even when she was an adult and could understand how hard it must have been. She knew she had to have been an accident.

Did her father ask any of her brothers to adopt her so she could be raised with children close to her age? Did any of them volunteer? That would have been logical, maybe better, to have her cousins as siblings and not be raised by nannies—not that her father didn't try his best.

Her brother William and his family lived on the Jersey Shore near the beach. Would she have still gotten polio if she had lived with them? Their exposure was less. Not that it was her father's fault. No doubt one of her nannies told him she was lonely and chafing at all the restrictions, so, with the best of intentions, her father took her to a public pool at the wrong time and probably blamed himself. She could still remember hearing him talk to her doctor outside her hospital bed, "My little BETTEkins, my poor little Bette. Will she ever walk again?"

Bette stopped herself. Where did all this come from? She did not believe in regret. *All life is a process*, she thought. Had she not grown up in such an adult environment, she probably would not have become so independent. Had she not had polio, she might not have learned to do needlepoint. Had she not gone to B. Altman to buy a book on needlepoint designs, she would never have met George.

George, dear George. How she missed him. Her focus shifted to memories of his final years. As trying as he could be, and patience was not her strong suit, she was glad she had been there for him. He had always been so involved in his work, so it was like the first time she had had him to herself, day and night.

Well, not exactly to herself. He and Claire remained close as ever, but the things they had done together in the past, such as play tennis and go for long walks, were no longer feasible. Instead Claire sat with him and watched television.

As the years went by and George's mind started to dim, he became totally dependent on her and her alone. "Bette," he would call out, "Where's my Foxy?" She had to limit his contact with others as George could not keep up with the conversation, making it awkward for everyone and hard on him. And on her.

Per his doctor's suggestion, she did simple games with him to activate his mind. She pushed him to show her and Rosie card tricks and acted as if he had guessed the right card, although he rarely did. Rosie always made a big deal out of it as if he were the most clever magician she had ever seen. The same with card games. Over time, it went from poker to gin rummy to Go Fish. Bette did jigsaw puzzles with large pieces and sometimes played backgammon, but more often than not, all he was up to was checkers, and then not even checkers.

George was often restless and would wander through the apartment. Occasionally he got out, providing him—and her—a brief respite. Bette kept tabs on him and made sure that either she or Rosie knew where he was, whether it was roaming the hallway or dropping in on Gertrude or Dariush. Jimmy, the doorman, knew that if by chance he got into the elevator and came downstairs, he should let her know right away.

Then he died, and it left a huge void in her life. Bette felt totally adrift. Against her wishes, Claire hired a personal trainer who came to the apartment three times a week. Bette hated every minute of it and wanted to quit, but Claire kept telling her that staying fit was the only defense against aging, which Bette knew was right but didn't care. Why fight old age? Claire never once asked her mother what she wanted; she just sprang into action.

Why, Bette wondered, *was Claire so invested in keeping me alive? She saw what had happened with her father. Old age wasn't pretty. Or easy. Doesn't she know that at my age, life is just a waiting game?*

Bette had little interest in seeing what few friends she had left; their conversations mostly centered on their health. Boring. She had been a competitive bridge player, part of a league, but had resigned when George retired. Nor was she interested in computer literacy. To what end? Certainly not to share photos of herself on Mega or whatever that computer site was called that Jia loved so much. Whenever she visited, Jia would insist that she look at videos of all sorts of crazy stunts. They horrified her, insane thrill seekers. What was wrong with people these days? No, she had television and the newspaper and the phone and her books and, above all, her needlepoint.

Bette's mind hopscotched over to Jia. What was going on with her and Kenny? They had been together more than five years. Were they having problems? Or did they not believe in marriage like so many young people these days?

Bette recalled how impressed she was with Kenny the first time they met; George was still alive then. He addressed her as Mrs. Gartner, none of this first-name business. But what struck her most was how he handled George, who had been sitting at his desk scribbling on a legal pad. Kenny waited with Bette by the doorway while Jia went over to tell George she had someone special she wanted him to meet.

George turned to look at Kenny. "Father?" he asked.

Jia looked at Bette, her eyes wide as saucers, but Kenny, smiling, just walked over to George. Putting his hand on George's shoulder, he looked at the legal pad. "What've you got there, sir? A brief?" Kenny asked as if the scribbling made sense.

George stared at him a moment, a puzzled look on his face, then looked at the pad, then back at Kenny.

"I'm Kenny Peterson, Jia's boyfriend," Kenny said, then added, "I'm a lawyer, too."

A moment later George stuck out his hand. "George Gartner."

"A pleasure to meet you," Kenny said, shaking his hand. "Jia has told me so much about you."

George nodded, clearly pleased.

But as much as Bette liked Kenny, Bette knew that you can never know what anyone else's relationship is really like. Perhaps Jia had doubts. Bette suddenly felt concerned that Jia might think she was more invested in her marrying Kenny than in her happiness. Bette resolved to have a talk with her before the day ended.

Then there was Claire, another major concern. Ever since Jia left home, Claire had been without a focus, unless you wanted to call yoga and running a purpose. She had so much talent. When Hope died, she gave it up for a time. Bette understood. She was distraught over losing her only child, then had to get herself together to raise her granddaughter. But as Jia grew older, there was no reason Claire couldn't go back to painting full-time. Instead she dabbled with art classes, refusing to take it seriously. Or ran. Run, run, run. When you have a God-given talent like that, you need to pursue it. But whenever she even hinted about it, Claire shut down. Well, too bad. She needed to speak her piece.

As a rule, she tried not to interfere with their lives, but now, believing that she had to, Bette made a mental note of what she wanted to say to her nearest and dearest. It was up to them whether they listened or not.

She picked up the intercom and called out, "Rosie. Bring me my lunch. And tell Venera I need her."

TWENTY-FIVE

The Old Lady's Night Aide

VENERA'S HAND WAS ON THE CELL PHONE IN HER POCKET—set to vibrate in case she got a text—as she stood in back of Mrs. Gartner, watching her write invitations on thick ivory note cards with the name Elizabeth Amelia Fox Gartner engraved at the top in black. Mrs. Gartner used a black fountain pen, and Venera marveled at the elegant if wobbly handwriting. The message was short and direct: Come to dinner. Tonight at eight. Formal.

Having seen the guest list, Venera knew that she was included. This would be a story to tell her grandchildren. She would keep her invitation as a souvenir. But why was she invited? And what would she wear? What was formal? Was she supposed to wear a ball gown like Cinderella, then go back into jeans at midnight? Hopefully Rosie would know.

After she wrote each card, Mrs. Gartner then wrote the name of each guest on a matching ivory envelope—including her daughter, son-in-law, great-granddaughter, and her boyfriend. *Imagine,* Venera thought, *being that fancy with your own family. Was this what she had always done when she had them for dinner in the past? Maybe this is how it's done when you are rich.* Venera had to stifle a laugh thinking about the reaction it would have back home if her mother were to send invitations to family dinners and expect everyone to dress up.

Rosie entered the room, cell phone in hand. "Jimmy said Dariush's last name is Rouhani. *R-o-u-h-a-n-i*. Also I googled Citarella's catering menu. Do you want to hear the options?" Rosie asked Mrs. Gartner.

"In a minute," Mrs. Gartner said. "Did you order the flowers?"

"Yes, ma'am."

"Use the Royal Doulton china."

"The Royal Doulton china," Rosie repeated. Turning to Venera, she said, "It's gorgeous. Gold-trimmed with different colorful flowers in the middle and rarely used."

"Make sure I have enough left in mint condition, and use the Baccarat glasses, but first run your fingers along the tops to make sure none is chipped."

"I know the drill, Mrs. G. It hasn't been all that long."

"When is the last time you polished the flatware?"

"I don't remember, but it's on the list."

Venera listened as if they were speaking a foreign language. *Royal Doulton? Baccarat? Flatware? What was that? Good thing Rosie knew what it all meant.*

"Done!" Mrs. Gartner announced as she wheeled herself around and handed Venera the small stack of envelopes. "I want you to hand deliver them. Rosie can give you Claire and Jack and Jia and Kenny's addresses, and the others go to people in the building. I have put the apartment numbers beneath their names."

Venera handed the top envelope to Rosie.

"Thank you," Rosie said, sounding uncharacteristically shy. When she opened the envelope and read the invitation, her face fell. "Seriously, Mrs. G.? Formal? That rules me out."

"Not at all. I have a closet full of gowns you can choose from."

"I can't wear one of your dresses."

"You can, and you will."

"Look at me," Rosie said, her hands curling down her body. "Does it look like I could fit into anything you ever wore?"

"I have several caftans I bought on my travels that are one size fits all."

"Can't I just serve? I would be so much more comfort—"

"No! I want you at the table. In my lovely caftan."

Venera, who had been flipping through the envelopes as Rosie and Mrs. Gartner talked, stopped cold when she came to one. "Mrs. Gartner, I think this may be a mistake." She showed her the envelope.

"No. No mistake."

Venera showed the envelope to Rosie.

"What's the problem?" Mrs. Gartner asked. "I didn't realize I needed a committee to decide who to invite."

Rosie laughed, but Venera was embarrassed. "No problem," she said while thinking, *Yes problem*. Knowing that Miss Sidenstriker would be at the dinner took all the pleasure away for Venera. Now she dreaded it. "Should I go now?"

"Yes. Take taxi money from the petty cash envelope in my desk drawer. Where were we? Oh yes, the menu, and before I forget, do we have any unused candles for the candelabras?"

"I'll check," Rosie said, then started reading a list of menu items from Citarella as Venera got the cash she needed and left the room. Once she got into the foyer, she took her cell phone off vibrate so she would hear the ping of a text or ring of a call.

Venera stood in front of Miss Sidenstriker's apartment door, not sure whether to ring the bell or slip the envelope under the door. She was pretty sure Mrs. Gartner wanted her to literally hand the envelope to the old witch. The longer she hesitated, the harder it became to deliver it. Mrs. Gartner was so excited about the dinner, and Venera worried that Miss Sidenstriker would spoil it for her with her poisonous attitude toward people. Besides which, since when were they friends? Or even friendly? *I doubt Mrs. Gartner is even on Miss Sidenstriker's radar.* Finally Venera decided she just couldn't do it. She would tell Mrs. Gartner Miss Sidenstriker was unable to come.

Just as she was about to leave, she heard the sound of approaching footsteps within Miss Sidenstriker's apartment.

"Who's there?"

How does she know someone is there? Venera wondered. *What is the name of those dogs in movies who sniff people's trails? Bloodhounds. Yes, the old bitch is a bloodhound. Always out for blood.*

Miss Sidenstriker shouted, "Who's there?" a few more times, each time louder.

Venera made a dash for the back stairs before Miss Sidenstriker had a chance to open the door. She went down enough stairs to be out of sight, then waited to see what would happen. The silence made it feel like a game of cat and mouse, each waiting the other out. Finally Venera heard the sound of the door being unlocked.

Venera tiptoed down the remaining stairs to the safety of the floor below, confident that the bloodhound was not up for a chase. But if she were, Venera was ready, willing, and able. However, it was not to be. Venera heard Miss Sidenstriker's door close, then lock.

She wasn't sure who the person was to whom the other envelope was addressed: Dariush Rouhani. *Was he young?* she wondered. *Middle-aged? Old? And what was his connection to Mrs. Gartner?* The name sounded Middle Eastern. *I wonder if he's the man I almost knocked over earlier today.*

As she rang the bell, she hoped he would answer so she could apologize, but alas, he was not home. She slipped the envelope under the door.

When she got to the great-granddaughter's building on 12th Street, the doorman told her neither Ms. Kahng nor Mr. Peterson were home.

She handed him the envelope, then took a cab to Mrs. Haight's home in Chelsea.

Having never been inside a townhouse in Manhattan, she was hoping to be invited in. She was surprised by how narrow it was; it looked almost like a dollhouse. Mrs. Haight answered the doorbell dressed in tights and a leotard. At first she didn't recognize Venera—they had only met a couple of times.

"Hi, Mrs. Haight. It's me, Venera."

Claire looked panicked. "Is Mother all right?"

"Yes, she's fine. She sent me," Venera answered, handing her the envelope addressed to Mr. and Mrs. Jack Haight.

"This is Mother's handwriting. What the hell?" Mrs. Haight said, taking the envelope.

"She's giving a dinner party."

"She's what?"

Opening the envelope, Mrs. Haight stared at it in disbelief. "Has she lost her mind? Who else has she invited?"

"Your granddaughter and her boyfriend and Rosie and me and her neighbor Miss Sidenstriker and—"

"Okay, okay. I'll put an end to this little flight of fancy when I get there. Excuse me, I have to get dressed and get uptown," Mrs. Haight said, practically closing the door in Venera's face.

That was rude, Venera thought. *And so much for seeing a townhouse.* Maybe so much for the dinner party too, although she doubted that Mrs. Gartner was about to drop her plan.

She decided to walk back on the path alongside the Hudson River rather than take a cab. It would give her time to think.

She needed to think. She didn't know what to make of Jusef's silence. It had been hours since she sent the text. She thought about what she had written—"let me know where I stand"—and wished she could erase it. She knew she owed him an apology, but she had already apologized—many times. After all the years they had known each other, couldn't he at least have written something like, "Why did you do that" or "I hate you"? That would be better than totally cutting her off. *That's not right either*, she thought. *But then, he's the silent type. A macho man. He used to think for me as if he knew best. Like, if it makes him happy, it will make me happy. And I went along with it. But a house full of kids? No thank you.*

Venera's thoughts switched to wondering what she would do if he said, "I forgive you, come home." She needed to be prepared for that. She couldn't just jerk him around, but neither could she leave her fate all up to him. She needed to make up her mind about what she wanted.

TWENTY-SIX

The Old Lady's Daughter

CLAIRE WAS ON THE VERGE OF TAKING A SHOWER WHEN her mother's night aide showed up at her door with the ridiculous invitation. Now she needed to get uptown and put a kibosh on her mother's dinner plan, but first a quick, cold shower. She loved cold showers, a habit she shared with her father.

"Nothing like a cold shower to get your blood flowing," her father loved to say to goad her mother.

"Nothing like a hot tub to relax you," her mother would respond. Her mother made her take baths every night, but once she was old enough to bathe alone, Claire took cold showers.

As Claire got out of the shower, she eyed the scale. Dare she check her weight? She knew she was too thin. At 5'10" she had the body of a young boy and the face of a woman in her early seventies. Her hair had turned white almost overnight after Hope's sudden death, and she had never wanted to dye it: it represented her grief.

Closing her eyes, Claire stepped on the scale and took a deep breath. Looking down, she saw she weighed 120 pounds, down five pounds from her normal weight, which was already low for her height. It was probably due to the additional spin cycle class she had begun a month or so ago. So be it. Exercise was good for body and mind.

Tomorrow I'll Google the research on night terrors, she thought. *There has to be a way of using mind control to stop them. Mother is the queen of mind control; I must have some of that in my DNA. After all, I've read about miraculous cancer cures using guided imagery. Night terrors should be far easier.*

She got dressed in a sweatsuit and running shoes, having decided she would get there faster if she jogged north along the path by the Hudson River rather than taking the subway. The way the subways had been running lately, she might have to wait half an hour for the C train.

Claire was heading out of the bedroom when she noticed a few pieces of paper lying on the floor by the wastebasket next to her side of the bed. She picked them up and was about to put them into the bin when she saw the brochure from the Yale Art School summer program in Paris that had come the previous day. She could never fathom why her name was still in their data bank, but it was—she got regular mailings. She had thrown it away without reading it.

She removed it and slowly read the text, then studied the photos. Suddenly her heart started racing. Feeling flushed, she got up and opened a window to get some air, then flopped down on her bed. She grabbed the brochure and waved it as if it were a fan. She knew she was having a panic attack.

Claire forced herself to slow down her breathing, inhaling slowly through her nostrils—counting to ten—then exhaling through her mouth—again counting to ten. After a few minutes, she felt better. She remained in place a few more minutes, then studied the brochure in her hand.

On the cover was a photo of the Louvre. *Paris,* she mused. *Oh my, would that I could. But I'm too old to start anew; my proverbial ship has sailed. Right now my job is to take care of Mother, and I do the best I can by overseeing her care. If something happened to Rosie, Mother would be okay. If something happened to me or I left for a few weeks, she wouldn't.*

As much as Claire felt burdened, she also hated even to think about her mother's eventual demise. Despite the fact that her own daughter had died, Claire took for granted that her parents would always be there for her. As a result, she was unprepared for how hard her father's death had hit her. He was one hundred—it wasn't like it was tragic or unexpected—but it triggered in her a fear of her own mortality. She didn't share her mother's belief in an afterlife. As far as Claire was concerned, this was her one life, and while she had experienced the worst tragedy a mother can have, she wasn't ready to check out or, for that matter, for anyone in her orbit to die. If she had the power, Claire would freeze time.

When her father died, she worried that her mother would die soon after as so often happens with long marriages. However, her mother surprised them all with her resilience, especially given that during the lockdown, she was almost totally isolated after years of being with her husband day and night. Claire was in awe of her stoicism and resourcefulness. She never complained. She kept herself busy designing and needlepointing eyeglass cases and giving them to everyone she knew. If they weren't the quality of her earlier work, what did it matter? It was still an impressive achievement.

It heightened Claire's fear of losing her mother. She knew rationally it was silly, this sense of needing her mother. She was seventy-two, her mother ninety-five. But aside from loving her mother, she was also Claire's "job," and Claire needed a job.

Stop, Claire told herself. *This is too depressing to think about.* During her brief forays into therapy, the main thing she had gotten out of it was to learn the "art" of thought stopping. She slipped the brochure under the mattress, then headed for the door. She stopped midway. *Why did I keep it?* she thought. *It will just keep me in turmoil.*

She went back, slid the brochure out, and put it in the trash.

TWENTY-SEVEN

The Old Lady's Housekeeper

ROSIE WAS HELPING MRS. G. CHOOSE WHAT TO WEAR FOR the party when she got an inspiration. "Play dance music from the fifties," Rosie said, tapping the device.

As big band music started playing, Mrs. G. got right into the mood, snapping her fingers and swaying in her wheelchair. Rosie felt like a saleswoman in a vintage clothing store as she removed one beautiful evening dress after another to show her "client."

"I'd forgotten how many dresses I have," Mrs. G. said. "In the old days, George and I were both involved with various charities that held formal dinners." She paused, then added, "George was such a good dancer."

"I bet you were too, Mrs. G.," Rosie said.

"With my limp?"

"Oops. Sorry."

Laughing, Mrs. G. said, "I wasn't, but Claire was. George started teaching her from the time she was around eight. He would put on a record, take her hand, and the lessons would begin. How I loved watching them."

"I can imagine."

"They could've competed on one of those dance shows they have on television these days—they were that good."

"I know. I had just started working for you when you gave a dinner party, and after dinner he and Mrs. Haight got up and danced around the dining room table. What a show it was! I almost poured coffee on one of your guests, I was so busy watching."

"Which guest?"

"I don't recall her name . . . pale-blue dress . . . short blonde hair . . . maybe . . . Mrs. Shepherd?"

"You should've let it spill. She was all over George throughout dinner."

"Mrs. G.," Rosie said, "your husband only had eyes for you."

Mrs. G. didn't respond.

Rosie removed a V-neck silver gown with a shimmering beaded top and a chiffon skirt from its hanger.

"That one," Mrs. G. said.

"I knew it," Rosie said as she slipped the dress over Mrs. G.'s head.

"George loved it."

"No wonder. It's gorgeous."

Mrs. G. moved forward so Rosie could zip up the back. "It's way too big," Mrs. G. said, pulling the fabric away from both sides of her waist. "This is a waste of time. None of my dresses are going to fit."

"It's not like anyone's going to see the back, but I can make it look like it fits perfectly," Rosie said as she removed the gown. "I just need to get my sewing box."

"Forget it. Last time I wore it, I was young, or at least younger, and still had my looks. Now I look like one of those old, wrinkled apple-head dolls."

"Mrs. G.!" Rosie scolded. "What a thing to say."

What set her off? Rosie wondered as she left the room. *Did I say something wrong?*

When she returned with the sewing box, she noticed her boss was staring blankly ahead.

"Mrs. G., are you okay?" Rosie asked.

"No," Mrs. G. said.

"What's wrong?"

"What?" Mrs. G. snapped. "Nothing." And just like that, she was back. Rosie pinned the back of the dress, then carefully removed it and set it aside to fix later.

"Now, it's your turn," Mrs. G. said.

Rosie went to the closet and quickly selected an aqua caftan she had always admired. It had an elaborate bib embroidered with gold thread. Not wanting to undress in front of her boss, Rosie put it on over her clothes—Mrs. G. did not need to see her rolls of fat.

"I love it," Rosie said, smoothing the caftan down over her body.

"George bought it for himself at a bazaar in Marrakesh many years ago, but I loved it so much, I swiped it. He never knew it was missing."

"I can't picture Mr. G. in a caftan," Rosie said.

"It was one of those purchases you make when you're away somewhere and think you'll wear it when you get back—you know, like buying a cowboy hat in Santa Fe."

"Oh yeah?" Rosie said, thinking, *How would I know?* For her, it was more reminiscent of the costumes Bob Hope wore in the old movie *Road to Morocco* that Mrs. G. loved to watch whenever it came on. Mr. G. had loved it, too.

Attempting a belly dance, primarily with her hands, that looked more like a hula, Rosie started singing, "We're off on the road to Morocco—" when she got a beep signaling an incoming text message.

"Excuse me a moment," Rosie said and left the room.

Standing outside Mrs. G.'s bedroom, Rosie read a text from Frank: "Do you know where Patty is? The school called to say she's not in class. I tried to call her, but she doesn't answer."

Rosie wrote back: "Did you drop her off at school or tell her to get there on her own?"

Frank wrote back: "I dropped her off, thank you. She's probably home, but she isn't answering my calls. You need to go there. I have back-to-back clients all day."

"I'm working," Rosie shouted in anger.

"Everything okay?" Mrs. G. called out.

"It's just—give me a moment."

Rosie texted Frank back: "I can't just leave Mrs. G. And this is a parental week that you fought so hard to get when I wanted full custody. She's probably home sleeping or with her barista."

Frank wrote back: "WTF. What's the bastard's name? I'll have him arrested for having sex with a minor."

Rosie wrote back: "Calm down. I didn't say she was having sex. Text her that you're going to call the super to see if he's seen her if she doesn't answer. That will get her to call you back."

Rosie put the phone in her pocket and had just gone back into the bedroom when the beep went off again with another text from Frank: "You were right; she's home."

Rosie texted back: "Did you tell her to go back to school?"

Frank's return text: "No. She was crying, so I told her she could stay home."

Rosie responded: "With the fucking cat?"

Frank: "He's in my bedroom with the door closed."

"Do you want to tell me what's going on?" Mrs. G. said.

After filling her in about the cat bite, Rosie asked, "What should I do? Patty's home alone, probably in a lot of pain, and her father won't be home until after work."

"Tell her to come over. She can help you. It'll take her mind off her pain."

"Are you sure?"

"Rosemary," Mrs. G. said.

"Okay, okay."

Rosie sent a text to Patty and Frank telling Patty to come to Mrs. G.'s instead of being home alone. As she waited to see if Patty would surface, she felt on the verge of tears. Needing a moment to gather herself, she told Mrs. G. she had to go to the bathroom and left.

Outside the bedroom, Rosie leaned against the wall, her mind running over the call she had received yesterday morning. She had slept late, this being Patty's week with Frank, when the phone rang. Sure it was Frank calling with some excuse not to take Patty to her after-school orthodontist appointment, she groped for their landline.

"What do you want?" Rosie yelled into the receiver.

There was a pause, then the caller asked, "Is Mrs. Holt there?"

Oh great, Patty's teacher, Rosie thought, recognizing the voice. "This is Mrs. Holt. Rosie. I apologize. I thought it was my ex."

"No need to apologize," the teacher said. She told Rosie that Patty's grades had slipped this semester, and they needed to discuss what to do.

Ever since that call, all Rosie could think was, *I totally fucked up in high school ruining my chance of a scholarship to college, and now I've fucked up my kid by leaving Frank.*

Rosie remembered the night she told him she had had it, questioning whether she had been wrong. She had gotten home late, and Patty wasn't there. Frank was sitting on the edge of the sofa watching an MMA match on TV.

"Get him, get him down," Frank yelled at one of the wrestlers.

"Where's Patty?"

"What?" Frank asked.

"Patty. Remember her? Our daughter."

"She's at some concert."

"What! You let her go to a concert, knowing she had a paper due tomorrow that's half her history grade?"

"Big fucking deal. She's smart; she'll ace it."

"Yeah? How? She's only halfway through the research."

"She can bullshit her way through it. What's it about, anyhow?"

"The impact of overturning *Roe v. Wade* two years later."

"Best decision ever made."

That did it. *You do know you have a daughter?* Rosie thought, but knew it was a waste of breath.

Thinking about it now, Rosie wished she had stuck it out. Patty wouldn't be spending half her time with him, and Rosie could have monitored her schoolwork more closely. *Two more years—it wouldn't have killed me. Although I might have killed Frank. Too late now.*

God, she thought, *I never cry. I'd better get it together before Patty gets here.*

Five minutes later, she got a one-word text from Patty: "Okay."

She was about to go back to Mrs. G.'s bedroom to tell her Patty would be coming over when the doorbell rang.

Rosie opened the door for Mrs. Haight, who was holding a garment bag. She took one look at Rosie in the caftan and went berserk. "What are you doing in that?" Mrs. Haight demanded.

"Claire, is that you I hear?" Mrs. G. called out.

Rosie started to reply. "She told me I could—"

Mrs. Haight stormed past her, not waiting for an answer.

TWENTY-EIGHT

The Old Lady

"MOTHER, WHAT ON EARTH ARE YOU UP TO?" CLAIRE SAID as she entered Bette's bedroom.

"No 'Hello, Mother, how are you feeling?'" Bette asked.

"And why are you wearing a dress?"

"I went out this morning."

"That's insane. I can't believe Rosie took you out on such a windy day. It's like asking for pneumonia."

"Rosie does what I ask. Don't blame her."

"Was it a doctor's appointment? Why didn't I know about it? I would've arranged a car and—"

"Claire. Stop. I'm back, and I'm fine."

Claire dropped the garment bag she was holding on the bed.

"What's that?" Bette asked.

"Some dresses I thought Venera might like."

"Dear, you are about a foot taller than she is."

Claire hesitated a moment, then grabbed the bag. "You're right." She fumbled in her pocketbook to find the invitation and waved it at Bette.

"Yes! I'm having a dinner party," Bette said.

"So I see."

"You seem angry," Bette said, genuinely puzzled.

Claire responded, her tone and nervous pacing belying her words, "I'm not angry. I'm just perplexed. Your night aide shows up at my doorstep and hands me an invitation from my own mother for a formal dinner party the same night. And then Rosie answers the door wearing Dad's caftan."

"My caftan."

"Whatever. It's disturbing."

"What's disturbing about it?"

"Seriously, Mother? It's so unlike you—besides which, all your friends are dead."

"I don't need reminding—"

"And having family for dinner doesn't qualify as a dinner party. Formal at that."

"It's not just family."

"So I've heard. Who else aside from Jack and me and Rosie and Venera and Jia and Kenny and your neighbors?"

"After dinner, I've asked Mavis Jane Robbins to stop by. You remember her?"

"You mean the medium?" Claire asked, her voice rising. "This is getting worse by the second. Don't tell me you are having a séance. Oh my God. Mother. No!"

"Stop yelling. I'm not deaf."

"What is this about?" Claire whispered.

"You'll find out tonight."

"What does that mean?"

"You'll find out tonight."

"Is there something I don't know? Are Jia and Kenny getting married but for some reason leaving me out of the loop?"

"Don't I wish they were, but no."

"Then what?"

"I want to. It's as simple as that."

Claire paced around the room, then stopped by the bedtable and picked up the photo of Bette and George in costume. "Where did this come from? I've never seen it."

"Last night, I found it in a drawer in your father's desk in the study. I think he may have hidden it."

"No wonder. Why is Dad dressed like Tarzan?"

"I asked him to."

"How on earth did you get him to agree?"

"Never you mind," Bette said with a wink.

"Who's with him?"

"Me."

"You?" Claire asked. "Mother, you were Cheetah?"

"I was. I decided to give a New Year's Eve costume party. It was during the Korean War," Bette said. "Your father was depressed; you know how he hated any War, and I thought a party might distract him."

"Where did you get those costumes?"

"A costume rental place. Now enough with the third degree."

"Would that I had been there."

"You were, but you were too young to remember it. I was worried that if you saw a chimp running around the apartment, you'd get scared, so I took you with me to the rental place so you could see them. However, on the night of the party, when you saw me, you screamed your head off," Bette said.

"I must've been terrified." Claire was not amused.

"Dad, dressed as Tarzan, came running to see what happened," Bette continued. "He scooped you up in his arms, then peered through the eyes of my mask and said, 'Whoever you are, please leave or take that goddamn costume off. You are scaring my child.'"

"He didn't know it was you?"

"No, I wanted to surprise him, so I dressed in the bedroom off the kitchen."

"Mother, that is so you. So, then what?"

"I was laughing too hard to talk when your father said, 'Did you hear what I said?' But then you started laughing and said, 'Put me down. It's just Mommy.'"

"'What?' George had said. 'It's your mother?'"

"I could smell your perfume," Claire said. "Then I remembered. Did Dad laugh?"

"When he saw you were okay, yes."

"Do you have another copy of this picture? I want one."

"Take it."

"Mother, no," Claire said. She got out her iPhone and took a photo of it. "Problem solved."

"Do it your own way," Bette said, sounding annoyed.

Claire headed for the bathroom, saying, "Mother, why did you give Rosie the caftan Dad bought in Morocco?"

"I hate it when you walk away in the midst of a conversation."

"Sorry. Nature calls."

"I'll wait."

When Claire returned, she picked up where she left off. "You gave Rosie the caftan you promised to me."

"I just loaned it to her for tonight," Bette said. "Loaned."

"She's going to serve dinner in your caftan?"

"No. It's a buffet. And she's a guest. Remember?"

Just then Claire spotted Rosie standing by the door. "How long have you been standing there listening?"

"I wanted to change out of this and put it back where it belongs," Rosie said.

"You will do no such thing," Bette said. "I want you to wear it tonight." Rosie backed out of the room and closed the door.

"That was so rude. All Rosie has been doing is helping me get this organized."

"What *this*? I still don't get it."

"Please calm down and stop acting like I'm committing some kind of a crime."

Claire put the garment bag back on the bed, then dropped to the floor and assumed a lotus position. Closing her eyes, she started taking deep breaths. Bette watched, wondering how she had missed her daughter's jealousy of Rosie all these years. She never wanted Claire to feel that she was a burden and thought Claire would be grateful. Obviously she was wrong.

"Okay, Mother," Claire said, opening her eyes. "I'm calm."

It took Bette a moment to respond, aware that she needed to tread carefully. "When I woke up this morning, I decided—" Bette paused.

"You decided what?"

"Just come, honey. You and Jack. Don't make such a fuss about it. Please. Citarella is catering, and I want you to be a guest. That's why I put Rosie in charge and not you. I was trying to be considerate."

"So that's it? You're not going to tell me." Claire waited a minute, then got to her feet. "I guess not. At least can I stop at the flower market on the way home and—"

"Rosie already called the florist."

"You've thought of everything, haven't you?" Claire said, sounding petulant.

The doorbell rang, startling them both.

TWENTY-NINE

The Old Lady's Daughter

A MOMENT LATER, THERE WAS A KNOCK AT THE DOOR.
Claire opened it. "Yes?" she asked, staring at a teenage girl with green hair.

Rosie stepped out from behind Patty. "Mrs. Haight, you know my daughter, Patty."

"Patty? When did you get so tall?" Claire said, giving Patty a once-over as Patty looked down at the floor.

Looking past Claire, Patty said, "Hi, Mrs. G." Bette opened her arms, and Patty flew into them.

"What happened to her hand?" Claire asked Rosie.

"Her father's cat bit her," Rosie interjected.

"That's terrible."

"I agree. He needs to be put down."

"Mom! It wasn't his fault. I tried to take a chicken bone out of his mouth."

"I give up," Rosie said.

Claire stood awkwardly by the door for a moment, taking in the scene, then said to Rosie, "I can see you and Mother have everything taken care of, so I'm off," and left the room.

Claire went into the living room, anxious to get away before she snapped. *Here Mother is planning a party, her first in years, for God knows what reason, and apparently she doesn't need my help, not when she has Rosie to do everything for her. Not when only Rosie knows how she likes things. You would think Rosie was her daughter.*

Pressing her thumbnails into the skin at the top of her index fingers, Claire told herself to stop. Once her thoughts became negative, it was hard to turn them around, and it got her nowhere.

As soon as she got a lid on her anger, her thoughts turned to concern about her mother's behavior. The spontaneity of it was completely out of character. In the past, she spent days planning a party down to the smallest detail, but ever since her father died, her mother's social life had been almost nonexistent—and since her fall, completely nonexistent. Could this have a medical origin, like some kind of last gasp that wasn't that unusual or a sign of incipient dementia? *God, I hope not,* Claire thought. *It was stressful enough with Dad, and to go through that all over again. And Dad had Mother there to monitor him.*

She was hesitant to call her mother's doctor to ask about it. Her mother would be furious if she knew, humiliated. All Claire knew for sure was that something was up. Realizing that she needed to alert Jack before he made other plans, sure he would be as shocked as she was, especially if there were a séance, she called him at work.

"Good for her," Jack told Claire. "Maybe it's the last hurrah."

"The last hurrah?" Claire said. "That's all you can say? No, it's not the last hurrah. She's healthy as a horse."

"I've never understood that metaphor—are horses so healthy? If she were a horse, she would have been euthanized when she fell."

"Jesus, Jack. Please!" Claire said. She hung up, pissed, before she had a chance to mention the possible séance. Just as well. If he knew, he might find some excuse and not come.

Next Claire called Jia to fill her in. Just thinking about her granddaughter improved her mood. Jia's phone went to voice mail, so Claire left a message. "You're not going to believe this. Granny is planning a dinner party. Tonight. Formal at that. I just wanted to make sure you and Kenny are free. I assume Kenny owns a tux. Call me when you get this. We may be in for quite an evening. Oh, and prepare yourself for a possible séance. Mother invited a medium."

Resigned to the party, Claire wanted to do something for it, even if her mother didn't want her to. She would make a cake. A carrot cake with cream cheese frosting, her mother's favorite. She would make it a work of art to commemorate the occasion, whatever that might be. That would show her mother who knew her best. That would show Rosie, too.

When she got home, she would call Citarella and cancel the dessert. She didn't want Rosie to know she was bringing a cake; she wanted it to be a surprise. If she told Rosie, Rosie would tell her mother—they sure were awfully tight these days.

The only positive thing Claire had gotten out of the visit was the understanding that the idea of giving Hope's clothes to Venera was a mistake. She did not want to have to explain whom they belonged to, least of all with her mother present. And now the thought of seeing Venera in them—seeing anyone in them—was painful beyond words. She decided she would donate them to the thrift shop in her neighborhood, but first she needed to retrieve the garment bag from her mother's room.

Claire heard laughter coming from the bedroom. *Guess they're having a party in there*, she thought, sensing her negativity returning. She didn't feel like interrupting their "fun." She would have to remember to get it tonight after the party.

Claire was halfway out of the living room when her attention was diverted by the photo of her parents' wedding in an engraved silver frame with their names and the date inscribed on it.

"That's it!" she said. "That's it."

THIRTY

The Old Lady's Housekeeper

ROSIE LOOKED AT HER DAUGHTER AS SHE KNELT ON THE floor besides the wheelchair, her head in Mrs. G.'s lap, laughing about the cat bite. Laughing. As if it were funny.

As Mrs. G. stroked Patty's hair, Rosie marveled at the connection between them. Mrs. G. had known Patty since birth, quite literally, having come to the hospital the day Patty was born. Maybe it was because her only grandchild had died, although she did have Jia, whom she adored. But for whatever reason, Mrs. G. took a special interest in Patty.

"Seriously?" Patty said. "Mom, did you hear that?"

"Hear what?" Rosie responded, having been so caught up in her thoughts that she hadn't heard what they were saying.

"Mrs. G. invited me to the party and said I can pick out any dress I want to wear."

"And keep," Mrs. G. added. "Take as many as you like."

"Do you mean it?" Patty asked.

"Honey, it's your dad's week. You have to go there before dinner. And you have midterms coming up."

"Mom," Patty whined. "I want to come to the party. Mrs. G. invited me."

"I don't want to cause trouble," Mrs. G. said.

"She's always on my back about school. Always."

"I'm sorry honey, but no," Rosie said.

"I hate you," Patty said, as she ran out of the room crying.

"Oh dear, I'm afraid I did cause trouble," Mrs. G. said. "I should know better. Claire used to hate it when I asked Jia to do anything without asking her in advance."

"I can't be flexible with scheduling, or he'll do the same with me."

"She'll get over it."

Rosie went to the door and looked out to make sure Patty wasn't there, then came back. "Can I tell you something, Mrs. G.?" Rosie said in a hushed voice.

"Of course," Mrs. G. said. "Have a seat."

Rosie pulled a chair close to the wheelchair before continuing. "I'm wondering if I should sue for full custody. Her father bringing a feral cat into the apartment—it's reckless endangerment. Cat bites can be really serious."

"Rosemary," Mrs. G. replied, putting her hand on Rosie's arm. "You don't want to do that. It could turn her against you."

"She's already started. Watching her laughing with you, I realized that we rarely have fun together anymore."

Mrs. G. turned away from Rosie and looked out the window. After what seemed to Rosie like ten minutes, Rosie got up. "Where are you going?" Mrs. G. asked.

"I thought the conversation was over."

"You're pushing Patty away."

"How?"

"Sit back down." Rosie did as she was told. "Let me ask you this," Mrs. G. said. "Is Patty a motivated student?"

"Mrs. G., she's so smart, she's college material, but not if she doesn't apply herself. It doesn't help that Frank considers college a waste of time and money and tells her so."

"That's not what I asked. She needs to have her own dreams, her own goals, not just your goals for her."

"She's barely sixteen; how does she know what she wants? When I was that age, I was smart too, but I threw away my future."

"I understand how you feel, but the way you are going about it is counterproductive."

Just then Rosie heard the beep of a text message. She slipped her phone out of her pocket to see who had written, expecting it to be Frank. But instead it was Jia: "I need you to pick me up ASAP. Take an Uber."

"Everything okay?" Mrs. G. asked, and Rosie realized that her face must have registered her concern. She frantically tried to think of a good excuse to leave, then came up with it.

"It's Venera. She was just wondering if we need anything before she gets back."

"Maybe more champagne."

"Venera won't know what you like. Since Patty is here, I'll go out and get some."

"Go ahead, then," Mrs. G. said, "but first send Patty in. I'll let her choose any dresses she wants to keep—kids these days like vintage clothes."

"Maybe you can remind her that Mr. G. started her college fund and would be disappointed if she didn't go."

"Rosie, didn't you hear—"

"I know, I know. I just thought if it came from you . . ."

"Wait," Mrs. G. called. "Claire left some clothes she didn't need in the garment bag on the bed, thinking Venera might want them but forgetting how much taller she is. Maybe she has something Patty would like. They'd need to be hemmed, but they might be more her size. Open it, and let's see what's in it."

Rosie, anxious to get to Jia quickly, removed a few dresses from the garment bag and tossed them on the bed. They were feminine and youthful, making Rosie wonder at what period of her life Claire had ever been that "girly."

Rosie was halfway to the door when Mrs. G. yelled, "Get them out of my sight!"

Rosie grabbed the bag and dresses and took off, totally thrown.

THIRTY-ONE

The Old Lady's Across-the-Hall Neighbor

AN HOUR AND A HALF AFTER ARRIVING AT THE HOSPITAL, twenty frustrating minutes of which were spent waiting at the pharmacy to get a prescription filled, Miss Sidenstriker emerged from the emergency room in a wheelchair, holding a cane across her lap.

"Is someone waiting for you?" the nurse who was pushing the wheelchair asked.

Surveying the area, Miss Sidenstriker said, "Apparently not. I can manage on my own. Just help me get a cab."

But then she spotted Dariush pacing back and forth. "There," she told the nurse, pointing her cane at Dariush. "There's my ride."

"Hey, I need a cab," she told Dariush, as if he were a doorman.

The ride back to their building was nauseating as their driver was the kind who alternately pumped the gas or put on the brake. Miss Sidenstriker kept muttering, "Ugh."

"Driver, could you take it easy on the pedals? My companion here just came from the hospital."

"Yeah, I know. That's where I picked you up."

"Just . . . slow down, please."

Using the cane, Miss Sidenstriker reached out and tapped Dariush's arm. "It's okay," she whispered.

"You sure? We could get out and switch—"

"No, no. We're almost there," she said. She started fumbling in her pocketbook.

"I got it covered," Dariush said, removing his credit card from his wallet. As they rode in silence, Miss Sidenstriker was desperately trying to think of something nice to say since he had gone out of his way for her.

"By the way, how are your parents?"

"Not good," he said. "My dad's in prison, and my mom can't leave without him."

"I had no idea." Neither one said anything for a moment. "How long is his sentence?"

"It doesn't work like that. It's all arbitrary. It's already been seven years."

"What did he do?"

"Do?" Dariush asked, sounding angry. "Nothing. He's a Bahá'í, a religion that's banned in Iran."

"Oh my. That's terrible. I'm so sorry. You must miss them."

"I do," Dariush said, his tone softer.

"I think of my parents every single day," Miss Sidenstriker confessed. It just popped out, and she was embarrassed. It was far too personal, but thankfully Dariush didn't respond.

When the cab pulled up to the building, Jimmy came to open the door to help her out. Dariush handed Jimmy the cane.

"I can manage," Miss Sidenstriker said, grabbing the cane away from Jimmy's hand. Tucking it under her arm, she grasped the side railing and hobbled up the stairs and into the building without a backward glance, but then stopped at the front desk.

She hadn't considered how, with her injury, she would manage the long corridor to the elevator without help. Nor was she used to using a cane. She felt off balance and needed some support as it was hard to put any weight on her injured knee. She did not want to fall again.

She called Jimmy back, yet another insult to her dignity. He offered her his arm, and she had no choice but to take it. How she hated touching other people!

"I am so sorry, Miss Sidenstriker," Jimmy said as if he meant it—or was he angling for a tip? "What happened?"

Miss Sidenstriker could not bear sympathy right now or she really would break down, so she said nothing. To her relief, Jimmy took his cue from her and didn't probe. When they got to the elevator, he asked her to wait. A package had arrived for her.

As he ran to get it, she wondered what it might be. Then she remembered that she had ordered a rice cooker from amazon.com. She had been an online shopper for close to thirty years. Jeff Bezos was her real-life hero. Little did he know he had saved her life, at least figuratively speaking. She avoided stores at all costs, all those people with God knows what kind of germs coughing and sneezing and touching things—and staring at her face.

As Jimmy went to get the package, Venera quietly slipped into the elevator. A moment later Jimmy returned with a small box.

"Here you go. Gertrude Sidenstriker," he said, reading the label.

"Miss Sidenstriker."

"Sorry. Miss Sidenstriker," Jimmy said, holding out the package. "From the Westside Veterinary—"

"No!" she said with an anguished cry. She snatched the package out of his hands.

"Do you need help getting into your apartment?" Jimmy asked, holding the elevator open.

Venera frantically motioned at him with her hands to let the door go, but Jimmy was too busy helping Miss Sidenstriker into the elevator to notice. Venera moved to a back corner and tucked her arms around her body as if trying to make herself invisible.

The minute the doors closed, Miss Sidenstriker hugged the package, then burst into tears. "O Captain, My Captain," she whispered. Just then, she sensed that she was not alone. Swiveling around, she saw Venereal. *One humiliation after another*, she thought. *Well, fuck her. Let her think what she thinks.*

When the elevator reached the fourteenth floor, to her surprise, Venereal held the door open for her to get off.

"Can I carry the package for you?" she asked.

Clutching the package against herself with one arm, afraid Venereal might take it away, Miss Sidenstriker said, "No!" and limped out. When she got to her door, she realized with alarm that there was no way she could get her key out of her bag without the risk of dropping the package.

Without looking back, she said, "Okay, if you insist."

"Okay?" Venereal repeated.

"You can hold it."

She even had to allow Venereal to come inside the apartment with her. "Just put it there," she told her, motioning to the foyer table. Venera did what she asked, then left.

Once she was alone, Miss Sidenstriker made her way into the living room and collapsed on the sofa, totally bereft.

She had never had nor wanted a pet, especially dogs who licked their privates, then people's faces. But about fifteen years ago, on a cold, wintery night in Boston, Miss Sidenstriker was just getting into bed when she heard a loud and pitiful screeching sound coming from somewhere outside her building. She tried to ignore it to no avail. As the noise continued, she considered tossing a bucket of water out the window, but that seemed mean on such a cold night, even to her.

Finally, afraid she would never get any sleep if she didn't bring the annoying creature in, she donned an overcoat and leather gloves and went outside. It was snowing lightly and bitterly cold. Teeth chattering, Miss Sidenstriker cursed the animal who was nowhere in sight and now silent.

"Where are you, you little bugger?" she called into the darkness. "First you wake up the whole neighborhood, then disappear? Think you're Macavity?" Concerned that her angry tone might frighten the creature away, she began again, this time softly. "Here, puss, puss, puss. Here kitty, kitty." She felt like a fool and prayed that none of her neighbors were watching, but no lights had come on in the windows, so she was probably safe.

She was frozen to her core and afraid she would get pneumonia if she didn't go in when she saw an orange-and-yellow face peer out from under a bush. A face with a beak. *How can that be?* she wondered. *But then, I'm not wearing my glasses; I could be mistaken.*

"You," she began, ready to throttle the animal. But then it ventured toward her. Miss Sidenstriker stayed as still as she could so as not to scare it away. When it came within arm's length, she swooped down and grabbed it with her gloved hands. "Bite me, you little bugger, and I'll bite you back."

To her astonishment, when she looked down, she saw the creature was a bird, a shivering bird that resembled a parrot, but seemed too small for a parrot. She knew little about the species. Aside from yellow and orange, the bird also had green feathers under his wings. Miss Sidenstriker figured it must have escaped from a pet store or a cage in someone's home.

Back in the warmth of her apartment, she was at a loss. She didn't want it peeing or defecating on the furniture her parents had bought for her. The bird started squawking again. Miss Sidenstriker reflexively held her hand away from her body. That was when she noticed the bloody stump where one of its back claws had been.

"Oh no, you poor thing, who did this to you? No wonder you were crying."

Without realizing what she was doing, she held it to her chest and started rocking, gently stroking its back feathers. The bird quieted down immediately. When she looked down, she saw it had fallen asleep.

You hear all the time about love at first sight. Whatever dormant instincts Miss Sidenstriker may have had for contact with a living being were unleashed that long ago night. She was in love. She named her beloved Captain Flint after Long John Silver's parrot, which decided his gender.

The following day she reported in sick at work. Then, after wrapping Captain in a towel and tucking him into a shopping bag, she walked more than twenty blocks to buy whatever he might need, hoping it was not the probable owner's neighborhood store.

She found the clerk friendly enough when she asked where to find things for a parrot, although she may just have been nice to get her to buy more than she needed. When Miss Sidenstriker looked at the prices of the items, she was shocked. She would have to spend far more than she ever imagined a bird could cost, having gone all out to buy a big cage and many toys and accessories for it along with bird food and several books on the care of a parrot. But then she didn't have children to send to college, why not splurge on Captain?

"Miss," Miss Sidenstriker started to say as the clerk checked out her purchases.

"Melody's my name," the clerk interrupted. "Yes?"

"Melody. Lovely name. Can I ask you a question?"

"Of course," Melody said. "That's what I'm here for."

Miss Sidenstriker reached into the shopping bag and withdrew Captain, holding the toweling tightly against her chest. "Have you ever seen a parrot that looks like this?"

"What a cutie," Melody said. "That's a Conure. Where'd you buy him?"

"Ah, ah, I, uh, my friend gave him to me as a gift. Yes, such a wonderful gift for my birthday. My friend is so kind. She knew just what I wanted. But even so, I was so surprised." Tucking Captain back in the bag, Miss Sidenstriker rambled on for a full minute, elaborating on and almost believing her own lie, reluctant to tell the truth since for all she knew, Captain might come from this shop and Melody would know the real owner.

"Well, you're lucky to have such a wonderful and generous friend. Conures make great pets, although they often bond only with the owner. You will have to warn your friend—all your friends in fact—that their bite really hurts. We have a few in back where we keep our birds. Would you like to see them?"

"No," Miss Sidenstriker blurted, anxious to leave.

Laden down with paraphernalia, she cabbed it home. When she arrived, she saw a man taping a poster to a lamp post outside her building. As she started to exit the cab, she noticed it was a wanted poster showing a photo of Captain in all his splendor along with tabs at the bottom with a phone number and reward.

She experienced a brief moment of guilt before deciding that the man didn't deserve Captain, not with that injured foot that he might have caused or, at the very least, neglected.

She waited until the man had moved on before getting out of the cab, then hurried inside.

She had real separation anxiety the next day when she left to go to work, and for the first time ever had a tiny inkling of why being away from their children was hard for working mothers. Coming home at night, she could not wait to see Captain.

After reading up on Conure behavior, she felt comfortable taking him out his cage where he remained until she went to bed. She fed him off her plate and talked to him as if he were a person. And while he was not a person, he was a companion who became her emotional port in the storm brewing at work as technology took over.

Capable and smart, as much as Miss Sidenstriker tried to keep up, she knew little about all the many ways people communicated electronically. Most of the people in the company were much younger, and half the time she had no clue what they were talking about. Facebook? Tweet? Tinder? And when she did understand, she was usually aghast. *Social media?* she mused. *No thank you. People discuss the most intimate things, including details about their sex lives as if it were as ordinary as talking about the weather. And the way the women dressed, with half their breasts exposed? Did no one have a sense of privacy anymore?*

She knew her co-workers talked about her behind her back and was pretty sure it was just a matter of time before she would be asked to leave, even though everyone she had started with was long gone, and she was now the longest standing employee in the company. She wasn't really sure why she hadn't already been fired; her bosses had to know she was dead weight in this new electronic age. But then her salary was a drop in the bucket of their business. Maybe they pitied her: a mortifying thought. Not wanting to be kept on as a charity case, she asked for and received an early retirement package and bid adieu to Boston.

There was nothing or no one tying her to the city other than the Gardner Museum, that lovely gem of a museum with the wonderful Sargents that she visited most weekends. But New York had museums housed in old mansions, too. And there was MOMA and the Met, not to mention the theater. Her parents, then in their eighties, welcomed her and Captain back home with open arms. The timing was ideal as both were in failing health, and within two years, dead.

With George, her only friend, gone, and now with Captain just ashes, she had no one. She reached into her pocketbook, removed the bottle of painkillers she had gotten at the pharmacy, and downed two.

THIRTY-TWO

The Old Lady's Night Aide

WHEN VENERA HEARD JIMMY MENTION THAT MISS Sidenstriker's package had come from a veterinary hospital and saw the look of pain on the woman's face, she suspected that her horrid bird must have died.

The sobbing confirmed it. Venera was not surprised. A few weeks ago, when Venera came out to empty the garbage, she saw Miss Sidenstriker exit her apartment holding a pet carrier. Her eyes were red-rimmed beneath her glasses, and Venera assumed the bird was ill. She never saw the bird again and had all but forgotten it until today when she put two and two together.

She knew what it was like to lose a pet. Heartbreaking. When Toto, the dog she had grown up with, had to be put down, Venera cried for days. But a bird—can you bond with a bird, especially a vicious bird? *I guess Miss Sidenstriker could*, she mused. *They were a perfect pair.*

Upon entering the apartment, Venera was surprised to hear voices coming from Mrs. Gartner's bedroom. It did not sound at all like Rosie. Maybe the great-granddaughter whom Venera had yet to meet had come to visit.

Venera went into the kitchen to find Rosie and see what was needed, but Rosie wasn't there. Venera checked the dining room, the living room, but no sign of Rosie. She went to Mrs. Gartner's bedroom and knocked lightly. "Mrs. Gartner, it's me, Venera. Can I come in?"

"Yes, yes, come in," Mrs. Gartner said.

Mrs. Gartner was seated in her wheelchair in the middle of the room, smiling as a pretty girl, about fifteen or sixteen with green hair, paraded in front of her in a matronly floor-length floral chiffon gown. She had her right hand on her hips and held the left one, which was bandaged, up in the air.

"Yes? No? Maybe?" the girl asked.

"The No pile."

The girl slipped out of the dress, letting it drop to the floor. Down to her underwear, she picked up the dress and dropped it on top of one of three mounds of dresses on the bed, then headed back to the closet. Venera was reluctant to interrupt. Mrs. Gartner was clearly enjoying herself, but she wanted to be useful.

"Mrs. Gartner—"

"Come find a dress for yourself for tonight."

"What do you mean?"

"I'm guessing you didn't bring a formal dress with you."

"Does formal mean a party dress?"

"Well, yes, I guess."

"Then, no."

The girl returned. This time she was wearing a red dress with ruffles around the neck and ruffled layers from waist to hem on the skirt. "Venera, have you met Rosie's daughter, Patty?" Mrs. Gartner asked.

"Patty! Your mother has said so much about you. I'm so glad to meet you."

"You, too." Patty turned to Mrs. Gartner. "How do I look?"

"Venera, what do you think?" Mrs. Gartner asked.

Venera eyed Patty, wondering what to say. Aside from the dress being too old for her, it looked like something she had seen in that movie about the old days in the South, *Gone with the Wind*. All that was missing was a wig with sausage curls loosely tied with a ribbon.

As if she could read Venera's thoughts, Mrs. Gartner said, "I don't know what I was thinking when I got that."

"What's it for?" Venera asked Patty.

"Mrs. G. told me I can have any of her dresses I want." She twirled around in a full circle, fluffing the ruffles with her right hand. "It's dope."

"It's what?" Mrs. Gartner and Venera asked at the same time.

"Dope," Patty said, laughing. "Cool. Awesome. Get with it, Mrs. G."

"What happened to your hand?" Venera asked.

"It's nothing. Just a cat bite."

"That's not nothing," Venera said. "Did you go to the doctor?"

"I did. Honest, I'm fine. It just hurts."

"You might want to get a scarf to hold it up. It will hurt less."

"Are you a nurse?" Patty asked, sounding impressed.

Venera laughed. "Hardly. There were a lot of street cats in my town, and I've seen what can happen."

"Venera is smart. You should do what she says," Mrs. Gartner added. "Now, Venera, it's your turn to find a dress."

"Welcome to Mrs. G.'s Vintage Dress Shoppe," Patty said.

"Are you sure you've found all you want?" Venera asked Patty.

"Are you kidding? Look at my pile," she said, but then added, "Wait. Mrs. G., do you have clothes Mr. G. wore I could have? Even a tie."

"Go look in the closet in the hall. I gave most of it away, but I think we stored a few things."

As Patty ran off, almost tripping over her "new" gown, Mrs. Gartner turned back to Venera. "What are you waiting for?"

Venera, having already gone through Mrs. Gartner's closets, knew that whatever she found would look equally silly on her. However, not wanting to be insulting, she said, "Actually, I forgot. I did bring something I can wear."

Venera was relieved that Mrs. Gartner appeared to believe her. Now she would have to go to the thrift store on Columbus Avenue and find something, but that would be fun.

"Where's Rosie?" Venera asked.

"She went out to buy champagne," Mrs. Gartner said.

"What can I do to help?"

"When Rosie gets back, she can tell you."

Patty bounded in wearing a man's jacket that went almost down to her knees.

"I love it." Patty put her face against the lapels. "I can almost smell Mr. G.'s cologne. He always smelled so good," Patty told Venera. "He was so dope."

"So dope," Mrs. Gartner repeated, winking at Venera.

"Except whenever I saw him, the first thing he'd say was, 'How are your grades?' He and my mom, it's as if that's all that matters."

"What do you think, Patty?" Mrs. Gartner asked, her tone serious.

"Not you too, Mrs. G.?"

"I'm just curious to know if you've thought about what you want to do."

"Not a lot. Did you know what you wanted to do at my age?"

Laughing, Mrs. Gartner said, "Touché."

Patty started threading the fingers of her right hand through Mrs. Gartner's hair. Venera was surprised by the intimacy of the gesture.

"That feels so good," Mrs. Gartner said, making Venera wonder how long it had been since she had been touched. She started rotating her neck and shoulders. "Can you massage my scalp too, dear? Use your nails."

"I don't want to hurt you."

"You won't. My nanny used to do it for me all the time. We never took showers in my day. Just tubs. When I was a child, she would put me in the tub and pour water over my hair, then shampoo it. Her nails were long, and she would dig them into my scalp, and my whole body would tingle."

"How old were you?" Patty asked.

"Four, five at most."

"Why did you have a nanny?"

"My mother died in childbirth."

"No," Patty exclaimed. "That's so sad."

Venera felt a pit in her stomach. *Poor Mrs. Gartner*, she thought. *That's tragic.*

"She had preeclampsia, which was fairly common back in ancient times. I was lucky to have survived."

"Is that her?" Venera asked, referring to a period photo on the bureau of a young girl wearing a middy dress.

"Yes. Let me see it."

"She was so pretty," Venera said, handing Mrs. Gartner the photograph.

"Yes, she was," Mrs. Gartner said, smoothing her hand over the picture.

"Mrs. Gartner, I'm so sorry. I had no idea," Venera said.

"Don't waste time feeling sorry for me. I was doted on by my father and older brothers," Mrs. Gartner said, giving the photo back to Venera. "Now, what were we talking about?"

"Mrs. G. Let me do your hair for the party. It looks awful."

"Don't hold back," Mrs. Gartner said, laughing. "What would you do? I don't want green streaks."

"Why not?"

"But, Patty, how can you do it with your hand bandaged?" Venera asked.

"I once saw a video of a one-armed hairdresser on Instagram, and it was amazing." Patty turned to Mrs. Gartner, pleading, "I can give you a cut and blow-dry it if you have a dryer and brush. And if not, I can run home and get one."

As Venera waited to see what Mrs. Gartner would say, she wondered if Patty knew how to style hair for an old woman and if she really would be able to manage. "Well, I sure could use a cut, and I do want to look my best," Mrs. Gartner said, relenting.

"Trust me, you will," Patty said, sounding excited. Mrs. Gartner winked at Venera, at which point Venera realized it was beyond her control—they were in it together.

"I have a blow-dryer. I'll go get it," Venera said.

"First, bring me the needlework pillow I was working on last night in the living room."

As she left the bedroom, Venera started laughing as she tried to imagine what Mrs. Gartner's hair was going to look like.

Patty had said, "Trust me." That's an awful lot of trust to put on a one-armed fifteen-year-old kid in an evening gown that swam on her and whose idea of looking good is green hair.

THIRTY-THREE

The Old Lady

WHEN VENERA RETURNED WITH THE HAIR-DRYER AND the needlework, Patty got to work sprinkling Bette's hair with water, then combing it through. She used the forearm of her right hand to hold Mrs. Gartner's head in place.

"How short do you want it?"

"About here," Bette answered, cupping the back of both hands just beneath her ears. As Patty started snipping away, Bette retreated into her mind. Her vanity had disappeared when George died, not that she had ever been that vain. But George was proud of her looks, so she made an effort. Standing weekly appointments for a shampoo and blow-dry with Marceline, who had been her hairdresser for many years. Her hair had been styled in what she and Marceline deemed appropriate for a woman her age: cut below the ears with the front swept to one side. Born a strawberry blonde, Bette was not happy when it kept getting darker and darker, until by forty, she was a practically a brunette. Finding it dull, Bette got highlights to brighten it. She stopped doing it after going to a seventieth birthday lunch for her old college friend Helen.

Helen had always been a beauty, and still was, albeit faded. At the party, when Bette looked around the table at their contemporaries, she realized that she and Helen were the only women there who had not had some kind of work done on their faces. One woman, the second wife of a renowned plastic surgeon, had skin as tight as a drum thanks to three face-lifts. In Bette's view, while some looked younger, no one there looked anywhere near as good as Helen, gray hair, wrinkles, and all. Bette wondered who they thought they were fooling—their veiny hands were a dead giveaway.

As Bette's highlights grew out, she discovered that her hair had turned mostly gray—not an especially attractive gray, but nor was it as mousy as gray can be. She decided to embrace it. As she told Claire, "I've earned every white hair on my head and every wrinkle on my face." George was less happy with it. He preferred a younger-looking wife. But when he grumbled, she suggested that he look in the mirror. That shut him up.

She hadn't looked in a mirror since her fall and didn't know what she looked like anymore. She could feel that her hair had grown long and sparse, but she didn't care until today.

"What're you making?" Patty asked.

Picking up her needlework, Bette told her that it was a pillow for her great-granddaughter's boyfriend.

"I love autumn colors," Patty said. "And the zigzaggy design. It has so much energy."

"I used to do petit point when I was younger."

"What's petit point?"

"Needlepoint with small stitches. I did all the dining room chairs many years ago. I designed them based on plates that had belonged to my mother."

"What do you mean you designed them?"

"I sketched the images of the plates on the canvas and—"

"I have to see them." Scissors in hand, Patty ran out of the bedroom.

"Don't run with scissors," Bette shouted after her.

Patty returned a few moments later. "I can't believe you did them. You're an artist."

"Nonsense. I was just copying something."

"Well, I am super impressed, Mrs. G.," Patty said. "Did your mom teach you? I mean—"

"One of my nannies. She was English and—"

"I forgot you said she died." Patty paused, before adding, "I can't imagine not having a mom. Who did you have to give you grief?"

"Patty, your mother does a lot more than give you grief."

"She does; all I meant was—"

"I know what you meant, but, dearie, your mother wants what's best for you. She knows how intelligent you are, that you have what it takes to go to college."

"What if I don't want to go?" Patty asked as she started blow-drying Bette's hair. "It doesn't always help anymore in the job market, and it saddles you with debt for years and years."

"You sound like you did some research."

"Mark Zuckerberg didn't finish college; Steve Jobs, Bill Gates, Oprah Winfrey, John D. Rockefeller—"

"It's true, a degree doesn't guarantee success, nor does the lack of one prevent it."

"The way I look at it, if I wanted to be a doctor or a lawyer or a teacher, some profession where a degree is both mandatory and useful, I'd go for it, but right now I'm not sure."

"Ultimately it's your choice, but you need to understand why your mother is pushing you. She wants you to have more options than she had."

Patty started laughing.

"Are you doing something crazy with my hair?" Bette asked.

"No. Something my mom said just popped into my head."

"You can't say that and then stop."

"Okay, but don't get mad at my mom. She said your husband sometimes called you Foxy, and then, when he thought no one was looking, pinched your butt."

Bette smiled, relishing the memory.

"He'd call me Foxy when he thought I was trying to take over or when he was feeling a little—" Bette paused, then added, "Frisky."

"Frisky? You mean like wanting sex?"

"Frisky. Let's leave it at that, you impertinent child."

Bette acted as if she were offended, but in reality, she was a bit in awe of the freedom of today's young people, or in any event of Patty, who felt comfortable enough to talk to her as if she were a peer. Times had sure changed.

Patty turned off the blow-dryer, then fluffed Bette's hair with her good hand.

"Hey, Mrs. G., you look pretty hot," Patty teased.

What on earth has this child had done to me? Bette thought, as she patted her hair.

"Where do you have a full-length mirror?" Patty asked.

"Heaven forbid! I haven't seen myself in years, and I'm not about to start now. Now, scoot; I need to finish Kenny's pillow, and with you here, it won't happen."

THIRTY-FOUR

The Old Lady's
Great-Granddaughter

A S SOON AS ROSIE ARRIVED AT THE DOCTOR'S OFFICE TO take her home, Jia bolted past her out the door. She could not get away fast enough. Rosie ran after her, calling, "Wait up."

Once settled in the car, Jia sank against the back seat. "You're scaring me, Jia," Rosie said. "Was it bad news?"

"More like no news. The nurse said he was doing other procedures and would call or text me tonight."

"Well, that sucks," Rosie said. "To leave you on pins and needles."

"Tell me about it."

Once they got to the building, Jia told Rosie to take the car back to Granny's. "I'll go up with you," Rosie said. "You're a bit wobbly. What did they give you?"

"Some sort of an IV drip."

As they entered the building, the doorman handed Jia an envelope. Thanking the doorman, Jia headed for the elevator without looking at it.

Once inside the elevator, Jia said, "I'm going to take a Melatonin and try to sleep."

"You may not have much time."

"Why?" Jia asked, as she turned the envelope over to see who it was from.

"How odd. It's from Granny."

"Open it!"

"Why would Granny send me a note?" Jia said.

When she saw the invitation, she was stupefied. "A dinner party? Formal? Are you kidding? Okay, I don't get it. Is this some kind of a joke?"

"No," Rosie said. "She woke up this morning and decided to have a party."

The elevator stopped at Jia's floor, and Rosie followed Jia out. As soon as Jia put the key in the lock, Arnold could be heard barking.

"When did you get a dog?" Rosie asked.

"Don't even ask," Jia said. Rosie followed Jia into the kitchen so Jia could let Arnold out of the crate. The dog jumped all over both of them.

"Sit," Jia said in a sharp tone of voice, pointing to the floor. Arnold sat.

"Impressive," Rosie said.

"That cost about a thousand dollars."

Rosie bent over to pat Arnold. "I wonder if I should get a dog for Patty."

"Don't." Then, "Why?"

"She loves animals. She even loves Frank's vicious cat, even though it bit her, and she wound up in the emergency room at Roosevelt early this morning. Getting a dog would earn me major brownie points as a mom, and at the moment I could sure use them."

"Is she okay?"

"They gave her antibiotics, and it hurts like the dickens, but yeah."

"Rosie, don't waste your money on a dog. Owning a pet can be very expensive."

"I'd get it from a shelter."

"It's the upkeep. So far Arnold has cost us close to two thousand dollars, and that doesn't include what Kenny paid for him."

"Then forget that idea."

"Better bond another way. Maybe you should take her away with you when school ends. Log some quality mother-daughter time," Jia suggested.

"I can't. Your granny depends on me, and I depend on the income."

"I'll speak to Granny. Between Venera, Nana, and me, we can cover for you."

"You can't speak for your grandmother. Jia, please, leave her out of it."

"She owes you. Without you, her life would be very different."

"Honey, I'm the hired help. Without me, your family would find someone else."

"Don't say that. You're family."

Rosie didn't say anything, and Jia knew that Rosie was right, you don't pay family to work for you, but Rosie was so much more than just a housekeeper. Jia felt like they were friends, but were they?

"And as for Venera," Rosie said, as if unaware of the impact her silence had had on Jia, "she could get deported or decide to—"

"She isn't legal?"

"Truthfully, I'm not sure, but forgetting that, she could decide to return. And then what? You know your granny doesn't like new people."

"Well, leave it to me. One way or the other, you are taking Patty away with you."

"I better get back. I said I was picking up more champagne."

Jia thanked Rosie for picking her up and was at the door when she turned back. "Why don't you call Kenny to come stay with you? I hate leaving you alone like this."

Jia didn't feel like involving Rosie any further in her business just then. Rosie's matter of fact way of saying that she was not family had really bothered Jia. She never thought about their hierarchy and realized that only when you were the one on top could you be that clueless. She was embarrassed by how oblivious she had been.

"Good idea," Jia told Rosie. "See you later."

Jia had no intention of asking Kenny to come home, but she did need to tell him about the party. Hopefully the doctor would call soon so she didn't have to spend the day on pins and needles. The thought of going to Granny's not knowing, or worse still, knowing she had cancer. . . . This had to be the worst day possible to go to Granny's.

Jia lay down on the living room sofa, feeling scared and alone. She wondered why she hadn't asked Rosie to stay with her until she nodded off. Or she should have told Kenny. It was her own fault she was alone.

Ever since the moment she spotted blood in her stool, her thought processes had been clouded by panic. Normally, she was rational, but no matter how much she tried to tell herself that no one in her family had ever had colon cancer so the likelihood of her having it at her age was small, she couldn't stop wondering why the doctor scheduled a colonoscopy based solely on a phone visit. Something she said must have sounded suspicious, but what? She didn't think she had hemorrhoids. She hadn't eaten beets. What else could explain it? Why had she gone along with it? Above all, why hadn't she checked him out? Maybe he had a kid about to enter college and needed the money or three kids all in college at the same time. Or a spendthrift wife. Stupidly, she had Googled for a doctor rather than ask her internist for a referral. But she and Nana had the same doctor; Dr. Howland might tell Nana. Not meaning to, Dr. Howland might say something like, "I'm glad Jia has such a good gastroenterologist," assuming that Nana knew.

Jia never, ever wanted her family to know.

The more she obsessed about it, the more certain she was that she had cancer. Why else wouldn't the doctor have called? He probably wanted to wait until the end of the day when he had time to let her down gently.

"Cut it out," Jia screamed at herself. Arnold barked, which made Jia laugh. "Come here, my little service pal," she said, patting the sofa. Arnold jumped up next to her. Cuddling the dog, she soon drifted off to sleep.

THIRTY-FIVE

The Old Lady's Downstairs Neighbor

SINCE HE HAD TOLD HIS ASSISTANT THAT HE WOULDN'T BE back, Dariush decided to walk to Zabars.

Heading north, he thought about his parents. Yes, he missed them, but their absence was screwing up his life. They had asked him to stay in the apartment until they returned, none of them imagining it would be this long or, God forbid, never. Since his sisters lived in other states, it was all on him. How long was his life supposed to remain on hold? At times he was angry that his mother didn't realize the toll it was taking on him, but then he felt guilty. She had so much on her mind—it was like she had forgotten that he was now an adult.

They had left when he was just starting a BA degree program at The Bernard and Anne Spitzer School of Architecture at CUNY, even though what he really wanted to do was go to the Culinary Institute of America to become a chef. It had been his dream since childhood.

As a boy he would do his homework at the kitchen table while his mother prepared dinner with his sisters as sous chefs. He loved everything about it: the chatter, the laughter, the aromas, the tastes. He became their designated taster, as early on he developed a knack for identifying just what was missing. As each of his older sisters left home, he took over her place until finally it was just his mother and him preparing meals.

However, Dariush was nothing if not a good son, and his father, an architect, made it very clear that he expected his only son to follow in his footsteps. Dariush dropped out in his junior year when money became tight without telling his mother. Instead, he kept up the pretense of talking about his classes, but as time went by, he told her the truth. A friend's father arranged for him to get an entry-level job in development at the Museum at a salary that covered the cost of maintaining the apartment. But he hated living there by himself, especially when most of his friends lived either in Harlem or Queens.

At his age, he should by now be living in his own home. Instead, he rattled around a seven-room apartment and slept in a twin bed like he was still a kid. It was embarrassing to bring women home to Mommy and Daddy's apartment. He couldn't have sex with them in his parents' bed or even his own, not with his bedroom plastered with all his childhood memorabilia.

Thinking about how life can change on a dime, he remembered the day the call came for his father from his grandmother in Tehran that changed everything. Both his parents had been sent to boarding school in America in their teens and had not gone back after the revolution.

As he and his mother listened, his father kept repeating, "Oh no, not Papajan. Oh no, oh no." Then finally, "*Chashm*, okay, I'll be there."

"Did he die?" his mother asked the minute his father hung up.

"No, but he had a heart attack, and I have to go."

"I'm so sorry, Arya, but you can't go," his mother said. "You know they've been cracking down again on the Bahá'ís. It's too risky."

"BitaJan, it's my father. I haven't seen him in person in close to forty years."

"You see him on WhatsApp almost every day."

"That's not the same."

"He wouldn't want you to come."

"But he does. Maman said he keeps calling for me."

"What about Dariush and our daughters and their families? What about me?"

Dariush's father pushed his chair away from the table and stood up, angry. Dariush could see on his face that he was resolute; he was going. He glanced at his mother and sensed that she saw it, too.

"If you must go, I'm coming with you," his mother said. "I need to see my family too."

Even though his parents planned to return in a few weeks, fearing the possibility of being detained, they gave Dariush, not yet nineteen, power of attorney over their relatively limited assets.

Dariush's grandfather passed away a week after his parents arrived. They were planning to come home shortly after the funeral, but Dariush's father was arrested for protesting after being informed that the only place a Bahá'í could be buried was in a communal plot at the Khavaran Cemetery. His mother stayed to try to see what she could do to get him out of prison, never imagining that seven years later, her husband would still be in Evin, and she would still be in Iran.

During the pandemic, she got COVID-19 and was very ill. Then, as she was considering a return, her mother-in-law was diagnosed with lung cancer, and his mother didn't feel right about leaving.

A honking car brought him back to the present. He was surprised to see that he had already reached 81st Street. When he got to Zabars, he decided that while he was there, he would pick up some nuts and frozen filo dough for baklava. He would make some for Mrs. Gartner. His parents had always invited the Gartners to their Persian New Year's parties, where they were introduced to all kinds of Persian cuisine. Mrs. Gartner especially loved baklava. He laughed to himself, thinking he might send a plate to Miss Sidenstriker if he was feeling benevolent. *Let's see if she can bring herself to thank me,* he thought.

The moment he opened the door to his apartment, he saw an envelope on the floor. He picked it up, opened it, and read the invitation. He had no idea why he was being invited, but he looked forward to seeing Mrs. Gartner, whom he hadn't seen since her fall. Whenever he delivered the baklava, it was Rosie who came to the door. It would be nice to see someone who knew and liked his family.

He reread the invitation and stopped. He didn't own a tux. He usually rented one when he went to a wedding, but the rental place was downtown. He could probably find something at History & Mystery, a thrift store on Columbus Avenue. He had often been tempted to go in but for some reason hadn't. It didn't matter if what they had was out of date as long as it was a tuxedo. It was just for one night. Last resort, if he couldn't find one, he would wear a dark suit.

When Dariush got to the store, he saw that it had a Spring Blowout Sale sign in the window—better still. He wasn't one for shopping, but the store fascinated him. It was indeed filled with history and mystery, with items ranging from designer clothing to teapots and potholders to just plain junk.

There wasn't much to choose from for what he needed. The only formal suits were a shiny, powder-blue tuxedo with dark-blue velvet lapels and a white tuxedo complete with vest. Two choices, prom wear or groom, neither one right. He removed both from the rack and took them to the tiny, curtained dressing room in back of the store.

He started with the prom tux. He knew he would look and feel foolish in it and was happy when the choice was made for him—the pants legs came halfway up his calf, and the jacket was a tight squeeze.

Dariush eyed the white tux. It looked like his size, and he saw by the tag that it had been marked down several times and was only seventy-five dollars, and no wonder. Who wanted a white tux from a thrift store? If he were getting married in summer, he might wear white, but then he would want to either buy something new or rent it from a custom tuxedo store. But it was stunning. Perhaps it had been worn as a costume in a movie or for a movie premiere.

Dariush opened the jacket and read the label: Brioni for Men. He recalled seeing magazine ads with movie stars promoting the brand. Brad Pitt, maybe, although that was years ago. He examined it carefully to see if it had a stain or hole somewhere, but if it did, he couldn't find it. He couldn't help wondering if he had whatever it took to carry it off. No matter what, he had to try it on—his movie-star moment—even if just for the fun of it.

When he put it on, it fit him to a tee. Brushing his shoulder-length hair back with his hand, he tied it into a ponytail with a rubber band he had around his wrist. Every time he did so, he could almost hear his father saying, "DariushJan, cut your hair. It looks terrible." Initially, as a teenager it was a kind of rebellion, albeit mild, but his parents had been gone so long now that it had no meaning attached to it. He just liked it.

He had to see how he looked. There was a mirror on a wall outside the small cubicle, so he pushed the curtain aside and stepped out. *Wham!* He smacked right into a woman wearing a low-cut black flapper dress with spaghetti straps and diagonal fringes, with a green feather boa around her neck. A brown braid hung down the right side of her chest.

She shrieked.

"I am so, so sorry," Dariush said, trying not to gape.

The woman brushed her arm as her breathing quieted down. "No one died," she said.

She had a charming accent Dariush couldn't place, and she looked really sexy, even with the silly green feathers around her neck. "Is your arm all right?"

"Yes," she said, rotating her arm in a circle. Dariush watched her as she fiddled with her dress, adjusting the length so it was even. He was mesmerized as she wiggled her torso around so the fringes swished.

"Wait a minute," she said, eyeing him in the mirror. "I think I know you."

"You know me?" Dariush replied, staring right back.

"From the building. The Stevens on West End. I almost knocked you over this morning."

"That was you?"

"I'm afraid so. I'm really sorry." She turned away from the mirror. "Your turn."

Dariush felt a little foolish as he examined his reflection in the mirror with the woman as his audience. Now it was his turn to talk to her via the mirror.

"Do you live in the building or were you just visiting?" he asked.

"I work for Mrs. Gartner on the fourteenth floor."

"Did Rosie leave?"

"No, no, I'm the night aide. What floor do you live on?"

"The floor below."

"Oh." She paused. "I think I left an invitation for you this morning under your door."

"Someone did."

"It was me. Is that what you're wearing to the party?" the woman asked as she tucked the back of his jacket collar down.

"Do you think it's appropriate?" Dariush asked, thinking, *She must think I look ludicrous.*

"I have no idea what's appropriate. I've never been to a formal dinner," she said, emphasizing the word *formal*. "But you look good to me.

I mean it looks good. Not so sure about the ponytail. It's pretty out of date."

Dariush was amused by her forthrightness. It was refreshing and for some reason didn't seem judgmental. He turned around to face her, thinking he would like to ask her out, maybe even cook dinner for her.

"And my dress? I know," she said, playfully waving the feathers at his face. "The boa is a bit much, but I love it. I couldn't decide between the boa and a long strand of pearls. I could always wear pearls, but when would I ever get another chance to use the boa?"

"You look amazing." Then, "You're invited to Mrs. Gartner's party, too?"

"Excuse me, can I get by?" a customer said.

Dariush moved quickly out of the way, then back. He did not want the conversation to end.

"Please, would you like to get a coffee or tea? By the way, my name is Dariush."

"I know. I read your name on the envelope. Dariush Rouhani. I'm Venera."

THIRTY-SIX

The Old Lady's Night Aide

WHEN SHE BUMPED INTO DARIUSH—OR RATHER, HE bumped into her—Venera was looking at her reflection in the full-length mirror. She panicked for a moment, which was embarrassing, but she quickly recovered. She hesitated a moment before telling him he looked familiar—she had to remind herself that she was engaged. He had to be there looking for something to wear that night.

She always looked for meaning in such happenings. Were the fates trying to send her a message as she waited to hear if her fiancé would have her back? That Jusef had moved on and so should she? Was her attraction to him an indication that she was already pulling away from Jusef? It was very confusing—and a little exciting.

Then Dariush asked her out for coffee. As silly as it seemed to her, she felt like it was cheating. But she said yes anyhow. She wanted to know more about him.

When they got to the little café adjacent to the store, Venera told Dariush that she wanted a skinny grande latte, then found a table while he got in line. As she waited for him to join her, she wondered what had gotten into her. Here she was, waiting to hear from Jusef about her entire future, and she was having coffee with a man she didn't know.

He looked like an old-time movie star in that white tuxedo. She surreptitiously snuck a look at him in line waiting to pay. Dressed in tan chinos, a button-down shirt, and navy jacket, presumably what he wore to work, he looked damn good. He was at least 5'10" and had a nice build. He looked smart, but maybe it was the glasses. Venera always associated people who wore glasses with intelligence, although she knew it was irrational. He didn't look American; he looked more Middle Eastern, yet he spoke without any accent. Maybe he was American-born? He was swarthy, and she had a thing for swarthy men. *Damn*, she thought. *I better leave.*

The moment Dariush got to the table, Venera jumped up. "I'm so sorry, but I can't stay. I promised Rosie I would help with the party."

"Surely fifteen minutes won't matter," Dariush said. "Please. You're not going to let me drink my tea alone."

Venera hesitated before sitting back down. "Fifteen minutes," she said, determined to stick to it and act more reserved. She wanted to find a way to let him know she was engaged to disabuse him of the notion that she was interested in him—or did she? She had brought it on herself. One minute waiting to hear from Jusef, the next flirting with a stranger. She could tell that he liked her; she wasn't oblivious to the sparks—his or hers. She hated the kind of girls who needed guys to fall for them whether or not they were involved with someone else, as if to test their own attractiveness. She wasn't like that. Either she was engaged, or she wasn't. Enough dillydallying.

"Where are you from, Venera?" Dariush asked.

"Croatia," she said, trying to act diffident.

"I love Croatia. I went there once on holiday with my parents. Which city did you live in?"

"Jelsa. I'm planning to go back soon if my fiancé will have me." There, she said it.

"Oh, so you're engaged."

There was a pause before either one spoke again.

"What do you mean, if your fiancé will have you?" Dariush asked.

"It's complicated—and I should be getting back to see if Rosie needs help."

"Would it take more than fourteen minutes to tell me?"

"I guess not," Venera said.

She began by telling him how she had secretly gotten a passport, then left Croatia and her fiancé without a word of warning for what she hoped would be a grand adventure before settling into domesticity. She left out how she had paid for it. Leaving as she did was bad enough.

"All right," Dariush said. "I could see how he might be angry. But how angry?"

"Angry enough not to answer any of my calls or texts."

"I'm sure he'll cool down."

"There's more."

Despite her concern about limiting her time with Dariush, Venera launched into everything that had happened since she arrived on the doorstep of her close friend Anika.

Anika had been shocked when she opened the door and saw Venera standing there, but she was happy to see her and insisted she stay with her, which is what Venera had hoped since she didn't have much money.

"You got lucky," Dariush said.

"Yes, for a while at least. During the day while Anika was at work, I visited all the places I had dreamt of seeing until I was almost out of money. Then I took the subway to different boroughs and just wandered around, looking at the buildings, the shops, the mix of people, the traffic, the noise . . . everything."

"You could probably be a tour guide."

"But then Anika met a guy, Tomás," Venera said, ignoring Dariush's comment, "and it became awkward. She lived in a studio apartment."

"I get the picture."

"I either had to go back home or find somewhere else to live . . . and get a job, even though I was here on a visitor's visa."

Venera paused, her attention focused on a woman who had just entered carrying a squirming baby in her arms who reminded her of her younger sister's baby. *She must be walking now*, Venera thought, *and here I am, an ocean away.* Feeling a wave of homesickness, she turned back to Dariush.

"Before I figured out what I was going to do, Anika came home from work one night. Tomás was with her. I was on the sofa bed watching the news. Anika said she needed to take a shower and went into the bathroom. The minute the shower started running, he sat down next to me and asked if I needed any favors. At first I didn't understand. 'You know, what with your fiancé so far away.' I still didn't get it. Then he got more graphic. I told him to go to hell, and he laughed. Next thing I knew Tomás turned the TV on high and tried to kiss me."

"No!"

"I pushed him away yelling, 'Stop!' A moment later, Anika came out of the bathroom. Tomás leapt up.

"'What's wrong with your friend? She's crazy. She told me she loved me and tried to kiss me.' He's lying, I told Anika. He was the one who tried to kiss me. But Anika believed him. She told me to pack up and get out, calling me all sorts of bad things. As I packed, all I could think was what a pig he was, but I was also thinking, if she really believes him, the news will spread back to Jelsa, and everyone will think I'm a—I didn't know what to do," Venera said, her voice almost a whisper. "Or where to go. It was getting dark, and I never liked walking alone in that area at night. It wasn't a great neighborhood."

"I'd like to find the bastard and give him what's coming to him."

"You don't even know me, Dariush."

"I wasn't really serious, but I hate injustice."

Just then her cell phone beeped, startling both of them. Venera looked at the number, then picked up. "Sorry, Rosie," she said, standing up. "I'll be back right away."

"Just tell me what happened next."

Venera sat back down.

"I remembered I had the phone number of my friend Jelena's American cousin Brigita tucked in my wallet, so I called her and told her what happened. She gave me the address where she worked and told me to come there, that I could sleep on her bedroom floor. It turned out she was Mrs. Gartner's night aide. She was about to move to Chicago, and her replacement had not yet been found."

"So that's how you got the job."

"Brigita introduced me to Mrs. Gartner, telling her I needed work and was trustworthy, and I was hired. I got the feeling that because of her age, Mrs. Gartner didn't think she would live that long, so she didn't ask if I was here legally. Actually, the more I think about it, the more I'm sure she knows I'm not because she pays me in cash."

"I'm sure she was far more concerned about finding someone she could trust than your immigration status."

"So now you understand why, if my fiancé doesn't already have enough reason to tell me not to come back, he also probably thinks I go around hitting on my friends' boyfriends. Not just Jusef, but no doubt my parents also heard the rumor. It just gets worse and worse."

"They know you. They know that's not who you are."

"I don't even know who I am anymore." She had no idea why she had opened up to this complete stranger, but she was done talking about herself. "I really have to go."

As they headed back home, Venera asked him where he was from. Dariush told Venera the story of why his parents went back to Iran, how his father had been sent to Evin Prison, how he hadn't seen them in several years, and how he couldn't go back without risking his life.

That's terrible, Venera thought. *At least if I go back, I won't be facing jail or death.* She noticed that his whole demeanor had changed when he talked about his family, and she couldn't blame him. *I would feel guilty all the time if I knew my family was living under the threat of death and I was partying. In fact*, she thought, *I shouldn't go to the party either. I don't deserve to have a good time. Not only did I abandon Jusef, but I stole from him as well.*

When they got to the building entrance, Dariush told Venera that he needed to make a quick stop by his office to see if he had any urgent messages. As she headed inside, she couldn't help wondering if he was planning to return the tuxedo.

THIRTY-SEVEN

The Old Lady's
Across-the-Hall Neighbor

M ISS SIDENSTRIKER AWOKE WITH A START. SHE HAD NOT intended to fall asleep—she never slept during the day; that was for boring people with no interests—but when she got back from her disastrous outing, she went to lie down for a moment. Next thing she knew, she came to with searing pain in her knee. Then she remembered. From the moment she had been jolted awake at the crack of dawn by the little Croatian bitch Venereal to her humiliating fall on 77th Street to the moment Jimmy handed her the package containing her beloved Captain's ashes, it had been one horrific incident after another. *Why?* she thought. *Was I Genghis Khan in a previous life? Not that I believe in all that karma nonsense.*

Her knee hurt like hell, although at least she knew her kneecap wasn't broken. And she felt a little woozy. Using the cane, she hobbled to the kitchen to get an ice pack from the freezer. She knew she should have done that first thing when she got home, but at that moment, the trauma of receiving Captain's ashes had predominated over the physical pain.

Miss Sidenstriker sat on a folding chair in the kitchen and placed the ice pack over her knee, then held it in place with a dish towel. She stared at the kitchen clock. Five-thirty. Time to make dinner, but she had little appetite. Or energy. She felt depleted.

Then she spied the package containing Captain's ashes on the counter where she had left it when she got home. *Oh no*, she thought, *I can't let my poor baby be all closed up in a box within a box unable to breathe. Time to fix his final resting place, his so-to-speak altar.*

She was really nervous to find out what ashes looked like. Even though both her parents had been cremated, she had never seen their ashes. She had read that burned bodies became like chipped pieces of dried clay, a ghastly thought. When her father died, rather than spreading his ashes someplace where he had been happiest like most people did, she put the package under her mother's bed so they could somehow still be together. By then, her mother was in ill health and unable to cope with arranging the cremation. She never even asked about the ashes, but Miss Sidenstriker enjoyed knowing that they were still together in some way.

When her mother died, Miss Sidenstriker moved the package with her father's ashes from under her mother's bed to hers. And when she received her mother's ashes, she put them under her bed as well. It gave her comfort just knowing they were there.

Perhaps it was because she already had Captain that she didn't feel quite as alone when they were both gone. But Captain's death left her more bereft than she had ever been. She thought the expression *passed* or *passed on* was pure hogwash. Passed on to where? In her view, people passed into the oven or were buried in a box six feet underground as a last stop. However, despite her beliefs, she was prepared to suspend doubt about an afterlife in service of keeping Captain "alive" and present, albeit in an altered form.

She got the package, and then, taking a deep breath, pushed herself to open it. There was a plastic bag inside that was wrapped in old newspaper. As Miss Sidenstriker removed the newspaper, she was struck by the headline of a story: Socialite Elizabeth (Bitsy) Bingham Dexter Hammond, 71, Killed in Freak Accident. Could that be Bitsy Bingham, her old nemesis? There couldn't be two Bitsy Binghams.

Momentarily forgetting about Captain, she read the text. "Bitsy died tragically while on a horseback-riding safari in Botswana with her second husband, sportsman Bob Hammond, when, backing away from the overhanging branch of a jackalberry tree, she hit her head and fell off her horse into crocodile-filled waters."

Maybe there is a God, Miss Sidenstriker thought, coughing and laughing so hard she could hardly breathe. As she fought to get air, her right hand slammed on top of the plastic bag making a popping noise. Startled by the sound, it brought her back to her grim task.

Carefully opening the bag, to her dismay, she saw that the ashes did indeed look like specks of clay. It was a mere handful. Nothing about them conjured up Captain. She had to trust that these were really his ashes, her Captain's, not someone else's pet or, worse still, Bitsy Bingham's.

Forgoing the cane, she held the plastic bag in both hands like it was a divining rod and slowly dragged herself from room to room murmuring, "Where, Cappie, where do you want to spend eternity?" as if the ashes could somehow communicate the dead bird's wishes.

She cocked her ear like she was listening.

"Yes, yes, I hear you. . . . Oh yes, I want to be near you, too," hoping that he would "choose" her bedroom. And miracle of miracles, he did, which she knew from the vibrations she felt coming from the bag when she came near her bed. "Dear Captain, dear, dear Captain." She left the bag on top of her bedspread for safekeeping.

Next Miss Sidenstriker retrieved a box from her closet that she had put aside when Captain died. It contained his favorite toys along with a pair of bronze candlesticks she had bought from a Met Museum catalog, some paper flowers, and a beautiful vintage Chinese porcelain bowl that her maternal grandmother had given her when she graduated from college. It was quite valuable, but nothing was too good for her Captain.

She put the box on the floor next to her dresser. Even though the top of the dresser was covered with knickknacks she had picked up at museum shops over the years, some quite delicate, some quite meaningful, she swept them all off and into a shopping bag with the back of her hand and put the bag in her closet.

Next, Miss Sidenstriker assembled all the items in the box on top of the dresser, then tried to place them. The porcelain bowl belonged in the center with a candlestick on each side, but the paper flowers and Captain's many toys took more time. Again she elicited Captain's help.

"How would you like them, dear heart? Should they be spread apart? Piled up?"

It took a good thirty minutes of arranging and rearranging in "consultation" with Captain before she felt satisfied.

She then carried the bowl to the bed next to the plastic bag and slowly emptied the ashes into it, careful not to touch them. A few specks spilled on the bedspread. Miss Sidenstriker froze, not sure what to do. If she brushed them onto the floor, they would be vacuumed up and gone forever. The same if she washed the bedspread.

Finally she picked them up with the tip of her fingers and rubbed them between her breasts. She knew it was weird and suddenly worried that someone might be watching, which was impossible given that she was alone in her small, windowless bedroom.

Carefully picking up the bowl containing the precious contents, she limped toward the dresser. Just before she got there, her injured knee buckled, and she fell forward. The bowl dropped out of her hands. It crashed to the floor, sending the ashes flying everywhere, including all over Miss Sidenstriker.

Horrified, Miss Sidenstriker fled the bedroom, limping and screaming.

THIRTY-EIGHT

The Old Lady's Night Aide

AS THE ELEVATOR APPROACHED THE FOURTEENTH FLOOR, Venera heard the sound of a woman screaming as if being murdered. Chills ran down her spine, and her first instinct was to press the emergency button to stop the elevator, but then she thought that if it was Rosie—who else could it be?—she needed help.

The minute the elevator stopped and Venera stepped out, she was pushed against the wall by Miss Sidenstriker, who was babbling incoherently. A film of gray dust covered her face, and she was as white as a ghost. Venera was frightened, sure that Miss Sidenstriker had gone crazy and was attacking her. She tried to escape her clutches, but then Miss Sidenstriker burst out crying and let go. Venera heard her say, "My bird," and understood immediately that the ashes must have dropped, hence the dust on her face. Realizing that the nasty, grief-stricken neighbor had been traumatized shifted something inside Venera; it was hard to hate someone so pathetic.

"I'm sorry, Miss Sidenstriker," Venera murmured, gently brushing ashes off her arms.

"The bowl—I dropped—I dropped Captain's ashes," Miss Sidenstriker said, sounding almost like a child. As she slowly calmed down, Venera wiped the ashes off her face as well.

"I'm so sorry," Venera said again. She wanted to mention the bird's name but wasn't sure what it was.

"Would you come with me, Ven—" Miss Sidenstriker began, her voice low, her tone gentle. "I need help."

Venera offered Miss Sidenstriker her arm, and together they went back into Miss Sidenstriker's apartment and into Miss Sidenstriker's bedroom.

"This is your bedroom?" Venera asked, mystified as to why she would live in the maid's room when there were other bedrooms in the apartment. But Miss Sidenstriker didn't answer. She dropped down across her bed, face first.

Venera saw the broken remains of a bowl and ashes on the floor and then understood that the help Miss Sidenstriker needed was for her to clean up the mess, not assist her back inside. She went into the kitchen and found a broom and dustpan as well as a cereal bowl. When she returned to the bedroom, she saw Miss Sidenstriker's shoulders shaking—she was obviously crying.

Venera swept the ashes into the dustpan, then emptied them into the bowl. Glancing around for a place to put them, Venera noticed the display on top of the dresser. Since Miss Sidenstriker didn't seem aware that she was there, Venera looked around the room. Aside from furniture, the only other objects in the room were a stack of books on the bedtable, an empty carton, and a bag full of knickknacks. It could be the room of a nun.

Venera felt herself tearing up. *The woman denies herself in every way possible. She pushes people away so all she had was that bird. And now she has no one.*

It was so sad. Venera wanted to say to her, "You have to make your life," although she knew it was too late for Miss Sidenstriker. But not for her.

She wasn't sure whether to ask Miss Sidenstriker where she wanted the cereal bowl that now held the ashes. She had stopped shaking, and Venera thought she had probably fallen asleep. Venera put the bowl on the dresser, then picked up the broken pieces of the bowl, the broom, and dustpan.

She was tiptoeing toward the door when she heard, "Thank you, Venera."

"You're welcome," Venera said.

Just before she got to the front door, Venera remembered that she hadn't delivered Mrs. Gartner's dinner invitation to Miss Sidenstriker. She removed it from her pocketbook, then, seeing a pen on a table by the door, scribbled a message on the envelope and left it on a table before leaving.

THIRTY-NINE

The Old Lady

Aﬀter Patty left the room, Bette worked on Kenny's pillow. She worked quickly, sloppily, but she wanted to finish it, even though she was concerned that to Jia it might seem like she was too invested in her marrying Kenny. But Bette had her own relationship with him and appreciated his kindness to her. He always came with Jia when she visited. Bette wondered how many young men would want to spend time with an old lady. He could have made excuses, but he actually seemed to enjoy talking to her.

When the pillow was done, Bette pressed the button on her Fitbit that lit up the time: 6:15. She wheeled herself to her desk so she could pay her bills. Next she watered the orchids using the can that Rosie left by the stand earlier in the day, a weekly chore, after which she poked food pellets into the soil with her index fingers. How she loved her orchids! George's office was in the thirties near the flower district, and he often bought Bette gorgeous and exotic plants, knowing how much she loved them. Going to the annual orchid show at the Bronx Botanical Gardens together was one of the highlights of her year.

She went into the bathroom to wash her hands, then opened a drawer on the plastic bin and retrieved the bottle of Ambien her doctor had given her after George died. She checked the label for an expiration date but couldn't find it.

As she wheeled herself back toward her bed, Bette realized that she had forgotten to get a manicure. George had always taken pride in her hands, with her long thin fingers that were still relatively nice, albeit veiny and dotted with age spots. She hadn't had her nails done since George's death; she had had no need for it. But tonight she did. However, she didn't own any nail polish.

Bette pressed on the intercom that connected her to Venera's room. "Venera? Are you home?"

"Yes, Mrs. Gartner," Venera answered, her voice sounding nasal.

"Do you think you could give me a manicure?"

"Okay."

"Do you have polish?"

"I do."

A few minutes later, Venera came into Bette's bedroom carrying a small basket filled with various shades of polish, none pink or red. Bette had never seen such an assortment. In the days when she had a weekly manicure, she always chose red. She removed all the bottles from the basket and lined them up on her desk with a kind of childlike pleasure.

"What do you think?" Bette asked, amusing herself as she held up a bottle of black polish. "My daughter will think I've lost my mind."

"Do you need her permission?"

"No," Bette answered, "I do not. Let's do it."

"I'm going to start with a clear undercoat," Venera said.

"Okay." As she held out her hands, Bette asked, "Do you know if everything is all set?"

"I'm sure Rosie has it all under control," Venera said as she started filing the nails on Bette's right hand.

"You delivered the invitations to Dariush and Gertrude, right?"

"Gertrude?"

"Miss Sidenstriker. You did give her the invitation?"

"Yes, yes, of course." Venera answered so quickly that it gave Bette pause.

"Venera?"

"She didn't answer the doorbell, so I slid it under the door."

As Venera continued working on her nails, Bette felt sure there was more to the story. She obviously hadn't wanted Gertrude to come in the first place. But she would deny it. Bette opted to let it go.

"Mrs. Gartner, can I tell you something I've never told anyone else?"

"Well, my dear, I've confided in you. Now it's your turn."

"You will think badly of me, but I have to get it off my chest." Bette wondered if this was a ploy for sympathy to cover up what she had done, but the poor girl did look miserable.

Venera related the story of how she had "stolen" the money she and Jusef had received as wedding gifts to buy a ticket to America.

Bette burst out laughing.

"Why are you laughing?"

"You're a survivor."

"What do you mean?"

"You're very resourceful, my dear. And ambitious."

"What do you mean?"

"You go after what you want."

"But I betrayed Jusef's trust. You really don't think I did something terrible?"

"Well, of course it wasn't right, but he didn't give you much choice, did he?"

"Mrs. Gartner, you make it seem like I have nothing to be ashamed of. But I am so ashamed."

"That's a waste of time. What's done is done."

Bette had taken to Venera from the moment she met her. Her confession confirmed Bette's sense that this smart, lovely girl had a thirst for adventure that would probably lead her to do other things she needed to do with her life.

Suddenly overcome with a wave of fatigue, Bette closed her eyes, hoping Venera would consider the subject closed. But Bette could not turn off her mind as easily. Venera's "betrayal" of Jusef reminded her of the one dark patch in her marriage.

A memory surfaced that she had worked hard to quash over the years. It was during the mid-sixties. Like many Americans, they had front-row seats to the war in Vietnam via the television set. Ever since coming back from World War II, George had had periodic bouts of depression, usually short-term. However, the Vietnam War sent him spiraling downward. Obsessed with the stupidity of it, he ranted and raved nightly as he watched the news on television.

The day President Johnson announced that he was sending an additional fifty thousand troops to Vietnam, George was livid. That night at dinner, it was all he could talk about.

"Has the man no conscience? War is insane. Sending young American boys to kill or be killed in a senseless war?"

"You have to stop listening to the news. It's not good for you to get this upset." Bette got up and went behind George to massage his neck and shoulders. "Try to eat something. Your dinner's getting cold."

"That's enough, Foxy. I'm not hungry."

"Daddy," Claire chimed in. "What about the 'clean plate club' rule?"

"Young boys are dying in rice fields, not knowing who's an ally, who's the enemy—"

"George, she's just a child," Bette said.

"So are those boys," he yelled. He shoved his elbows back and pushed Bette away. She ran out of the room in tears.

After that, he often came home late. When he did join Bette and Claire for dinner, he had little to say. Bette reasoned, then pleaded, then nagged him to see a therapist, if only to get medication for his depression. His refusal created additional tension between them.

One day, Bette was going through one of George's suits before sending it to the cleaners and found a phone number scribbled on a piece of paper. Even now thinking back, she wasn't sure what prompted her to call the number, but she did. A woman answered.

"Hello? Hello? Is anyone there?" Bette was about to hang up, when the woman asked, "Georgie, sweetie, is that you?"

Bette hung up, her whole body trembling. Her feelings ranged from hurt and anger to fear. George was her life. She had always discussed everything with him, but now she was on her own. The only thing she felt sure about was that until her mind was clearer, until she knew what she wanted, she wouldn't say or do anything. It gave her a tiny measure of control.

Much as she tried to act as if nothing was wrong, she wasn't that good of an actress. She became distant, especially when George wanted sex. She used headaches, backaches, her period, every excuse she could think of to avoid sex. Initially, George would ask if anything was wrong, but then he gave up.

Basically a private person, she didn't tell anyone. The last thing she wanted was to be fodder for gossip, and she knew that once anyone knew, it would get around—it was just human nature. They would be watched. Was George flirting with some woman? Was she aware of it? Did she seem upset?

Instead, she poured everything she was thinking and feeling into a journal. As a child, she had never kept a diary, but for the first time in her life, she understood how a journal could be like a friend, a friend you could trust with your secrets.

A couple of months later, before she had decided whether to confront him or not, George surprised her with a diamond-and-gold tennis bracelet from Tiffany & Co.

"What's this for?" she asked, sure in her heart it was proof of his guilt.

"Because I love you."

As she thanked him, Bette wondered if it meant the affair was over.

She put the bracelet away and never wore it. After that, as much as she hated herself for doing it, she played detective for months. But George was on his best behavior, as if trying to make up for his indiscretion. He stopped coming home late, and he took Bette's advice and stopped following the news. In time, they got back to the comfort level they had had before it happened.

Ultimately, Bette concluded that it was a brief fling and not a love affair, probably based on a need to escape his existential pain. Had he been able to talk to her or anyone else about the war, ideally a therapist, he might not have needed the distraction of an affair, but that was not her George. He kept everything bottled up inside. They never spoke about it, nor did he ever ask her why she didn't wear the bracelet.

As she reflected on it now, she realized that he must have known she knew. He knew how much she loved wearing the jewelry he gave her. How much, for example, she loved the pearls she got when Claire was born. She almost—*almost*—felt bad for him, knowing that with his sense of integrity, he must have been ashamed of himself.

Bette opened her eyes, willing herself back to the present. *Damn those memories*, she thought. It was ancient history, a brief chapter in an otherwise long and happy marriage. In retrospect, she wished that she had worn the bracelet when George was alive so he could have known she had forgiven him.

She decided she would wear it tonight, but she wasn't sure where she had put it. When Claire came, she would ask her to see if it was in the safe.

Bette held out her hands, flicking her fingers upward. "I've changed my mind. They look perfect as they are."

"That's just the undercoat," Venera said.

"I know, but they look nice. George always preferred my nails like this. Now, go see if Rosie needs you."

FORTY

The Old Lady's Housekeeper

ROSIE ENTERED THE DINING ROOM CARRYING THE FLORAL centerpiece she had ordered per Mrs. G.'s instructions and carefully placed the arrangement in the center of the table, then stood back to survey her handiwork. She had set the table using Mrs. G.'s finest ivory linen tablecloth and her antique crystal candelabras. The sideboard held a stack of plates as well as a silver tray filled with flatware wrapped in linen napkins that matched the tablecloth. Rosie had put leaves in the table so it could comfortably seat ten people, which hopefully would be enough.

An array of garnished platters from Citarella on the sideboard looked inviting: poached salmon with dill sauce, chicken salad, potato salad, tossed salad, a cheese platter, cut veggies with three different dips, and a breadbasket.

She gave herself a moment of pride about how good it all looked, not that it was all her doing. The dining room was made for entertaining, with its ivy-covered wallpaper, pale green drapes, faded pastel-colored oriental rug, mahogany table and chairs, sideboard, ornate framed mirror above the fireplace, and crystal chandelier above the table. Mrs. G. had made the needlepoint cushions on all ten chairs.

Imagine having that much time, much less patience, for such an undertaking, she thought. Rosie wondered which one she would pick if she had to choose between being someone with money who hired others to do for them or someone like herself who was the worker bee. She felt it would probably be the latter. She couldn't imagine what she would do if she didn't work—not that she aways liked working, but it gave her life structure. She didn't have talents or hobbies like Mrs. G. did. Nor would she ever want to be someone who put on airs—who thought they were better than other people just because they had money. No, she knew who she was and was okay with it most of the time.

Rosie went over to the sideboard and swiped a taste of the chicken salad with her finger. "Too much celery," she murmured as she gave the display a final once-over. The whole business of ordering in was new to her. In the old days, when Mr. and Mrs. G. entertained, she did everything—all the cooking, serving, and washing up. It was exhausting. A part of her was relieved that it had been taken out of her hands, while the other part felt she could have done it better had she been given more notice.

Rosie felt a sense of anticipation for the evening ahead. This would be her first fancy dinner party as a guest, and fancy it would be. She couldn't wait to find out why the medium had been invited after dinner. It could only be to provide entertainment, if that's what you could call it.

Suddenly she realized that Citarella had forgotten the dessert. She needed to call them ASAP.

She went into Mrs. G.'s bedroom to see if Mrs. G. wanted to inspect the dining room before the guests came.

"I'm sure it looks good," Mrs. G. said.

"You okay?" Rosie asked, noticing that she seemed a little downcast.

"Just tired."

"No wonder. What a day this has been."

"Yes," Mrs. G. said. "Indeed it has."

"I'm going to go change unless you need me to help you get dressed."

"Go ahead. Claire can help me when she gets here. Where did you put the dress?"

"I fixed it best as I could, then put it back on a hanger in the closet."

"Okay." Rosie was at the door when she turned back. "Mrs. G., do you mind my asking what you and Patty talked about?"

"We talked about vintage clothes, and how much more feminine they were than today's clothes."

"No, really?"

"Rosie, you have to give her room to figure out if she wants to go to college. All breathing down her neck is doing is making her want to rebel."

The doorbell rang.

"That must be Claire," Mrs. G. said. "Send her in."

When Rosie opened the door, Mrs. Haight stood there, towering over her in three-inch bone-colored heels. She wore a floor-length black suit accessorized with diamond stud earrings.

A small beige leather pocketbook held up by a slim silver chain hung over her shoulder. She held a large square box in her hands.

"Don't you look nice, Mrs. Haight," Rosie said.

She reached out to take the box from Mrs. Haight, but she held on to it, saying, "I got it."

"Whatcha got in there, Mrs. Haight?" Rosie asked.

"Um, just some old decorating magazines I had lying around," Mrs. Haight said, with such hesitation that Rosie suspected she was lying. "I thought Venera might enjoy looking at them."

"That's thoughtful of you," Rosie said.

Mrs. Haight looked around for a place to put the box. "Is Mother resting?"

"She's waiting for you to help her get dressed. By the way, she let Patty do her hair."

"Not with green streaks, I hope."

"She looks good. We need pictures tonight, although I guess we can use our phones."

"I'm surprised no one thought of that," Mrs. Haight said. *She means me*, Rosie thought, amused. *My bad.* "It's better if it's just one person; otherwise it's too disruptive."

Putting the box carefully down on a counter, Mrs. Haight said, "I'll call my husband and tell him to bring his Nikon. He's a good photographer. Everything else all set?"

"Citarella forgot to send the dessert. I was just about to call and read them the riot act."

"We don't need dessert. We have to make sure the night ends early, or Mother will be exhausted."

"But she wanted a dessert."

"Don't tell her," Mrs. Haight said.

"But—"

"Rosie, don't say anything. I mean it."

Whoa, someone is on edge, Rosie thought. *Maybe she's nervous about the party, wanting it to go well for her mother, but if so, why skip dessert? Mrs. G. will not be happy, and she'll blame me. Oh well, tomorrow's problem.*

"By the way, you left a bag of dresses in your mother's room, but she asked me to get them out of her sight. What would you like me to do with them?"

"Oh God, she must have recognized them. They were Hope's."

"Oh, I'm so sorry."

"See if your daughter wants them. They'd have to be taken up, but they might fit."

"Thank you. She loves old clothes."

"Just make sure she doesn't wear them around Mother."

"Of course."

Changing the subject, Rosie told Mrs. Haight she wanted to give her a heads-up. In the morning she was planning to ask Mrs. G. if she could take two weeks off at the beginning of July. Jia's suggestion had resonated with her.

"Haven't you already taken your vacation?" Mrs. Haight asked, standing with her back against the counter as if she thought Rosie might grab the box.

"Yes, but I've been having issues with Patty, and Jia thought—"

"Jia? Where does she fit into this?"

"She thought that maybe you and she, between the two of you, could fill in for me for part of the time if Venera can't cover for me and has to go back to her country."

"Part of the time? I don't know my plans. If Venera is gone? God, is she leaving? Why didn't anyone tell me?"

"I just said, if she has to go; it could happen. She could be deported, or her fiancé could ask her to come back."

"Oh, my God. Someone needs to sponsor her. I'd hate to lose her."

"That's a great idea. Maybe you can—"

"What's a great idea?"

"Didn't you just say someone should sponsor Venera?"

"Mother can."

"Seriously, Mrs. Haight? Your mother? It can take a few years to—"

"I don't want to think about that right now. We were talking about you taking time off. No. Mother won't be comfortable with strange aides."

"But if you and Jia are here, and possibly Venera will still be here, you won't need—"

"Don't badger me, Rosie. No."

You are not my boss, lady, Rosie thought. *I'm going to take it up with Mrs. G. tomorrow. She will understand. And if you aren't willing to sponsor Venera, maybe I can. I could argue that I need her to take care of my daughter. I need to look into what that entails.*

"You just sprung this on me. Do not discuss it with Mother. I have to think of what's best for her. That's all I ever do."

Rosie couldn't believe Mrs. Haight actually believed that. *All she ever did? A daily call and a few visits a week didn't exactly seem like all that much effort. Why can't rich people ever think of anything but their own needs?*

"Claire?" Mrs. G. called out.

"I'm here, Mother."

"Come help me get dressed."

"Case in point," Mrs. Haight said.

"Do you need anything before I get changed?" Rosie asked.

"Why change? You look fine just as you are," Mrs. Haight said as she headed toward her mother's bedroom.

Patty, who had been showing Venera her haul from Mrs. G., joined Rosie in the kitchen. "Dad's just called. He's home, so I gotta go."

"Do you need taxi money?"

"Mom, I can take a bus."

Rosie fished in her pocket and removed her credit card. "Use this."

"You feeling all right?"

"Shut up," Rosie said, laughing. Patty was almost out the door when Rosie remembered the garment bag.

"Wait," she shouted. She retrieved the bag from the hall closet and brought it to Patty. "Mrs. Haight says you can have these dresses. They belonged to her daughter."

"The dead daughter?" Patty asked.

"*Shhh*. She's here." Rosie motioned toward Mrs. G.'s bedroom.

Laughing, Patty whispered, "That's creeeeeeepy," as she unzipped the bag and peeked in. "These are cool."

"Not too creepy for you?"

"Bye, Mom!" Patty kissed her mother lightly on the cheek. She was almost out the door when Rosie ran after her and pulled her into a bear hug.

"I can't breathe."

Rosie released her. "I'm sorry."

"Sorry about what?"

"Everything," Rosie said, close to tears. "The divorce, going back and forth between two homes—"

"Are you crying?"

"Me? No."

"Liar. Mom, I'm fine. I get it. I love Dad, but I know he can be an asshole. Enough with the guilt trip."

"I hassle you about school—"

"If I listened to Dad, I'd flunk out."

"Say that again."

"I have to go," Patty said, fingering the credit card. "Maybe I'll make a pit stop at Bloomie's."

"Yeah, right. Just you try," Rosie said as she opened the back door and pushed Patty out.

FORTY-ONE

The Old Lady's Night Aide

AFTER FINISHING THE MANICURE, VENERA WENT BACK to her bedroom to get ready for the party. She pulled her suitcase out from under the bed and removed a pair of strappy high heels that would work well with her outfit. As she shoved the suitcase back, it bumped up against the bottom of the bed and something dropped.

Fishing under the bed, Venera removed a notebook. *I guess Brigita must have forgotten to take it with her*, she thought, *but why hide it? It must be very personal.* She considered throwing it away but decided she could mail it to her.

She wasn't planning to open it, but she wanted to make sure it was Brigita's and not a previous aide's before sending it. She assumed that Brigita or whomever it belonged to would have put her name on the first page. To her great surprise, Venera recognized Mrs. Gartner's handwriting. *Now, that is a mystery. Why would Mrs. Gartner hide a journal under the bed off the kitchen? Had Brigita or Rosie found it and snuck it to the bedroom to read, assuming it was a diary of sorts?*

Venera knew the right thing to do would be to bring it to Mrs. Gartner. But then, if she had actually hidden it herself in what she thought was a safe place, whatever was written must be very private. Tonight was not the night to show it to her; she would give it to her tomorrow.

The first thing she noticed was that the paper had turned yellow and crinkly. *Mrs. Gartner must have hidden it a long time ago,* she thought. *Whatever it was had to have been upsetting. Hopefully she had forgotten about the journal and whatever it was that it contained.*

Partly to protect Mrs. Gartner or so she convinced herself, but mainly out of curiosity, Venera opened the journal to a random page.

Why didn't G tell me he didn't want children before we got married? Other men came back from war and got married and had big families. Not G. He was so scared of having a son who could one day be drafted, he would rather have no children at all. That goddamn war. I practically had a nervous breakdown when he told me how he felt. G finally relented, and I had Claire. But then the Korean War started, and I wanted a second child, but G was adamant. He said we gambled once and got lucky, we had a girl, but he won't risk it again.

Venera flipped ahead.

How could G destroy our family like this? Is it my fault? Has my nagging pushed him away? Does he still love me? Did he ever? Does he love her, whoever she is? Who is it? His goddamn secretary? Is it all about sex? Don't I satisfy him? I never say no like other women I know, even if I don't feel like it. Is he planning to leave me? Do I want him to stay? Should I tell him I know, give him an ultimatum? Her or me? What would I do if he chose her? I don't want to be divorced. A single mother. I can't do that to Claire. And besides, I love him so much. But how can I overlook this? Pretend I don't know? Am I that good an actress? If he so much as tries to touch me, I don't know what I will do. How do I figure this all out? I feel so alone.

Venera closed the journal, her head spinning. Before learning that Mrs. Gartner had grown up without a mother, Venera had assumed that Mrs. Gartner's life was perfect. She had a family who loved her, she lived in a beautiful apartment, and she had money. Now this revelation about her husband, about whom she always talked so lovingly. Venera didn't think Mrs. G. stayed with her husband just because divorce was frowned on when she was young. She made a conscious choice to stay in her marriage despite his betrayal, despite his refusal to have more children.

My problem is the opposite. In a way, I betrayed Jusef by leaving, and I'm the one who doesn't want a big family. Mrs. Gartner accepted having only one child because she loved her husband so much, but I don't love Jusef enough to agree to his terms. I don't even know if I love him anymore, at least not as a husband. When I was in my teens I did, but people grow up and change.

Venera shifted the journal up and down in her hand, trying to decide what to do with it. She felt certain there was no way Mrs. Gartner would ever want anyone to read it or to even read it herself. It would be too painful.

She went to the incinerator and tossed it in.

When she got back to the bedroom, she put on her party dress and braided her hair. She eyed herself in the mirror, then took out the braid and brushed her hair. She bent her head over and tossed it back so her hair hung down her back. Still not satisfied, Venera parted her hair down the middle and made a loose bun. Then, pulling a few strands from the top, she reached for her nail scissors and cut them until they were about five inches long. She wet the strands, then moussed and whirled them into a spit curl, which she more or less cemented in place with hairspray.

She couldn't believe she was about to go to a party in a costume, a first for her. She had to show Jimmy how she looked—he would get a good laugh.

As she headed out the kitchen door to get the elevator, she thought about how Mrs. Gartner had laughed when she told her how she had taken the money to come here. Laughed and called her a survivor. Was that good or bad? She also called her ambitious. How was she ambitious? Was that good or bad? Based on Mrs. Gartner's response, Venera believed she thought it was good. *Maybe I am ambitious,* she thought. *I am. I may not know what I want, but I am starting to know what I don't want, and that is to marry Jusef. We would both be miserable.*

FORTY-TWO

The Old Lady's Daughter

As she headed to her mother's bedroom, Claire was preoccupied with her conversation with Rosie. She hoped she had put out that fire. There was no way she was going to allow her to go on another vacation.

But there was another possible problem brewing—Venera. Could she be deported? Or might she just pick up and leave without giving decent notice? Could Mother sponsor her or would she be considered too old? Kenny could do the legal work, but what else was involved? *Maybe if I offer to raise Venera's salary she might be induced to stay.* Yes, she would do that. And since Venera would undoubtedly tell Rosie, she would also give Rosie a raise. No need for Mother to know any of this. Time to quietly retire her as overseer.

When Claire entered the bedroom, her mother was busy burrowing through her desk drawers.

"At your service," Claire said.

Her mother closed the drawers and turned around. Claire did a double take. Her mother's hair had been cut to below the ears with a side bang and was all teased. *Good thing Mother never looks in the mirror*, Claire thought. If she hadn't been so upset by her encounter with Rosie, she might have laughed, but instead she was angry.

"Well?" her mother asked.

"It's . . . interesting," Claire responded, knowing her mother knew her well enough to know what "interesting" implied, but she hated that her mother looked foolish and prayed that no one would make her feel self-conscious.

"That bad?"

"No, no, Mother. It's just . . . unexpected."

"Oh well, too late to do anything about it now."

Claire spotted the silver evening gown laid out across a chair.

"Is that what you're wearing?" she asked, trying to hide her shock.

When Claire read that the dinner was formal, she assumed that it meant cocktail attire for the women. Not a ball gown. What was this party? As a rule, her mother hated being overdressed.

"Yes," her mother answered. "Isn't it beautiful? Your father picked it out."

"What?" Claire said, wondering if her mother was losing it.

"I don't mean today," Mother snapped. "I mean, he went shopping with me when I got it. It was for the opening of a Broadway play he invested in."

"It's lovely," Claire managed to say, totally relieved.

"Help me put it on."

Claire helped her mother into the dress, careful not to disturb her hair. Once the dress was on, Claire thought her mother's hair didn't look all that bad, certainly better than it would have looked had she left it flat and stringy.

"I miss Dad so much," Claire said. "This will be our first real dinner party without him."

"I know, I know. I've been thinking about him a lot today. You know he died on his hundredth birthday."

"Yes, Mother, I know. That was such a coincidence."

"Coincidence? No, dear. He chose that day."

As if people could have that much control over their fate. Only Mother could think such a thing, Claire thought. *Ever an alpha.*

"Hand me the perfume bottle, will you?"

"I remember how Dad always used to buy it for you for your birthday."

"We both loved the scent."

When Claire handed her the bottle, her mother put her right index finger to the stopper, then turned the bottle upside down. After dabbing perfume on the back of her neck, she dabbed it between her breasts.

"Whew," Claire said, waving her hands in front of her face. "That was enough for all the women in New York."

"It's not for you, dear."

"Who is it for?"

"Never you mind."

Claire couldn't help laughing. Her mother was full of surprises today.

"Now. I need my pearls. They're in the top dresser drawer."

Claire removed the blue velvet pouch that hosted the pearls and handed them to her mother. As her mother attempted to attach the clasp by herself, Claire watched, knowing that if she offered to help, her mother would be annoyed. She never wanted to ask for help if it was not absolutely necessary.

Finally, after several failed attempts, her mother snapped, "Well, don't just stand there."

After attaching the clasp, Claire did a few gentle stretches to ease her tension. For some reason, she had a sense of foreboding about what lay ahead. Why was the medium invited? It was very strange.

"When did you get that suit?" her mother asked, interrupting Claire's reveries.

"You've seen it before. I bought it at Loehmann's years ago."

"Get a shawl from the bottom dresser drawer. That should solve the problem."

"What problem?"

"The fit isn't right. It hangs on you."

Damnit, Claire thought. *I am in no mood for a put down. I think I look pretty damn good.* Her suit had the kind of shiny veneer that worked well against her fair skin and hair. Even if it was twenty years old, it was timeless, the kind of suit that many New York women had in their closets for such occasions. It worked for cocktail parties or formal events. A shawl could become the focus, which is why Claire had chosen not to adorn it. This was her mother's night. But Mother knew best, or at least thought she did.

"Claire! Stop daydreaming. Get that shawl," Mother said.

For a moment Claire wanted to lash out, "Stop being so bossy," but she knew her mother would see her as a child until her dying day. And in a weird way, it was comforting.

Claire found a deep red pashmina shawl and wrapped it around her shoulders. "Better?" she asked, her tone mildly sarcastic. But her mother didn't pick up on it.

While she was in front of a mirror, she removed lipstick from her bag and applied it. It was the same color as the shawl. Looking at her reflection in the mirror, Claire smeared her lips together. She could see her mother watching.

"You have to admit it looks better," her mother said. "You're so skinny, you don't need black to make you look even thinner."

Claire kept her mouth shut, but the remark annoyed her.

"I think I need more sparkle."

"That dress is pretty sparkly, Mother."

"Can you go to the safe and bring me my diamond-and-gold tennis bracelet?"

"When did you get a tennis bracelet? I never saw it," Claire said, heading out of the room.

When her mother didn't answer, Claire figured she hadn't heard the question and wondered if maybe her mother's hearing was going. Better book an appointment for her with an ENT.

The safe was under the bottom shelf of the hall closet. Claire tried the combination, but it didn't open. She tried again, then shouted, "I've forgotten the combination."

Her mother called back. "The last four digits of my phone number."

When Claire opened the safe, she saw several bracelets, but no tennis bracelet. "Mother, it's not here," Claire said, loudly, but not shouting, testing her mother's hearing.

"It might still be in the Tiffany box," her mother called back.

When Claire returned with the box to the bedroom, she said, "Mother, you have to change the combination. It's too obvious."

"You can do it when the time comes."

"I hate it when you say that," Claire said, genuinely upset.

"Let's be realistic. I am ninety-five."

Tearing up, Claire reached for a tissue on the bedtable. Her mother watched, a solemn look on her face.

"Oh honey," her mother said. "Come here."

"Mother, I'm not a child. It's okay. It's just I don't like it when you talk about dying. I can't imagine my life without you in it."

Her mother didn't say anything, which left Claire wondering what she must be thinking. They had never talked about her dying. Aside from her being old, it wasn't like she had cancer or a weak heart and any other reason to discuss her impending death or either of their feelings about it. But now it was on the proverbial table.

Claire went on. "I don't know how I would have gotten through Hope's death without you and Dad. I'm so used to you being there for me. Mother, I'm over seventy, but at times I still feel I need my mommy."

"Nonsense. You have your husband and Jia and—"

"I know. I'm just being silly."

"Your life has not been easy, and I admire the way you have handled it with grace and fortitude. The way you committed yourself to Jia could not have been easy. You had so much potential for a promising career as an artist—"

"You thought I had potential?"

"My dear, you had enormous talent. I mean have—you have enormous talent. Why do you think I hung your painting in the living room?"

"To remember Hope?"

"That too, but also because I was so proud of your work."

"You were?" Claire was stunned. Had she projected her own lack of confidence onto her mother?

"One reason I hired a full-time housekeeper to help with Jia was to give you time to paint. Don't you remember? I kept asking you if you wanted Rosie to babysit Jia. I even asked if you wanted Jia to come here after school so you would have more time to—"

"Yes, but I just thought you wanted more time with her—"

"I did—of course, I did—but I couldn't understood how you could walk away from your art."

"You never said anything."

"I didn't want to interfere with your marriage. I thought perhaps Jack didn't want you to work, afraid you would overshadow him."

"Oh, Mother," Claire said, floored. "I can't believe we are having this conversation now. Just this morning, I threw away a brochure from the Yale School of Art about a summer program in Paris."

"Go! It's not too late."

"Leave for a month?"

"Absolutely."

"I can't leave you and Jack."

"Yes, you can."

"What's gotten into you today?" Claire asked.

Moved, she hugged her mother, who held on tight. When they finally separated, mother and daughter both had tears running down their cheeks. Claire had no idea why her mother was crying, but she knew why she was. There was no way she was going to leave her and go to Paris.

"Good thing nothing is planned for tomorrow," Claire said, grabbing another tissue from the bedtable for her mother. "You're going to be very tired."

"Don't worry about me. I'll be fine, my dear. Just fine. Now help me fasten the bracelet."

FORTY-THREE

The Old Lady's Across-the-Hall Neighbor

E VER SINCE SHE SAW THE ENVELOPE ON THE FLOOR BY THE front door and opened Mrs. Gartner's invitation to dinner, Miss Sidenstriker had been agitated. Why had she been invited? No one invited her to dinner, much less a dinner party. No. One. Was it some kind of a trap? Did Mrs. Gartner know her husband used to visit and suspect she and George had—no, that was preposterous. Was it possible that Mrs. Gartner actually liked her, even though they barely knew each other? It was her parents who had been friendly-ish with them. It was so odd.

She had limited experience with parties of any kind. When her parents were alive, their holiday gatherings were just the three of them. Even during the most social period of her life when she was in Boston and at times had to attend company events, she was uncomfortable and would make excuses to leave early. Not that she imagined that anyone cared or missed her.

So why start now? She had a built-in excuse with her knee, but then maybe it would take her mind off Captain.

While she was still standing by the door, she heard the elevator door open. She looked through the peephole at Venera dressed as a flapper girl, of all things, complete with a feather boa. She must be going to a costume party later on.

But then she looked back at the envelope and saw "See you later, Venera" written on it. Is she going to serve in that outfit—or could she be a guest? Who else was coming? If she were to go, whom would she be seated next to? What on earth would she talk about? Charlotte Brontë?

Then there was the dress code. The invitation said formal. Now she was really confused. Was it formal or a costume party? She could go as a librarian, a librarian with a cane. She had the clothes for that, and she would at least be comfortable. But no, there was no way she could imagine Mrs. Gartner expecting her guests to come in costume. Venera definitely must have other plans, despite the note.

The more she obsessed about it, the later she knew she would be if she went. There was no way she would get there before 8:15, which meant she would make an entrance, and everyone would stare at her.

As she mulled it over, she decided that she would get dressed before making a final decision about whether to go or not. But she didn't own an evening dress. Her clothes were all sensible working clothes. Maybe she could add a print scarf to her outfit to spruce it up a bit. But none of her scarves were especially pretty.

Her mother had been somewhat fashionable. Having never given her parents' clothes away, Miss Sidenstriker decided to look through her mother's closet, something she had never done before. It seemed so invasive, she had to hope her mother would forgive her if somehow, as unlikely as it was, she knew.

The moment she opened the closet, she saw a lovely mid-calf, pale-green jersey dress and matching stole, and it looked just her size. She tried it on. The lining was a little scratchy, probably because of aging, but so be it. She remembered seeing her mother in it at a dinner given for her father when he retired many years ago. She had thought it classy then and classy now.

The next hurdle was shoes. Miss Sidenstriker didn't own dressy shoes, and now she had an injury that affected walking. However she wouldn't want to stand out by wearing oxfords with her mother's fancy dress. She owed it to her mother's memory to wear shoes that became the dress.

Since she and her mother both wore size ten, she tried on a pair of black pumps with two-inch heels. Using the cane, she practiced walking around the apartment until she got the wobble under control. She knew it was dumb to do with her knee hurting the way it did, but she reasoned that she would be sitting most of the time.

Using the mirror above her dresser, she fixed her hair as best she could, redoing the bun. Miss Sidenstriker picked up an old lipstick that was lying in a silver tray on top of the dresser. She removed the cap to see the color. It was a pale pink, not at all showy. Aside from concealer for her birthmark, she never wore makeup, but this was an occasion.

Holding the lipstick half an inch away, she traced the shape of her lips, then closed her eyes as she mulled whether to wear lipstick or not. She inhaled deeply, then opened her eyes and put the lipstick back on the tray.

Dressed and ready, the time had come to decide if she was going.

"Well, Captain, what do you think? Go or stay?" She repeated "Go or stay" several times. Her stomach rumbled, and she realized she had barely eaten all day. She chose to take it as a sign.

"You're right. I will go and get a proper meal, and maybe I'll get a chance to take a closer look at that portrait I saw."

Heading for the door, she realized that she needed a gift for her hostess. Wasn't that what people did? But what? Then she got a brainstorm. She would give Mrs. Gartner the book her husband had so enjoyed when he came over, *Old Granny Fox* by Thornton Burgess. It was a first edition with wonderful illustrations by Harrison Cady. Hopefully Mrs. Gartner, who was presumably well educated, would recognize the value of such a gift.

If only George was still alive. Just sitting next to him would make the evening so much easier, but then even if he were alive and she had been invited for dinner, there is no way she would have been seated next to him. She wasn't family; she was nobody.

Just as she was about to leave, she had an urge to go to the bathroom. All the stress was playing havoc with her bowels, not the solution she envisioned or wanted for her constipation. She also needed to take more pain medication. Above all, she needed to rethink going. She belonged in bed with her leg elevated, her knee iced. It was very kind of Mrs. Gartner to have invited her; it was a first, and she was truly flattered. But at the moment it seemed akin to climbing Mt. Everest.

FORTY-FOUR

The Old Lady's
Great-Granddaughter

JIA, DRESSED IN A JUMPSUIT AND BLACK SNEAKERS, AND Kenny, in a tux, decided to take their car to the garage by Kenny's office, then walk the rest of the way to Granny's building in the hope that Arnold would get the piss and all else out of his system. Kenny held the leash as the puppy stopped, sniffed, and christened any and all scents about five times every block, which made for slow going.

Jia started fast-walking ahead of Kenny, having little interest in being alone with him until she knew the result of the colonoscopy. The fucking doctor still hadn't called.

"Seriously, Jia?" Kenny called out. "You can't walk with me so we can talk?"

Turning around, walking backward, Jia replied, "It's not that. I haven't gotten any exercise all day."

"Whatever," Kenny said, sounding annoyed.

Kenny probably thinks I'm being distant because of our fight about Arnold, Jia thought, *but it won't be much longer, and I can tell him everything.*

Jia got to within a block of the building well ahead of Kenny. As she waited for him to catch up, she decided that when he got there, she would make pleasant small talk so as not to worry Nana or Granny about any tension between them. Their radars were sharp, especially Granny's, so she needed to sound sincere.

"How was your day?" she asked Kenny when he finally caught up to her.

"You mean other than—"

"Kenny, please. Let's table that for now. I'm sorry if I was too—"

"Was? Jia, I feel a chill just standing next to you. You tear away—"

"I'm trying. Come on. We can deal with this later. How did it go today at work?"

"Great, just great. How about you? Did you get your article written?" Kenny said in an impersonal tone of voice.

"Yes, thanks for asking."

As they walked in silence, Jia wondered how she would get through the evening. "So, are we keeping the dog?" Kenny asked.

"Later," Jia said, again sprinting ahead of him to avoid saying something she would regret. It would be so easy to say yes, but what if she had cancer? Caring for Arnold would be an added burden.

She got to the building just as Papa was exiting a cab, a camera bag slung over his shoulder. Jia dashed over to embrace her grandfather.

When Kenny arrived, he and Papa shook hands as Arnold jumped up on Papa's leg, his tail wagging a mile a minute.

Reaching down to pat the puppy, Papa said, "So Bette invited you too, pal?"

"Not my call," Jia said. "Do you think Granny will be angry?"

"At you, never, but better keep him off the Persian rugs."

Nana was in the foyer when they entered the apartment, a red shawl draped across her arm.

"Nana, you look Fan. Tastic," Jia said, bowled over by how beautiful her grandmother looked when she made an effort. Then she noticed her shoes. Whispering, she added, "I thought Papa hated it when you wear high heels. It makes you taller than everyone else, including him."

"Oh, yes?" she said with a shrug, avoiding her husband's glance.

"Liar!" Laughing, Nana told Papa and Kenny to go into the dining room.

"Not the living room?" Papa asked.

"No, that's where Mother wants us to gather. I'll be in shortly."

As Papa and Kenny headed for the dining room, Rosie entered from the kitchen carrying a bottle of champagne wrapped in a towel. Rosie mouthed, "Any news?" to Jia, who shook her head no.

Jia reached into her pocketbook for a Godiva bar. "Where did you get that fabulous outfit?" Jia asked Rosie, handing her the chocolate bar.

"It's not mine. It belongs to—"

Claire interrupted with, "Mother. On loan for the night."

"So, anyone have a clue yet what this is about?" Jia asked.

"Your granny invited Mavis Jane Robbins, the famous clairvoyant of West 67th Street, to come after dinner," Rosie said.

"So I heard," Jia said. "Maybe the reason Granny wants us all here is for a séance."

"She won't say," Nana replied. "Rosie, go into the dining room and pour champagne into everyone's glasses, and Jia, see if Mother's ready. She told me she needed a few minutes to write a speech."

As Rosie headed into the dining room, the doorbell rang.

"It's open," Nana called out.

An attractive man in his twenties with short black hair entered, wearing a white tuxedo and carrying a tray of pastry. *Who is he?* Jia wondered. *A magician? Is that what's in store? Or possibly a wedding? But whose? What is this fucking party? And why doesn't the doctor call me? I want to go home.*

"Dariush, welcome," Nana said. "Have you met my granddaughter, Jia Kahng?"

"Hi, I'm Dariush Rouhani. I live on the twelfth floor. Wait, the same Jia Kahng who writes for—"

"We're so proud of her," Nana chimed in. "Her grandfather and me."

"Nana's my publicist."

"I made baklava for Mrs. Gartner. I almost left it in my apartment," he added with a laugh.

The three of them stood awkwardly for a moment, then Jia said, "I'll take it."

Nana took Dariush's arm and led him into the dining room. Jia heard the neighbor/magician/groom tell Nana how he missed playing backgammon with Granddad. *So maybe he's here to teach us how to play backgammon,* Jia thought. *Or get married.*

After putting the tray of pastry in the kitchen, Jia went into Granny's bedroom. The back of the wheelchair was at the desk with Granny's body hunched over, her head bent down.

Jia froze, terrified.

"Granny?" Jia called, her voice quaking.

When there was no response, Jia tiptoed a few feet closer to the wheelchair, her heart in her throat. When she was three feet away, she called out again. "Granny?"

"I'm not deaf."

Jia screamed, which made Granny scream.

"It's me, Granny," Jia said, running to her side. "You scared the shit out of me."

"I scared you?"

"For a moment, I thought you were—"

"Dead? Well, I'm not dead yet," Granny said, slipping the pad on which she had been writing into a pocket of her wheelchair.

"I don't want you to ever die," Jia said, embracing Granny.

"Don't be stupid," Granny said, her tone angry.

"Okay, then. Die, you old grouch."

"That's more like it."

"Now, let me look at you."

Jia was bowled over by the transformation in her beloved Granny. She walked a full circle around the wheelchair. "Wow. Just wow. Granny, you look absolutely beautiful. Like a geriatric beauty queen."

"A geriatric beauty queen," Granny repeated, clearly pleased. "That's an oxymoron, if I ever heard one."

"I never knew you couldn't take a compliment."

"When it's not bullshit I can."

"Granny, such language! Seriously, you have to tell me what this party is for. You have everyone guessing. I promise I'll keep your secret."

Granny twisted her fingers around her lips, indicating that they were sealed.

"Is your neighbor from downstairs getting married?"

"What?"

"The attractive young man. He's wearing a white tux."

"A white tux?" Granny laughed. "Dariush. He is handsome."

"Is he getting married here tonight?"

"Could be," Granny said, sounding amused by the guessing game.

Jia studied Granny's face. "Are you planning a séance?"

"Could be," Granny said again.

"Granny, don't stonewall me."

"Don't you stonewall me," Granny said, tossing the ball back at Jia.

I can never get away with anything with her, Jia thought. *She knows something is bothering me.* What do you mean?"

"Look at me," Granny commanded.

"Granny, this is lousy timing. I'll come over tomorrow afternoon. We can chat then."

"No, this can't wait."

Resigned, Jia decided to tell her about her fight with Kenny instead of what was really on her mind. Granny listened intently as Jia spoke of her concern about how Kenny avoided conflict by just walking away or sulking.

"Pot calling the kettle black."

"Meaning what exactly?" Jia asked.

"You just related how upset you were when Kenny got the puppy without asking you, but you held it in. That's always been your pattern. Like a dog, you like to lick your own wounds."

"I do?" Jia said, stunned by the observation.

"I'm not judging you, my dear," Granny said. "My only worry is how it impacts your relationships, whether with Kenny or any other partner."

Jia walked over to the window and looked out. "It's such a beautiful night."

"Do you see what you just did?"

Jia turned back. "What?"

"You didn't like what I said, so you walked away instead of addressing it."

"That's not why, Granny. I was reacting to your statement, 'Kenny or any other partner.' It surprised me."

"Why?"

"I know you adore Kenny, and I thought you wanted me to marry him."

"Kenny's a lovely man, even if he spoils dogs, but you have to want to marry him, not me. All I care about is your happiness."

Sensing that Granny wanted her settled before she died, Jia was dying to let her know she planned to marry Kenny, but until she heard from her doctor, she couldn't say anything to reassure her.

"*Andiamo*! Let's get this show on the road," Granny said.

Jia started pushing the wheelchair toward the door.

"Wait! I forgot the pillow. Bring me the needlework I left on the bed." When Jia brought it to her, Granny tucked it by her side.

"Who's the lucky recipient?"

"Kenny. You need to take it to a seamstress to do the backing. Maybe a brown velvet."

"Granny, that's what I call a mixed message."

"What's mixed about it?"

"First you say you don't care if I marry Kenny, then you have me doing wifely chores for him."

"I see your point," Granny said. Then she added, "Okay, then, take it to a seamstress for Kenny while on your way to a date with a new man."

"Good idea," Jia said. "I will."

FORTY-FIVE

The Old Lady

AS JIA PUSHED THE WHEELCHAIR INTO THE DINING ROOM, Dariush stood up, and the others followed suit.

"Sit down, sit down," Bette said, but no one listened. She wasn't all that displeased, but then Jack ran in front of the wheelchair and, walking backward, started taking pictures. "Jack. Stop. What're you doing?" Bette snapped. "Put that damn camera away."

She hated having her picture taken. She considered herself unphotogenic, having never seen a good picture of herself, although it occurred to her that she might have an inflated image of how she really looked. A depressing thought, plus which she had not requested photos. Whose idea was that, anyhow?

"This is an occasion," Jack said. "Do you want me to make an album and include everyone but you?"

"Just one, then leave me alone. And make it quick."

After taking the shot, Jack turned the camera around to show it to Bette. Summoning up the courage to look, to her relief, she saw that she had not aged all that much in the last few years. The old woman she saw in the photo had a cloud of white hair around her face and wore a gorgeous evening dress adorned with pearls. *Not exactly a geriatric beauty queen*, she thought, *but pretty damn good for someone my age. Dear Patty had done an okay job. The pouf is kind of flattering.*

"You look great," Jack said.

"It's you, Jack. You can make anyone look halfway decent."

Jia leaned over the wheelchair and whispered, "Granny, for God's sake, take the damn compliment and admit you look good."

Oh my God, how I love that child, Bette thought as, suppressing a smile, she waved Jia away, then looked around and noticed that her guests were all still standing... and watching. *Now I'm a sideshow,* Bette mused. *My own damn fault. I should've just smiled and been gracious.*

"Please, sit down. Please."

As Jia pushed the wheelchair to the head of the table, Arnold, who was lying under the table at Kenny's feet, started barking.

"Is that a dog?"

"Kenny brought Arnold," Jia said. "He should've asked."

"I'm sorry, Bette," Kenny said.

"It's fine. Arnold is always welcome."

"Granny, that is so not true," Jia said, taking a seat next to Kenny. "When we brought him over to see you a month ago, you were panicked he'd pee on your rugs."

Jia was right; Bette had not been happy. She loved dogs, well-trained dogs, but Arnold was spoiled. Running all over the apartment with Kenny chasing after him, jumping up on furniture, not listening to commands. And her rugs were valuable.

"I can lock him up in a bathroom," Kenny said.

And have him whine the whole time and disrupt the party, Bette thought, but instead she said, "You'll do no such thing."

She removed the needlepoint pillow cover from her side and, holding it away from Arnold's reach, handed it to Kenny. "Don't let Fido chew this up."

"Is this for me?" Kenny asked.

"For your office. I didn't have time to add backing to it."

"It's beautiful, Bette. I'll treasure it," Kenny said. "And don't worry, Arnold will not get near it."

"He better not. It almost ruined my vision making it."

"Oh no, Bette. I'm so sorry."

"Granny, you old meanie," Jia said, laughing. "Kenny doesn't know your sense of humor well enough to know you're just teasing him."

Bette, though glad to see Jia spring to Kenny's defense, had too much on her mind to be bothered with more small talk. She needed to make sure Rosie had gotten everything just right.

Eyeing the table, she was glad to see that the flower arrangement was perfect, and the table looked great, set with the linens, flatware, and china she had requested. The plates were especially meaningful to her, a wedding gift from her father who had inherited them from his parents. They had rarely been used—she was too afraid they might be chipped—but today, as she thought about what plates to use, she remembered how George used to chide her about not using them more often. He loved the pattern with its bold colors and Asian feel to it. "What's the use of having them if they just sit in a cupboard?" he would say. Having been used so infrequently, they were all in mint condition.

Next, Bette looked to see who was sitting next to whom. In the old days when she had a dinner party, she always used place cards, but today she had completely forgotten to consider the seating arrangements. *Oh well,* she mused, *I'm out of practice. And from the looks of it, Claire probably told everyone where to sit and had done a good job of it.*

Kenny and Dariush flanked her. Venera was on Dariush's right, Jia on Kenny's left. Jack was at the end of the table closest to the door, George's official chair, with Claire at his right and Rosie at his left. There was an empty seat between Claire and Jia. Bette tried to remember who else she had invited. Then she remembered: Gertrude. Was it possible Venera hadn't given her the invitation, after all?

She was going to say something to Venera until she noticed how animated Venera was as she chatted with Dariush. Venera seemed a bit flushed, and Bette, a romantic at heart, didn't want to disturb them. She hadn't noticed Venera's flapper outfit until that moment and was confused by it. Was that her idea of formal? Very odd choice, especially when she had offered her the pick of one of her lovely gowns. Maybe it had belonged to her grandmother?

She turned her attention to Dariush. He, too, looked out of place in a white tuxedo, but he was nonetheless dashing. There was something in his manner, his charisma, that reminded her of a young George.

Bette's mind drifted to a long-ago dinner party. George was presiding over his end of the table, handsome as ever in the maroon velvet dinner jacket Claire had given him one Christmas, charming two pretty women friends with witty anecdotes while Bette listened to one of her dinner partners say to the other, "Trickle-down economics are the dumbest idea to come out of this administration."

Bette was no fan of Reagan, but as she recalled, it was a business dinner. These were George's new clients, wine had been flowing, and he had cautioned her to tread lightly.

"You don't know what you're talking about," the other man said. "It's brilliant."

Bette couldn't remember their names—just what happened next. "Reagan should have stuck to acting with Bonzo." With that, he picked up a handful of peas off his plate and threw them at his "opponent."

There was a shocked silence, then Bette stood up and announced, "Round one, the gentleman with the blue tie." Both men stared at her for a moment, and then George started clapping and everyone else joined in. A few moments later, George came over and whispered in her ear, "Score one for Foxy," which Bette knew meant that he was pleased with the way she had handled it and planned to thank her later in the bedroom.

"Mother," Claire called out across the table. "Mother," she repeated, clapping her hands loudly to get Bette's attention.

"What?" Bette looked at Claire, trying to shake off the memory. All day, and now tonight, she was flooded with memories of the past that came at her, unbidden, uninvited. It had to stop; she needed to be present. Like now.

"Did you really invite the medium?"

Bette realized that Claire probably thought the empty chair was for Mavis Jane Robbins, but before she could answer, the doorbell rang. Arnold tore out from under the table, barking.

"Arnold, stop! Kenny, damnit, get him," Jia said as Venera got up to open the door.

Claire gripped Jack's hand. "God help us, it's the medium."

"What medium?" Jack sounded alarmed. "Your mother invited a medium?"

"I was going to tell you."

"I'm not staying if there's a séance."

Bette was not happy about the chaos. The last thing she imagined was a puppy at the dinner party. Her mistake—she should have known that Jia and Kenny would bring Arnold, their spoiled baby. Imagine bringing a dog to a dinner party. She hoped that was the last surprise, the first being Jack's picture taking. She worried about the old superstition that bad things happen in threes. This was her party, and she had planned everything down to the smallest detail. She did not like being co-opted.

A moment later, Venera returned with Gertrude, who was leaning heavily on a cane.

"Is that her?" Jack asked Claire.

"I have no idea who that is."

The puppy started sniffing Gertrude's feet. Kenny tried to grab him, but Arnold was faster. "Someone catch Arnold," Kenny shouted as the dog stopped to get another whiff of Gertrude's shoes.

Gertrude froze as Jia jumped up and caught Arnold.

"I'm so sorry," Jia said. Tucking Arnold against her body with one arm, she reached out to shake Gertrude's hand.

"I'm Jia, Bette's great-granddaughter."

"Gertrude Sidenstriker. I live across the hall," Gertrude said, stiffly shaking Jia's hand.

"Welcome," Jia said. "Are you the medium?"

"Medium? What an odd notion. Most certainly not."

Claire turned to Jack. "Maybe Mother was pulling my leg."

As Kenny sat down, Jia put Arnold in his lap. "Don't let him go."

"I won't."

Gertrude limped over to Bette and handed her a book-sized package. "Thank you for inviting me," she said.

"You didn't need to bring a gift, Gertrude."

"It's just a book George liked. I thought you might want to have it."

"Thank you, Trudy. How thoughtful. I'm so glad you came," Bette said. "Are you all right?"

"I fell," Gertrude said, her voice a little slurred. "This afternoon. On 77th Street, across from the museum."

"That's terrible. As I recall, that block has lots of cracks in the pavement. At least it did before my fall when I could still walk."

"Yes, it still does."

Bette suspected that Gertrude must have taken painkillers. If there were any leftovers, she needed to tell Rosie to give them to her. The poor woman was already wobbly; she didn't need another fall going out to buy groceries.

"I'm so sorry," Bette said. "If you need anything—an ice pack or some Tylenol—just let Rosie know."

"Thank you," Gertrude replied so quietly that Bette wondered if she was holding back tears. She hoped Gertrude didn't mind being called her by her nickname, but Gertrude was such an awful name.

"I hope you don't mind me calling you Trudy," Bette said.

Gertrude seemed surprised before answering, "No, not at all."

Watching her hobble to her seat, all Bette could think was, *Poor woman, so alone, and lucky me; I am so blessed.*

Bette clinked her glass to get everyone's attention.

"Dariush, I'd like to ask you to say the Bahá'í prayer your father used to recite when we had dinner at your parents' home."

Dariush seemed startled. "All of it?"

"We have time."

"It's been a while, so bear with me."

Dariush stood up. The others all bowed their heads. "Dear Lord, thank you for all our blessings. Our lives, our health, our loved ones, our needs, and the beauty of nature that surrounds us. We pray to become worthy of this by doing our share to make this a better world for all. We pray for wisdom for our leaders and peace and justice for all mankind."

He paused to take a breath. When he continued, his recitation became increasingly emotional. "We pray for the elimination of dreaded diseases that disable men for life or cause long suffering before death. And most of all, Lord, we pray that you strengthen our faith in you, for it is only though such faith that we can weather the inevitable storms of life with courage instead of fear and enjoy the most sublime of all pleasures, peace of mind. Amen."

Bette thanked him as he sat back down.

Venera, who had been listening with full concentration, seemed moved and whispered to Dariush, "That was beautiful."

"Now please, everyone, help yourselves to the buffet," Bette announced.

Jack got up first. "I'm starved," he said. Bette had a moment thinking he should be asking her if he could get *her* dinner. Then she saw him ask Gertrude what she would like. A moment later, Claire was at her side asking the same question.

"Thanks. I'll have some salmon and potato salad."

A cell phone went off, setting Arnold off again. Bette was annoyed as she watched both Jia and Venera search for their phones. *So rude,* Bette mused. *I should have thought of that beforehand—no cell phones allowed. At the very least they should be turned on mute at dinner.*

The call was for Jia. "Hold on a second," Jia said, then dashed out of the room. Bette's annoyance turned to unease, confirmed when she saw Rosie get up to leave.

"Rosie!"

"Yes, Mrs. G.?"

"Come here," Bette demanded.

"I was about to get more champagne, Mrs. G."

"Come. Here," Bette commanded.

Rosie went to Bette's side. "What was Jia's call about?"

"I'm sure it's nothing, Mrs. G."

"Swear on Patty's life that nothing is wrong."

"Don't ask me to do that," Rosie said.

"Then go find out and come back and tell me."

Kenny got up to follow Rosie, dropping Arnold on the floor. The puppy traipsed behind him. "Claire! Get your grand-dog. I don't want him loose in the apartment." Claire grabbed the dog and took him over to Jack at the buffet.

Bette heard Claire tell Jack to take Arnold for a short walk before he ruined one of her mother's rugs. Jack handed Claire the plate he was making for Gertrude, then left. Claire brought the plate to Gertrude, then went back to the buffet to get her own dinner.

Bette was left alone at the table with Gertrude, Venera, and Dariush. She knew that, as the hostess, she should try to draw Gertrude out, but she was more interested in the dynamic between Venera and Dariush, who were deep in conversation.

"I like your haircut," Venera said.

"You do?" Dariush asked, patting the back of his head. "It's going to take a while to get used to."

"It was time."

"Agreed. By the way, what happened to the green feather boa?" Dariush asked.

"Oh, did you like it? I can go get it," Venera asked.

"No, no, I just wondered why you weren't wearing it."

"I feel silly enough already."

"You look great."

Watching them flirt, Bette remembered Venera's fiancé, though she doubted he could compete with Dariush. *Whatever Venera decides to do*, Bette thought, *Dariush needs to move on with his life, too.*

Bette heard a little moan. She looked across the table at Gertrude, who had a pained look on her face as she removed a bottle from her bag and swallowed a pill. Just as Bette was thinking that Gertrude had better start eating, Claire put Bette's plate down in front of her.

Claire was on her way back to her seat when Gertrude got up. "Can you tell me where the bathroom is?" she asked Claire.

"There's a guest bathroom right off the foyer. I can show you."

"No need," Gertrude said. "I can find it." As she tried to walk, she stumbled.

Claire jumped up to catch her. "I'm coming with you."

Just then another cell phone rang. Another electronic interruption.

This time it was for Venera who, like Jia, ran out of the room. *Young people and all their drama,* Bette thought. *I have never experienced a dinner party before like this with everyone getting up and leaving the table. If this keeps up, when am I going to make my speech?*

She turned to Dariush, who was looking toward the door. "Don't worry. She'll be back," Bette said, sounding a bit abrupt. She softened her tone. "I'm glad I have you alone for a minute. How long do you intend to keep holding down the fort?"

"The fort?"

"Your parents' apartment. Not exactly my idea of a bachelor pad."

Bette knew she was being pushy, but there wasn't time to pussy-foot around, not with the people she cared about. Dariush took a bite of his dinner before responding as if to buy time as Bette continued. "I know in your culture families stay together and parents wield a lot of influence."

"I think of my parents as more American than Iranian. They've both lived here since college."

"Then they would understand."

"I don't know, Mrs. Gartner," Dariush said, putting his utensils down. "They lived in Iran during their formative years."

"Don't stop eating."

"Then you eat, too."

Bette had little appetite, but she took a bite of potato salad to be polite.

"Have you considered that, with you now an adult and your sisters all married, when they come back, they might want to downsize?"

"No."

"Well, they might. Most people do. Dariush, I know how important your family is to you, but moving out of their home doesn't mean abandoning them."

"I know that."

"Are you sure? Intellectually maybe, but I'm not so sure you do emotionally."

"I need to think about it. But if you don't mind, I'm going to go see where Venera is."

Bette understood his need to end the conversation. It was a lot to digest, and he might not yet be ready, but she felt that at least she had planted a seed.

With him gone, Bette was completely alone at the table. With all the earlier commotion, she was glad to have a moment to herself to reflect on how to get dinner back under her control, but first she needed to review her speech.

Wheeling the chair around, she moved toward a wall sconce for better light. Removing her speech from its hiding place, she began reading. It wasn't long, but she was worried that it might be a bit too—Bette searched for the right words to capture her concern—too on the nose. It lacked subtlety, she knew, but it was too late now to do anything about it. As trite as it might seem, it expressed what she needed to say.

Suddenly, Bette heard voices approaching from the foyer.

"Is that painting an original?" Bette overheard Gertrude say.

"Yes," Claire responded.

"I know it was supposed to be in a private collection, but I had no idea . . ."

"What private collection? It belongs to Mother."

Bette could tell by their footsteps that Gertrude and Claire had reentered the dining room. Curious to know where the conversation was heading, Bette felt that her presence might stop the flow, so she tucked the speech away, then dropped her head down so if they saw her, it would look like she had fallen asleep. The fact that she had moved to the corner would seem odd, but she could explain it later.

"Where is everyone?" Bette heard Claire say. *Good.* Claire hadn't noticed her.

"Maybe there was a fire drill."

Bette was astounded. *Gertrude making a joke? Whatever she's on must be powerful stuff.*

"Where were we?" Claire asked.

"We were discussing the painting. It looks like the work of William-Adolphe Bouguereau of—"

"You mean the French nineteenth-century artist? Yes, I know the painting you're referring to," Claire said. "That's what inspired me. I loved the serenity of the mother and daughter."

"You? You painted it? I don't pretend to be an expert, but I spend a lot of time in museums and believe I have a good eye. You are very talented, Mrs.—"

"Claire. Please." *Claire is warming up to Gertrude,* Bette thought. *That's good.*

"Who were your subjects?"

Bette held her breath. The last thing she expected to hear was what Claire said next.

"My late daughter, Hope, and my granddaughter, Jia. The young woman who was sitting on your left."

"Tonight, you mean?"

"Yes. I painted them over twenty-five years ago before Hope was killed."

Gertrude gasped. Bette didn't hear what Claire said next. She was too stunned by her openness with Gertrude. *Claire almost never talked about Hope. Maybe Gertrude had given Claire one of her pills?* Bette knew that was unlikely, but she couldn't fathom why Claire decided to confide in Gertrude of all people. *Maybe because Gertrude was such a loner—she had no one to tell it to.*

When Bette tuned back in, Claire was telling Gertrude that she stopped painting when Hope died.

"You are far too talented to give up," Gertrude said.

"I don't know about that. But just this week I received a brochure about Yale's Summer Arts Program in Paris that was tempting. However, there's no way I could go and leave my husband and my mother."

Hearing that, Bette realized that Claire needed more of a push. She was about to let them know she was there when Gertrude said, "I also cared for my elderly parents and never regretted it—it was the right thing to do as there was no one else—but your mother has help and you have a husband and a granddaughter. Can't they fill in for you for a few weeks?"

"I would feel so guilty."

"That's fixable; I live just across the way. I can look in on your mother. And your granddaughter and her young man can visit your husband and bring him dinners."

Miracle of miracles! Gertrude was doing her work for her. Hopefully Claire would be receptive to Gertrude's advice.

Just then Arnold started barking. Bette heard Jack say, "Take it easy, boy. Take it easy."

Bette took advantage of the distraction to wheel herself back in place, assuming that Claire and Gertrude would be looking toward the door and Jack's entrance.

Once there, Bette again bent her head down, feigning sleep.

Jack entered with Arnold, still barking and straining on a leash.

"What's going on?" Bette shouted, acting as if she had been woken up.

"Mother, how long have you been there?" Claire asked as she tried to shush the dog.

"What do you mean?"

"I didn't see you."

"I've been here all along. I must have nodded off."

She knew her daughter well enough to know that Claire was probably not entirely convinced that Bette hadn't overheard her conversation.

"Mother?"

"What?" Bette asked, yawning loudly. She smiled at Claire, a picture of innocence.

"Never mind," Claire said finally, apparently satisfied, then turned to Jack. "Did he do his business?"

"He did."

"Let me have him. It's my turn."

Jack unleashed the dog and plopped him in Claire's lap. Gertrude shied away.

A moment later, Jia and Kenny bounded in holding hands. Her face was red and splotchy. Rosie slipped in behind them holding a bottle of champagne wrapped in a napkin.

Standing in back of Jack's chair with Kenny at her side, Jia declared, "I have news."

After her earlier conversation with Jia, Bette was not expecting an engagement—or pregnancy—announcement, not that she would have minded either. But what else could it be?

"My news is . . . drum roll . . . I don't have cancer."

"Cancer?" Claire and Bette shouted at the same time.

Jack put his face in his hands, muttering, "Oh my God."

"It's okay, Papa," Jia said, putting her arms around Jack's neck. "I'm fine. It was just a scare."

Bette was in shock. The mere thought of losing Jia reawakened the memory of Hope's death, not that it was ever far away. For years after Hope died, Bette would wait until George was asleep, then go into the living room and "commune" with the portrait, filling Hope in on everything that was happening with the family, especially Jia. She stopped a few years before George died. There was no need for Hope to know that her beloved grandfather had become feeble.

For a moment, Bette considered telling everyone that the party was over, they could go home and come back another day. Then she told herself to snap out of it. Jia did not have cancer, and everyone she wanted at the table was already here. She needed to pull herself together and complete her agenda.

Bette tapped on the side of her glass with a fork. "Any other bombshells?"

Everyone laughed, but Bette was dead serious. Enough was enough. "Rosie, pour another round of Dom Pérignon," she said. "Jia, wait till we are properly 'armed' so we can toast your news."

Despite Jia's "good news," Bette sensed a pall in the room. She was clearly not the only one shaken. No one spoke until Rosie had filled everyone's glasses. Then Jia, flanked by Kenny, gave everyone a blow-by-blow account of what had transpired.

Although Jia insisted that she hadn't told anyone, as Bette listened to the account, she recalled the way Rosie had hurried off that afternoon, leaving her alone with Patty.

When Jia finished and was back in her seat, Bette called Rosie over.

"You knew about it, didn't you? Tell the truth."

"I just found out this afternoon. She needed someone to bring her home after the procedure. How could I tell you that?"

"That was when you said you needed to buy champagne?"

"Yes, Patty was with you, so I assumed—"

"Okay, okay," Bette said, still trying to recover. She turned next to Kenny.

"Kenny?"

"I swear, Bette. I didn't know a thing. She didn't want to worry me.

She promised she will never keep secrets from me again," Kenny said, his tone serious.

"My bad, Granny," Jia interjected. "Kenny and I are going to work on better communication."

"You better." In her distress, she sounded mad.

"Don't be angry with me. If the news had been bad, I would've told you, but why put you through that if it was just a scare?"

"I'm not angry. It was just very upsetting," she said as she fingered her pearls.

She felt so weary. She had spent a lifetime trying to look out for everyone, but there's only so much a person can do. Life can change on a dime; that was the terrifying truth. All you can do is your best.

Out of the blue, it came to her that Rosie had forgotten to put out the dessert. What a relief to have such a mundane problem to solve. But when Bette called Rosie over to tell her to serve dessert, Rosie informed her that Claire had canceled it.

Bette was furious. How dare Claire interfere with her instructions? Why would she do such a thing? There was no point in confronting Claire. It was too late to rectify now, and it would only spoil the party. But still.

Bette inhaled deeply to calm herself down, then told Jia to undo the clasp on her pearls. It was time to end things. And do it with grace, not anger.

"But why, Granny? They look so nice on you."

"Just do it."

Bette held her hands across her neck so the necklace wouldn't fall off when the clasp was released. She held the pearls a moment, then put them down on the table.

"George gave them to me the day your grandmother was born. We both wanted a girl. In those days, you didn't know ahead of time."

"Granny, I know. I love that story."

"When I am gone, you and Claire will have to fight over who gets them."

"There won't be a fight. They belong to Nana. Besides, I don't want to think about this now. It's morbid."

"Be good to your Nana."

"Granny, I always am. You're scaring me."

"Who's scaring you?" Kenny asked.

"Granny. She loves to talk about dying just to get a reaction out of us. You know, Granny, I think I figured out the reason for the party."

"Tell me," Bette said, confident that no one knew her plan.

"The magician and Venera are getting married."

It took Bette a moment to figure out who the magician was. "I think he looks more like a bridegroom than magician," Bette said, playing along with Jia's "discovery." It amazed Bette how Jia could always lighten her mood.

"Not in my book," Jia said.

"Oh yes?" Bette said. "What would your groom be wearing?"

"Hush," Jia said, laughing. Bette eyed Jia, willing her to always be happy, as if that were even possible. But no harm in wishing.

"What would your groom be wearing?" Kenny asked, picking up the refrain.

"Granny, look what you started," Jia said.

Things seems to be falling in place, Bette thought. *But what have I missed?* She looked away from Jia and Kenny and across the table at Jack. She sensed that he was also still getting over Jia's announcement. She needed to talk to him, not that she could heal his grief, but maybe in some small way she could help. She wasn't at all sure what she was going to say.

"Sorry to disturb you lovebirds," Bette said to Kenny and Jia, "but Kenny, go trade places with Jack for a moment."

"I'll help clear the table," Jia said. Then, whispering to Bette, she said, "Are you going to tell Papa that he also needs to stop holding everything in?"

"Take my plate into the kitchen, smarty pants," Bette said.

As soon as Jack sat down, Bette asked Jack if he was all right.

"Yes," Jack answered, seeming surprised by the question. "Aside from a little arthritis."

"Oh yes, that. I'm afraid it goes with aging."

She and Jack looked down the table at Claire deep in conversation with Kenny.

"Your family may soon be adding a new member."

"You mean two."

"Is Jia pregnant?" Bette exclaimed.

Laughing, Jack told her he was referring to Arnold.

"Do you mind?" Jack asked, picking up the camera that was hanging from a strap around his neck.

"Go ahead."

Jack snapped a photo of Claire and Kenny and showed it to Bette.

"It's really good. Somehow you've captured their rapport." The photo gave Bette the opening she was seeking. "Have you ever thought of taking your photography more seriously?"

"It's just a hobby."

"But you're good. Really good. Now that you're semiretired, you could take courses, join a club, submit your work—"

"Bette, you're getting a little carried away. My work is pretty pedestrian."

"It doesn't have to be. Go to Rome, to Florence, to Paris. Roam the streets, photograph everything that captures your imagination. The people, the buildings, the stores, the fashion—"

"How much champagne did you drink?" Jack teased.

"I'm serious, dear. It would be good for you, good for Claire . . . good for your marriage."

"Has Claire been complaining about me?"

"No. Not at all." Bette paused. "Something died in you when Hope died. It died in all of us, but in time we found a way to find joy in life."

She stopped to let her words sink in. He wasn't stupid, and she was relieved that he didn't try to defend himself.

Jia returned from the kitchen and sat down next to Jack.

"Why so serious, Papa?"

"What?"

"You look so serious. Like you're a million miles away."

"Do I?" he asked. "I'm good."

Jack picked up Bette's hand and kissed it, then went back to his seat.

"I never saw Papa kiss anyone's hand. What did you say to him?" Jia asked.

"It was private."

"Should Nana be jealous?"

"Oh my God," Bette said. "The way your mind works. No."

Jia started laughing.

"Don't laugh at me," Bette said.

"I love you Granny. You rock."

"I am not a rock," Bette snapped. She was hurt. A rock was cold, hard, emotionless. Was that how Jia viewed her?

"I didn't say you are a rock. I said you rock."

"I rock?" Bette said, her tone annoyed.

"Get over it, you old grouch. It's a compliment."

"What does it mean?"

"It means you're wonderful."

"That's better," Bette said.

"You are wonderful," Jia said. She got up and threw her arms around Bette. "The best great-grandmother who ever lived."

Tears sprung to Bette's eyes. If she spent one more minute in the arms of her beloved Jia, she might not be able to follow through with her plan.

"Okay, okay. Enough," Bette said, pushing Jia away. "Go see where Venera and Dariush are." She needed for the party to end. As soon as Venera and Dariush returned, she would make her speech.

Jia went to the door of the dining room and yelled, "Venera! Dariush! Granny wants you back at the table ASAP."

A moment later, they returned. "Where have you been?" Bette asked. "You've been gone about fifteen minutes."

Venera leaned across Dariush to speak to Bette. "You will think I'm terrible."

"Did you steal more money?"

"No. Jusef called to say he married someone else."

"And you're glad," Bette stated.

"He found someone who, in his words, wants at least six children."

"That doesn't seem so bad to me," Dariush said.

"Not you, too," Venera said, rolling her eyes at him.

I can only do so much, Bette thought. She looked at her Fitbit and saw that it was nine-fifteen; the medium should be arriving shortly. She needed to get her speech over with. But then she saw Claire leave the dining room.

"Claire! Come back! Someone, please. Tell Claire to come back," Bette said, her distress palpable.

"I will, Granny," Jia said. "I will."

Jia was at the door when Bette heard Claire tell her to turn out the lights. A moment later there were in the dark.

"Now what's happening?" Bette called out. The last thing she wanted was for Claire to take over the party.

A moment later, Claire entered the dining room holding a cake ablaze with a few sparking candles and humming the "Anniversary Waltz." She placed the cake in front of Bette. "Blow out the candles, Mother."

"What are they for?"

"Mother! Please!"

Oh God, Bette thought. *Just do it and get it over with, then I can make my speech.* She leaned over and started blowing. It took a few tries until they were all out. "Now will someone turn the lights back on and tell me what this is about?" she said, unable to disguise her impatience.

Jack turned the lights back on. Everyone eyed the cake, a carrot cake with cream cheese frosting, artfully decorated with red roses and vines, with "Happy Anniversary" written in the center.

"It's been a guessing game all day, but I finally figured out the reason for the party," Claire said, addressing everyone at the table. "When I got the invitation, I was totally mystified. And then I remembered. Today would have been my parents' seventy-fourth anniversary. Since for some reason Mother wanted to keep it a surprise, I went along with it."

Jia started clapping. "Give it up for Granny and Granddad."

Everyone applauded, and Jack took pictures as Claire cut the cake and passed the plates down the table.

"Is it really my anniversary?" Bette whispered to Claire.

"Mother, I can't believe you didn't remember."

"Well, I didn't," Bette said, her voice filled with emotion. "All day I've been trying to remember something—now I know what it was." But George had. The photo falling that morning was a sign that he remembered the date even if she hadn't.

"Go sit down," she told Claire. "I have something to say."

Bette reached into the side pocket of her wheelchair and removed her speech. As soon as Claire was seated, she tapped her glass.

"I know you're all wondering what the purpose of this party was. My daughter assumed it was for my anniversary, but that was not it. I just wanted to thank each of you for all you've done for me and George over the years. I don't know how we would have managed without you."

"What did I do?" Gertrude blurted out, then covered her mouth in an embarrassed gesture as all eyes turned to look at her. "Sorry," she whispered.

"I knew when George snuck off and you let him in," Bette said. "He needed to escape from time to time. And if his breath smelled a little of Scotch, well then, so what."

"It was just a sip," Gertrude said, sounding defensive.

"It made him happy; that's all that mattered."

Bette looked at her speech, then pushed it down the side of her wheelchair. She would wing it.

"I know the last decade has not been easy. I never wanted to be a burden—"

"Mother," Claire started to protest.

"Don't interrupt. After my fall, I had no choice. I had to depend on others. Claire is an only child, as is Jia. Our family is small; it was all on you and, of course, Rosie and now Venera."

"Where is this heading, Mother?" Claire said. "I don't like the sound of it."

"Can I continue?" Bette waited until Claire nodded okay.

"I hope what I want for each and every one of you is clear, and if I sound corny, there's truth in clichés. Pursue your own dreams. Follow your passion. Live in the present. Embrace every moment; embrace what you have."

Clutching Jack's hand, Claire whispered, "I don't like this."

"Now, enjoy the delicious cake Claire made and Rosie, let's have another round of Dom Pérignon before the last guest arrives."

Jack stood up. "Apologies to the hostess, but I am not staying if there's going to be a séance."

"Sit down, Jack dear. I promise you, there will not be a séance."

Bette looked down the table at each of her guests as if trying to internalize them. She felt a sense of peace, of closure. She had done her best. Now it was out of her hands. She was ready for the medium to show up.

FORTY-SIX

The Medium

WHEN HER LAST CLIENT OF THE DAY LEFT AT 4:00 P.M., Mavis Jane Robbins put a closed sign on her door and locked it. No one understood the toll it took on her to do what she did. It wasn't easy. She had seen three clients that day and was drained. After using so much mental energy, she had to give her brain a chance to restore before going to Bette Gartner's home later that evening.

She had little interest in going. She had already seen her once that day and saw no reason to meet again. She never did house calls, but the old lady insisted she needed her to remind her husband to show up. Then she broke into tears. Relenting, the medium was left with the sense that she was somehow being used.

She set her alarm for seven, turned off her phone, and took a nap. When she woke up, she made herself a small tuna fish sandwich—she could not work on a full stomach—then went into her bedroom to get ready.

She wasn't sure what to wear. Her wardrobe was limited and mainly consisted of tailored shirts and pants. As she looked through her closet, she was aware that most people assumed female mediums wore gypsy-style dresses with jangly bracelets and necklaces and colorful headscarves. She had no desire to fit that stereotype.

She also knew they viewed those in the paranormal field as phonies and charlatans who preyed on people in need, taking cues from how clients behaved or what they said to inform their feedback. In all likelihood their only experience with someone like herself came from books or movies. Whenever she thought about the doubters, she believed that their attitudes stemmed from their own lack of any psychic ability or imagination. It astounded her that anyone with any intelligence whatsoever wouldn't at least have an open mind. All life is a mystery. A lot of phenomena are beyond human comprehension, but that doesn't make it any less real. Anything is possible. There are over 1.5 million species of animals. How and why? How can time and space have no beginning or end? How do you explain coincidences—not garden-variety coincidences, but mind-blowing coincidences that happen all the time?

The notion that some people are born clairvoyant and from an early age can predict events, or that others can communicate with people beyond the grave, seems less of a mystery than that of life itself—or UFOs.

It also bothered her that so many people lumped together those in the field who had genuine talent with the phonies who thought that all they had to do was put a sign in the window, then set up shop. It wasn't fair, especially since they were often more visible. She couldn't understand why anyone would choose a field that was mocked unless they had a calling. It wasn't like it was a good way to make a living. She worked hard to make ends meet. She could have been an accountant, she was good with numbers, but she chose to use her God-given talent to help people in a different way. But the phonies probably had no backup plan—no ability to hold a regular job.

After all the soul-searching, she decided to wear what she had been wearing all day. She wasn't a performance artist; she didn't have to put on a show.

When she got to the appointment, she tried the door, hoping to enter unnoticed. Fortunately, it was unlocked. As soon as she opened the door, she could tell from the noise level where the dining room was and that alcohol had been flowing.

She peeked in to see where her client was sitting. When the time was right, she needed to make eye contact with her. She could not do her job with so many onlookers, many of whom would be skeptics whose negative energy could sabotage her efforts. She noticed that her client kept looking toward the door, clearly wondering where she was, so getting her attention should not be a problem.

But first she needed to find a quiet place to see if she could summon the client's husband for the second time in one day. It was a challenging request, and she wasn't entirely sure she would be successful.

Going into the living room, she felt drawn to a portrait of a mother and child. It struck her as having an almost spiritual quality to it. She looked for the artist's signature and found only initials: CGH. She went closer to study it, moved by the sense of love and connection between the subjects. It was just the kind of positive energy she needed to accomplish her purpose.

She closed her eyes and inhaled deeply through her nose, then exhaled slowly through her mouth. With each breath, she felt herself going deeper into the recesses of her mind. When she got the response she needed, she was ready.

The medium slipped into the dining room unnoticed and stood against the wall opposite where the client was presiding at the head of the table, hoping to blend into the leafy wallpaper. A young woman had her arms wrapped around her client's neck as everyone talked about the cake, how beautiful it was, how delicious it was. It was a warm scene, and the medium hated to do anything that might disturb it.

But then the client spotted her. The medium gave her a thumbs-up, and then she saw her client take a long, hard look around the table at her loved ones. A moment later, her head slumped down over her chest.

The medium was alarmed. Had she fainted? Was she playing a trick on her? She waited a moment to see if her client lifted her head, but she didn't. Had she fallen asleep? Or could she be dead? How? She thought all her client wanted was to summon her husband one more time so he could see all the family, not that she planned to join him. How could she have known? If she had, she would never have agreed to come.

She eased out of the room, praying that her client had just fallen asleep and that no one had seen her come. Before she got to the front door, she heard screams. "Granny! Granny! Someone call 911!"

Then, total pandemonium.

THE END

Acknowledgments

Writing is in my DNA. A late bloomer, I didn't discover the joys of reading and writing until in my teens thanks to the encouragement of a couple of English teachers at my high school. Since then I haven't stopped writing in one form or another.

This book has been a long time in the making. Many years ago I mentioned to my writer friend Jimin Han that I wanted to try my hand at writing fiction, and she suggested that I join a short story writing group that she led at our local library. I knew right away that I enjoyed the form and was encouraged by Jimin and the group to keep at it. As a result I owe an enormous debt of gratitude to Jimin and my fellow group members Jean Huff, Ed Baran, Siobhan Mitchell, Donna Seife, Gregory French, Lisa Vangundy, Dick Fitzhugh, and Nahal Motamed who all supported my writing and gave me great notes. (My apologies if I forgot anyone.) When the book was finished, Nahal also copy edited and corrected my typos and other errors.

I became part of another group of writers with whom I frequently write on Zoom as well as go on an annual week-long writing retreat. During said retreats, I started weaving together some of my short stories into what became this book. I can never adequately thank the group for making me believe I had ability, reading various drafts, and offering incredible feedback: Jimin Han, Pat Dunn, Barbara Josselsohn, Alexandra Soiseth, Marcia Bradley, Dan Martin, Michael Biello, Deb Laufer, and Maria Memaldonado. I also want to thank Lisa O'Donnell, my

Scottish writer friend, whose counsel helped me realize that a prologue I had written was a mistake. Kimberley Lim, a brilliant developmental editor, gave me detailed, in depth feedback that shaped the final draft.

Others whom I counted on for honest feedback included my sisters Susan Morrison and Victoria Cowal, my niece Leslie Morrison, who also helped brainstorm titles, and my longtime friends Joan O'Brien and Kathy Strickland. (Again apologies if I left anyone out.) Special thanks as well to my fellow Peace Board members Roberta Baskin and Lis Wiehl for finding the time to read the book and provide their very generous reviews.

Then there's my family, my raison d'etre. My husband, Fraydun, genuinely encouraged my writing. Some of my children and their spouses read and gave me notes on drafts; the rest better read the book! Kim Manocherian, John and Judy Manocherian, Jed and Yael Manocherian, Greg and Kim Manocherian, and Cara and Keith Hamlin, and all their children: Alex and his wife Laura Strelov, Nina Strelov, Nick Strelov and his bride-to-be Anna, Sarah Manocherian, Lindsay Manocherian, Jonathan Manocherian, Joshua Manocherian, Michela Manocherian, Ryan Manocherian, Lucas Manocherian, Malia Manocherian, Cordelia Hamlin, Lily Hamlin, Gianna Hamlin, and Cruz Hamlin.

Lastly, I wish my parents were alive so I could thank them for exposing me to a culturally rich childhood. If as a child I seemed disinterested, it was a form of rebellion. Thankfully somehow it stuck, and I absorbed it anyhow. When I got older, I greatly appreciated them and it.

About the Author

Author photograph by Christine Petrella

This is Jennifer's first novel. Much of her life experience personally and professionally went into writing it, having been a family therapist, divorce mediator, Broadway & Off-Broadway producer, musical book writer, screenwriter/producer, and screenwriting teacher. She co-wrote and produced the films *Family Blues* and *Boundary Waters*. She taught introductory screenwriting at the Sarah Lawrence Writing Institute and now teaches privately.

Regarding theatre, she wrote the book of two musicals that are streaming online: *Marry Harry*, a full-length musical, and *Cockroaches & Cologne*, a short musical. She is a proud board member of New York Stage & Film, The Peace Studio, and 18 by Vote. She is married with five children and many grandchildren—great source material!

Made in the USA
Coppell, TX
07 September 2023

21322506R00164